I0749188

"Sic Kend'hara i'michlus't vi yu grecht. Sic Kend'erus vi vey inacht. Frecas sol vey grecht. Oc'flieme, sepra, fliecht ste'gats frecasse. Ic nule vey carus. Ic Kend'hara fi erust."

"With open arms for to welcome, we greet you. With arms closed, we lay ourselves down. Only darkness greets us. One light, distant, shining upon darkness' gate. And nothingness surrounds us. And open arms forever close."

—final transmission of the starship Kend'hara,
Terran year 2360 A.D.

Positively Pornographic. One of the most obscene books we've ever read. I liked the nude mud wrestling in a vat of chocolate syrup, though.
—New Pork Thymes

Funny, except for that part where Adam kicks Eve's ass in a fist fight. That went a bit too far.
—Boston Probe

Guaranteed to make your penis three inches longer or your money back!
—Chelsea Clinton's ex-boyfriend's
former roommate

Quite possibly the worst piece of excrement we've ever read. It should be burned, you fool.
—My Editor

Quite possibly the best piece of excellence you've ever read? And you think it should be learned in school?
—Author's Response

What cat coughed up this hairball?
—San Francisco Chronic Cold

Ten thousand monkeys? No, it's... better than that in certain parts.... Maybe twelve thousand?
—Nashville Banana

Never before in the history of books has something like this been published. It truly shows what sort of a writer Mr. Gatwood is. In all our years, we have never had this sort of reaction to a book before.
—The American Society for the Study of
Subclinical Allergies

Patriots:
Traitors in Waiting

A novel by
David A. Gatwood

Published by Gatwood Publishing.

Printed in the United States of America.

ISBN: 978-1-940809-01-4

For Amanda... our only hope.

A Word from the Author:

This book is the first in a series of three. To tell the truth, I just woke up one morning and had the urge to write a novel. As I started thinking about it, the ideas just sort of fell into place at a high level, and I wrote the first few chapters in my spare time near the end of my graduate studies at the University of California, Santa Cruz.

As with any project during graduate school, though, in the end, with so many things competing for my time, my thesis won, and the book sat on a shelf (or more accurately, on a hard drive) for more than a year before I had time to work on it again.

Once things had settled down with my job at a giant fruit company, I had more free time, as well as a new inspiration for the book—one that would change its scope entirely. In the end, this single book turned into a series of three books.

The first book in the Patriots series, "Traitors in Waiting", explores the great colonial war from the perspective of military officers born and raised in a loyalist Earth colony.

The second book, "Enemies From Within", treats the story from the perspective of the colonists.

The third book, "Beyond the Veil", tells the truth behind the war.

After the book, be sure to read "Behind the Book", where I tell more about the thinking that went into various parts of the book. A word of warning, though: it's full of spoilers. Don't read it first. (Yeah, I know you're thinking about flipping to it right now. Go ahead. Spoil the book. See if I care.)

Special Thanks:

to my family and friends
for always believing in me,

to the UCSC Wind Ensemble
for a reprieve from the
drudgery of certain classes
(and life in general),

to Douglas Adams
for making me laugh and
thus inspiring this novel,

to Arthur C. Clarke,
the butt of at least
half a dozen jokes,

to all those who
employed me while I
wrote this novel,

and to my fellow writers for
their comments and critiques.
As usual, I'm still waiting
to get them....

May 5, 2363

THE musty air stung their noses as they walked through the abandoned ship, its uninviting halls dark and cold, but there was air. There was definitely air, and that alone was an improvement.

James Kurtz had seen many such ships in his day, but none more unique than the Kend'hara. She was a thing of beauty, her sleek lines swept back like your true love's hair, entrancing at first sight. Yes, he'd seen many ships adrift in his day, most not worth repairing.

But this one—yes, this one is different. She'll be a great ship again, he thought—*just the right ship for my grandson, Joseph. Sure, he's only a boy, but someday, he'll thank his old granddad for fixing up this junker.*

Ever since James had retired from the Allied Earth Force, he'd dreamed of rebuilding just such a ship. He came from a long line of engineers going back for generations—his father, Joe, his uncle, Tom, and his grandfather, Paul—and his only son, James, Jr., had been an engineer until he was killed in the battle at Kensington 7.

He only hoped that his grandson would carry on his legacy... but he'd never admit that it mattered to him. "It's not my life," he'd tell them. Of course it did, but he'd never admit it.

Yes, he had been a ship's engineer once, but that was before—when humanity was still new, that youthful optimism still glowing in its eyes—when nations banded together to leave the planet and explore space. They colonized star systems, made new discoveries, developed new technologies, realized that no one else lived within walking distance, and went back to what they did best: fighting amongst themselves.

These days, it seemed like every day's news was filled with stories about the Colonial Earth Alliance (CEA) slaughtering innocent civilians on planets siding with the Terrestrial Earth Reciprocal Retaliatory Alliance (TERRA). Of course, TERRA owned the local media, he realized, and he wondered what the CEA media had to say....

There he was, though, living at the heart of TERRA, Earth, with his daughter, her husband, and their nephew, his grandson.

It all began innocently enough—one colony demanding freedom from the home world. The transition of power seemed to be going well at first, but then things went terribly wrong.

Chapter Two

It seemed so simple; a new government was to be formed. Elections were held, and the day of inauguration was upon them.

The newly elected leaders of the Colonial Earth Alliance stood at the podium and thanked the people for choosing them. They pledged to support trade relations with the Terrans and to work together for the common good.

Yes, all of the newly elected leaders were there, save one. Robert Dumas, representing Lenora Prime, promised tough sanctions against Earth.

"Their government's tyranny can be tolerated no longer. We must rise up—rise up and tear down that government, and build a new one where it once stood—a government founded on the principle of equality for ALL of humanity," he had said.

Indeed, his absence was no surprise—he was to be sworn in privately at his home on Lenora Prime—so it was with some shock that the media greeted him as he pushed his way towards the platform. As Dumas neared the stage, though, his pace slowed....

That's when the bombs exploded—carefully planted explosives, designed to level the platform.

Three weeks later, in a prerecorded announcement, Dumas announced his succession to President of the Colonial Earth Alliance according to colonial law. During his term, he delivered on his promise of tough sanctions... but they hurt his people far more than they hurt Earth.

The colonies were in ruins now. Shortages of supplies led seemingly normal citizens to take up arms and fight for their very survival. While these men and women were labeled "rebels" and "terrorists" by the colonial government, they found favor at its highest levels. Through various laundering schemes, the CEA supplied them with weapons, ships, and financial backing.

After a few months of horrible atrocities against Earth and its allies, the Terran Alliance began organizing counterstrikes against CEA worlds. This quickly escalated into an all-out war—a war that James Kurtz would have no part of. He only hoped that the fighting would never reach Earth itself.

So far, they had been lucky—some terrorist attacks, lost shipments to the outer colonies, that sort of thing. Compared to the devastation below him on the surface of Lenora Prime, though, they had been very lucky, indeed.

But those were the galaxy's problems. There were more pressing problems now, like this ship—three years adrift in space, and she still had air.

"They sure don't make 'em like they used to," he said. In his arms, his sole companion just looked up at him and smiled.

Chapter Three

Twenty-seven years later (November 10, 2390)

WHERE *do we go from here?* Joseph thought as he stumbled out of the shuttle into shuttle bay three on Terran Command Station.

"He is remarkably strong for his age, mature, and intelligent—prime officer material," they said. Officer material indeed, he thought. He'd gladly give up this lousy job for a warm burger and a drink.

Joseph Kurtz was his patriarchal progeny, which is to say, his father's son—headstrong and sure of himself... and always hungry.

It was entirely coincidental that at that very moment, his grandfather was fixing dinner on Earth, but that's not important. What *is* important is that Joseph caught the scent of pizza in the mess hall and broke into a fast clip.

As he entered the mess hall, the smell of pepperoni was unmistakable—a far cry from the smell of burnt wiring that marked his arrival on the station—but as he turned to look for the source of the smell, he ran into a wall.

"Ow, that must have hurt," he heard someone say. He tried to turn to see who it was, but that only made him dizzy, and he fell to the ground.

When he came around, Joseph thought he must be dreaming.

"Hi. I'm Amanda."

It wasn't what she said that got his attention; it was the way that she said it. She could have said, "Hi, I'm Amanda and you look like crap," and he still would have found it beautiful.

More than that, though, *she* was beautiful—not beautiful in a Hollywood movie star sort of way, but beautiful in a "My stomach just jumped up into my throat and kept going and now resides three decks up in its own quarters" kind of way.

And so it was with great pain that he slipped into unconsciousness once again.

Chapter

November 26, 2390

More than two weeks passed before Joseph saw Amanda again. Then, one day at lunch, he was sitting there in the mess hall minding his own business when he heard a small commotion behind him. There she was—the girl of his dreams—her long brown hair flowing around her shoulders like a robe, her blue eyes glistening in the light like a distant star. And there he was—Mark Mitchell—every girl's dream and every guy's nightmare... and he was hitting on Amanda.

Joseph shook that thought off. *It shouldn't matter that he's hitting on her. After all, she wouldn't even know that I exist save for the dent in the wall.* As far as he could tell, there was only one way she would ever notice him.

He walked into a wall. Not just any wall, though. This time, he picked a short wall that would catch him just a little above the knees. What he didn't count on was the table on the other side slamming him in the chin, but somehow, he managed to maintain consciousness.

"Wow. What's that, twice in a row?" he heard her say.

And there she was again, standing over him, helping him to his feet. "Amanda, right?" he asked.

"Yeah, that's right. Amanda Jenkins. You?"

"I'm Joseph. Joseph Kurtz," he stuttered. "Would you care to join me for dinner?"

"Don't tell me you tripped over the planter on my account," she mused.

"I'd be lying if I said I noticed it was a planter," he replied. "A wall's a wall to me."

She laughed. "Sure, I'd love to."

With that, Mark's eyes narrowed to a slit, the whites barely visible from across the room. Suddenly, the room grew eerily quiet, not like the calm before a storm so much as like house pets before an earthquake.... Joseph only hoped the date he was going on tonight was worth the pummeling he would likely get tomorrow.

Chapter Five

Later that evening (November 26, 2390)

The hour had arrived—the fated moment awaited—the kiss that would end their newfound friendship forever and leave something different in its place.

That was the thought running through Joseph's head when he sat down beside Amanda at a table in the "Crew's Quarter" (that was what everyone called this section of the main concourse full of shops and restaurants), waiting for their meal. A heavyset, older gentleman eyed them from across the room, but they paid him no heed. They were in love, and that was all that mattered.

With a crash, their food arrived on their table in somewhat poorer condition than when it had left the kitchen, but it arrived, and that alone was an improvement, as it meant they could begin eating.

"My sincerest apologies, sir," the waiter said. "I'll get that cleaned up for you and get you a new drink."

"Thank you," Joseph replied.

The waiter left with a flourish. While it may not be entirely clear how a waiter can leave with a flourish, this one did.

So there they were—two longing hearts, each waiting to see into the other's soul—two young fools staring into each other's eyes over a burnt steak, a greasy cheeseburger, and a puddle of water and grape soda.

Suddenly, the commotion on the other side of the room grabbed their attention.

"This is mad!" a strange Frenchman shouted. "I demand to be heard. The Alliance is corrupt!"

The man passed within inches of Amanda as he ran out into the hall. The elite forces quickly surrounded him, and he screamed, "They're killing us! They're killing us! Their own people!"

As the security team wrestled him to the ground, he continued to struggle to speak. "You have to believe me! There are traitors in waiting!" And then he became suddenly *silent*.

The room slowly returned to its usual din, but Amanda remained quiet.

"Amanda? What's wrong?" Joseph asked after a few moments, his concern clearly showing.

"Nothing important.... No, I think someone just walked over my grave."

***

As Joseph walked Amanda back to her quarters, they passed an information monitor.

> "In Terran Alliance News," the female anchor said, "there was more scattered fighting along the borders as three unmarked ships claiming to represent the Colonial Alliance attacked and boarded the freighter Garden of Eden near the no-man's land. The crew was jettisoned out of an airlock. No survivors were reported."

"Cast out of paradise?" Amanda quipped.

"Mmm-hmm," Joseph replied, smiling.

> "In other news," the male anchor next to her said, "Secretary of State Tracey Armstrong is scheduled to appear at Terran Command Station tomorrow to make an announcement about her progress in the peace process. Reporter Milt Stevenson has details...."

"Do we care?" Joseph asked.

"Nope," Amanda replied, grimacing.

A few moments later, they arrived at Amanda's quarters.

"I'll see you tomorrow?" Joseph asked.

She smiled. "Count on it."

Chapter Six

Later that night (November 26, 2390)

JOSEPH awoke suddenly to the sound of alarm klaxons blaring in his ear.

Time to wake up already? Joseph looked over at the clock. It read 11:48. *That's P.M.*, Joseph thought. *Not the alarm clock. Damn. That means....*

Thinking quickly, he threw on his black jumpsuit, sprang for the door, and then stepped cautiously out into the hall.

Joseph coughed as the acrid air burned his lungs. Even with his emergency light, he could barely see the end of the corridor through the smoky blackness, yet he knew it was just a mere two or three meters away.

And through the din, one name rang in his head. Amanda! Her quarters were on the outer ring—an easy target for any invading space fleet.

Just then, his communicator sounded its chime. "Kurtz here," he shouted.

"Joseph, it's Amanda. What's going on down there? The security board is lit up like a Christmas tree."

That's when he remembered that she was filling in for someone on the night shift, had started work several hours ago, and was in C&C some eighteen levels above him.

"I... I don't know. I just woke up. There's a lot of smoke. Fire suppression doesn't seem to be activated."

"Joe, according to the heat sensors, the fires are all in crawl spaces. The smoke is coming from the secondary ventilation system."

He looked around. Sure enough, the vents in the hall were billowing smoke like a Michigan chimney in February. He quickly closed off the problem vents, and the air began to clear as the local area filtration system kicked in. Then, he pulled out his data pad and began a diagnostic.

"Amanda?" he asked after a few moments.

"Hello, Joe. Whaddaya know?"

"You've been watching my movie collection, haven't you...."

"Like I'd tell you if I had," she replied playfully.

He smiled, shook it off, and continued. "It looks like something burned through the hull plating. Half this deck is depressurized down the length of the arm. My cabin and the empty cabin across the hall from me are the only ones on this side of the pressure doors."

"That would explain why no one else answered my status request.... Can you get off the level?"

"No way. I can't get out into the arm because of a depressurized section, and I can't go inside the nexus towards the engineering arm for the same reason. And in the other direction, the hall ends in a docking port.... The lifts are on the other side of one set of pressure doors, and the nearest access ladder is behind another set. And the access ladder wouldn't help anyway because the levels above and below me are depressurized."

"Listen, get yourself to a pressure pod at evac station 19-dash-3 Alpha. We'll send a team in EV suits to clean up the mess."

"I can't do that. Those pressure pods are down for maintenance... and on the other side of the doors."

"Then we'll bring you an EV suit," Amanda offered.

"No time. The EV suits are only designed to handle a few hundred degrees. The ceiling above my head is... starting to melt. It's going to get hot in here pretty quickly."

Amanda paused for a moment before speaking. "Melting? Are you sure?"

"Just the plastic bits," Joseph replied, "but they're dripping in spots, so yes it really is that hot. My best guess is that someone torpedoed us with something that's catalyzing the oxidization of the hull plating itself. It won't stop burning until it runs out of oxygen. You're going to have to vent the deck."

"But you'll die. There isn't an EV suit nearby."

"I can reach docking port 19C from here," he replied, glancing down at the end of the hallway.

"There's no airlock at that port."

"I know, Amanda. Look, it's simple. Evacuate all the air on this section of the deck, then blow the hatch. I should remain conscious just long enough to jump free."

"And this will help you how?"

"Since I'm so close to the central hub, I won't have to overcome much momentum to remain stationary and get away from the crew quarters arm. Forty-two seconds later, the station's operations arm will fly by. Have someone tethered to it in an EV suit to pull me inside the nearest airlock."

"Are you crazy?"

"We don't have a choice. This stuff is burning through into my deck. Air or no air, I'm probably about to die. At least this way there's a chance."

A moment later, he felt a rush of cool air. Knowing that the pressure was about to plummet, he quickly took gasping breaths to oxygenate his tissues, waited as the air grew thin, then shut his eyes and exhaled quickly, his breaths becoming steadily more shallow, then stopping altogether.

Chapter Seven

COLD. *Silent.* Those were the first thoughts in Joseph's mind as he stared down the outer hall of the central nexus. Port 19C was just ahead, a largely useless relic left over from when the station was under construction.

For a fleeting moment, he wondered why the designers had chosen not to put stairs, ladders, or lifts inside the nexus near the crew quarters, then dismissed it as being a case of 20/20 hindsight. Somebody probably said, "Hey, I can build it for fifty million less if I put all the lifts in only two places and run them up the outside."

Just then, through the faint air, he heard a muffled explosion. He opened his eyes and blinked away the blood only to see the ceiling burst into flame. Suddenly, he realized in horror why the ceiling was hot. *The fusion reactor! It's right above me!*

Well, there's not much I can do about it now, he thought as he visually scanned the area around the docking port. He had to find the manual release handle and pull it.

It's a curious thing, he thought. *The light bulbs have a near total vacuum inside, yet they hold together under Earth's air pres-*

sure. Strange that they all blew out in a vacuum. Must have been the shock wave. Or the temperature change.

Then he began to wonder if the sky might really be green, and why they can't raise cattle on Mars, and *whatever happened to that green sweater I like so much, anyway?* He shook his mind clear. He had to concentrate.

It seemed like an eternity passed as the release handle slowly disengaged the lock mechanisms that held the door shut. The motors were no doubt whirring noisily, he thought, which made it all the more creepy to feel their vibrations on the soles of his feet, yet be unable to hear them.

The door swung slowly towards him. After a few moments, he pulled himself through it and shoved off against its frame.

It's truly a peculiar feeling to realize that you are alone in space with no air, no ground beneath you, no sound, and very little light—just the cold blackness and vacuum of space. And so, as he flew across the empty void towards the ship's operations arm and slowly slipped into unconsciousness, Joseph's final thought was wondering if he would ever see his Amanda again.

Chapter Eight

November 27, 2390

A bright light in the distance.... Joseph wondered if this was heaven. An angel's voice, a whisper in the silence... saying... what? He could not be sure.

The light slowly faded until he could see clearly. Amanda stood over his bedside in the infirmary.

"Joseph, you're awake," she said.

"You're here," he answered.

"Of course, I'm here," Amanda told him. "I'll always be here for you. I promise."

Joseph smiled. "How long was I out?" he asked wearily.

"Just a couple of hours," she replied.

"The reactor!" he exclaimed, suddenly struggling to sit up.

"Relax," she said, shoving him back down onto the medical bed. "Jonathan scrubbed it in time. If he hadn't, you'd be a cinder already."

Joseph was visibly shaken. "What happened?"

"Everything went as planned," she told him.

But something hadn't gone as planned....

***

"Everything went as planned," he said gleefully.

Vladimir Rejndorv was a burly man—five foot seven, 280 pounds—the kind of guy you really wouldn't want to make mad. He spoke with a cotton-ball voice like you might hear in an old gangster film. This, coupled with his "cheery" demeanor, had earned him the nickname Vlad the Unintelligible.

Across the desk sat Svetlana Rusakova. Her chiseled features reflected the light of the single lamp that hung overhead, in stark contrast with the dark, foreboding blackness that lay beyond. He thought he saw a gleam of... was it anger in her eyes? Then it was gone again, so he could not be certain.

"The station...." She paused, grinning gleefully.

Rejndorv chuckled.

"Was it destroyed?" she asked with a gleam in her eye.

There it was again—that bitterness that he had seen a moment earlier—and, much as before, it disappeared as quickly as it had come.

"No. Sadly, the reactor core was disabled before it could go critical," he replied, "but they have major structural damage and only emergency power. They won't pose much of a threat."

"Excellent," she replied coldly.

Chapter Nine

"Let's get away," Joseph said.

Amanda just sat there in the Crew's Quarter, jaw agape.

"We both have some shore leave built up," he continued. "Why not take a weekend for us?"

"Are you crazy?" she asked.

"Yeah," he replied. "Crazy about you."

Corny like a bad fruit cocktail, but still sweet.

As she reached across the table to take his hand, someone stirred behind her.

"Say, you two lookin' for adventure?" the man drawled.

Amanda and Joseph stared.

"Oh, sorry. I'm Jim. Jim Bowers. And you two are?"

"Joseph Kurtz."

"Amanda Jenkins."

Amanda stared at the newcomer with a mixture of concern and disgust. The anachronistic-looking cadet with brown, gel-slicked hair and cowboy boots exuded an air of smugness that she couldn't forgive, and definitely didn't trust.

“A bunch of us are gonna take a day’s leave and go to Iridia Prime to explore the ice caves,” he said. “I thought you might like to join us, since you wanted to get away for a bit.”

“I’d have to talk it over with my supervisor, but it sounds like fun,” Joseph said. “Amanda?”

“Uh... sure. Count me in,” she replied skeptically.

“Okay,” Jim told them. “We leave at 0800 hours on Saturday—shuttle bay 12. Don’t be late.”

“We’ll see you then,” Joseph replied.

Well, at least Joseph will be there, Amanda thought, *so it can’t be all bad, right?*

Jim stood and left, leaving his empty tray precariously balanced at the edge of the table.

As the tray crashed to the ground, Joseph scratched his head, puzzled.

“Why do I think this could get interesting?” he asked.

Amanda smiled awkwardly.

Right?

A moment later, the viewscreen across the room flickered to life, a news anchor’s face filling the screen.

> "This just handed to me," the anchor said, "Terran Command officials confirm CEA attacks on New Argentina colony. More than three hundred people were killed and thousands more were injured yesterday when a stryker missile plowed through downtown Cirrus, New Argentina's capital."
>
> "In a related story, the CEA has claimed responsibility for yesterday's attack on Terran Command Station. About sixty military and civilian personnel were killed and two hundred more left homeless when a magnetic mine attached itself

to the outer hull and exploded. The resulting explosion depressurized parts of three decks and caused an estimated five hundred million dollars in damage."

"We'll have continuing updates on the latest escalations in border fighting and terrorist attacks as more information becomes available."

"You're watching TANN, the Terran Alliance News Network, with news updates every hour on the hour."

Chapter Ten

Wednesday, November 28, 2390
0700 hours

JOSEPH awoke, a cheap alarm clock's shrill whine echoing in his ears. *Rine, rine, rine, rine, rine. Why did I have to put it on the other side of the room?* he thought.

Since the alarm clock had a proximity switch, he actually had to walk over and turn it off. Apparently that was supposed to keep him from falling asleep. It didn't; he didn't. Instead, he reached into his right sock, pulled out a small knife, and threw it across the room at the clock. Sensing the motion of the knife over it, the alarm turned off. The knife, meanwhile, impaled itself upon the soft wood trim and set off several more alarms by causing a slight breach of the inner hull. These alarms, in turn, woke him up.

Imagine his surprise when he realized he wasn't alone. He could feel the presence of someone else in the room—a misplaced shadow here, a slight hint of perfume there—but he couldn't place it, so he carefully stood and walked around the corner. Standing in front of him was Amanda, dutifully fixing breakfast.

"Good morning, sleepyhead," she said, smirking. "Come on. I made us pancakes."

Joseph groaned. As if the headache weren't bad enough, he couldn't remember how Amanda got in his quarters.

He groggily made his way over to the basin to wash his face with cold water.

***

Joseph woke up again, this time with a jolt. Confused, he looked around and began climbing out of bed.

Imagine his surprise when he realized he was alone after all. He walked over to the basin and wet his face.

Still here, he thought. *What an odd dream.*

"Computer, fix me some pancakes. I don't want to be late this morning," he said. It dutifully obeyed.

And so he ate and dressed in much the same way you'd expect, except that instead of wearing his uniform, he put on a mu'umu'u. He walked down the hall, proud of the status report he had written on his data pad.

As he approached his engineering lab, the doors opened for him. Admiral Skylarov stood waiting for him.

"Going casual, Lieutenant?" he remarked.

Joseph looked down, only to realize that, to his horror, he was wearing pajamas again.

"Uh... no sir, just a little confused." He handed the data pad to the admiral.

"Son, I think you need to work a little harder," he said.

Joseph looked at the pad and noticed that instead of his carefully written synopsis of how to fix a difficult engineering problem, he had recommended engaging the base self-destruct and calling for the crew to abandon ship in life-pods.

This is too weird, Joseph thought.

"I... I... I d-didn't write that, s-s-s-sir," Joseph stammered. "I don't know how that got on my pad. What I meant to say was 'Picture a pig swim butt naked through the night. It is mad.' Uhh... wait a minute, I mean flush the exhaust manifolds through your nostrils and tether the ship to Neptune... I mean...."

Suddenly, the admiral shape-shifted into a tiny three-toed sloth, then into a giant, hideous beast. Stunned, Joseph began running. The beast followed him. Joseph tried to run faster, but he felt like he was running through water. He kept getting slower and slower while the creature got faster and faster. Suddenly, he hit a dead end. As he turned around and slid down the wall to the floor, the beast grew huge and dove towards him.

"Aaaaaaaaaaaaaaaaaaaaaaaaaaaaaaaaah!"

***

Joseph woke with a jolt. "Dammit. I've gotta stop waking like this," he said.

Joseph noticed Amanda standing there again, making breakfast. He smiled as he picked up his uniform.

"Do you care if I change in front of you?" he asked.

She just smiled at him. He changed. She minded.

Suddenly, Joseph found himself in the engineering lab... naked.

Admiral Skylarov looked his direction.

"Didn't I eat you before?" he asked.

***

Joseph woke with a jolt. "All right! ENOUGH ALREADY!"

***

Joseph woke with a jolt. Thinking quickly, he went back to sleep. A few minutes later, he woke naturally and walked over to the basin, washed his face, threw on a uniform, asked the computer for French Toast, and carried the food and his data pad to the engineering lab.

Admiral Skylarov arrived a minute later. Glancing at the pad, he paused, then said, "I'll read it later."

Joseph shrugged.

"I understand you have some weekend plans," Skylarov said.

Joseph was a bit confused.

"Don't look so surprised, Joseph. Even the walls have ears here."

As Joseph turned, the flesh-colored wall mutated into a giant lobe.

***

Joseph expected to wake with a jolt, but he didn't. He wondered if he was about to awake with a tingle or a headache, but he didn't do that, either. Instead, he awoke with a mild sense of nausea.

As he looked around, things didn't seem right. He walked over to the basin, and was even more puzzled. *That's not my toothbrush. Hey, wait! That's not my hairbrush, and those aren't my nail clippers, either! Oh, my God! These aren't my quarters!*

As he turned, he saw Amanda standing in the kitchen nook making breakfast. *Oh. I'm in Amanda's quarters. How did* ***that*** *happen?*

"You fell asleep last night," Amanda said, anticipating his question. "I couldn't get you to your temporary quarters all the way up on deck 7, so I let you sleep in mine."

"Thanks," he replied. "That was sweet."

Wait a second....

"Umm... we didn't...."

"No," Amanda replied. "You've been asleep. That would have been kind of hard."

They both sighed, then chuckled at the other's sighs, then giggled at the chuckles.

"I made you some breakfast," Amanda continued. "Come on and eat it while it's hot."

Joseph smiled. "Thanks, A. Say, you wouldn't have a spare uniform, would you?"

She giggled. "I don't think they'd fit you," Amanda told him.

I bet it would still fit better than the mu'umu'u, he thought as she handed him a plate of pancakes.

"Thanks, Amanda. You're an angel," he said, then gave her a small kiss and picked up his data pad. "I'm off. I have to meet Admiral Skylarov at 0800. I'll see you tonight, 'kay?"

"Yeah. See you tonight," she said sexily.

A slight shiver ran up his spine, and for a moment, he wondered if he was dreaming again. As she stared into his eyes, he hoped that if this was a dream, he would never wake up from it, but of course, this time he wasn't asleep.

***

"I'LL read it later," Admiral Skylarov said as he took the pad. "For now, let's talk about your weekend plans."

Joseph stiffened. "Admiral?"

"Don't look so surprised," Skylarov replied. "Jim told me. Iridia Prime. Nice place."

"Yes, sir," Joseph said. "So I've heard."

That's when Joseph noticed something was a little bit different this time around. Admiral Jenkins was standing beside him.

"Have you also heard that it's right in the middle of a battle zone?" Jenkins asked.

Joseph stiffened again. "No, sir. I didn't know that."

"Well, it is," Admiral Jenkins said. "That's not a safe place... but the bigger problem...."

Admiral Jenkins paused.

"Yes?" Joseph asked.

"The bigger problem," he continued, "is that Jim is incompetent—not incompetent in an engineering sense, incompetent in an 'I don't know how to keep myself out of trouble' sense. He takes unnecessary risks for fun."

"So I take it you don't want me to go?" Kurtz asked.

"No, on the contrary," Jenkins replied. "I want you *to* go—keep him in check, be the voice of reason, that sort of thing. From your record, I'm sure you can take care of yourself."

Dizzily, Joseph wondered if the clock incident had really been a dream, and he vowed to check the wall for hull breaches when he got back to his quarters. Until then, though, he could study the ice caves and take notes about what areas to avoid.

"Any suggestions on where not to go on Iridia, Admiral?"

"Besides anywhere?" he joked. "Not really. I've never been there myself, but my daughter Amanda has."

Joseph's jaw dropped. *Daughter?*

"Your d-d-d-daughter?"

"You didn't know that?" Skylarov asked, laughing.

"No, sir."

"Somehow, I had a feeling she didn't mention it," Admiral Jenkins replied. "Oh, how I wish I had a camera right now. The look on your face is... priceless."

Joseph just stood there.

"Take care of my daughter," Jenkins continued. "Make sure you keep her safe."

"You know she's... like... ten years older than me, right?" he asked.

The admiral just stared at him.

"Don't worry, sir," Joseph answered. "I'll watch her back."

As he left the room, Admiral Jenkins muttered, "That's what I'm worried about."

***

A few hours later

"HEY, Joseph!" Amanda shouted.

"Amanda! Hey!" Joseph replied as he ran to her across the hydroponics bay.

Amanda hugged him.

Okay, now to go in for the kill....

"So, Amanda, why didn't you tell me Admiral Jenkins was your father?" he asked.

"I... didn't think it was important," she answered.

"It wasn't... until I got orders to watch your ass this weekend."

Joseph paused a moment for effect, then continued, "Hmm... now that I think about it, maybe that wasn't the best wording to use with your dad."

Amanda's eyes widened. For a moment, Joseph thought she was turning pale. Slowly, carefully, he let his frown erupt into a toothy grin.

Amanda began to laugh, her face a shade of red even darker than that of her father's uniform.

"Ooh, you," she said.

"So, are you ready for tomorrow?" he asked.

"I think so. I've picked out a couple of books to carry with me for the trip over. It's a twelve-hour flight, you know."

Oh, if only we could have gotten something with a folding drive, Joseph thought.

"Wow," he exclaimed. "I didn't realize that. What are you doing on the way back?"

"I have a sleep shift," she answered. "Compartment 2. You can... join me if you'd like."

Joseph sat for a moment, staring at her smile. Unsure what she meant, and terribly concerned that the walls might, in fact, really have ears, he said only, "We have a few days to discuss that."

She smiled and kissed him on the cheek as they walked together towards Joseph's temporary quarters. When they arrived, Amanda's father greeted her at the door.

"Dad!" she shouted.

"I went by your quarters. You weren't there," he replied.

Amanda blushed a deep lavender behind her blue rouge, while Joseph smirked at the notion that rouge could be blue.

"What do you need, Dad?" she asked, mildly annoyed.

Admiral Jenkins just stood and looked at her for a moment, then sighed.

"You know that I'm retiring soon, right?"

She smiled. "Of course."

"When you get back, I won't be here."

She nodded. "I know."

"I also won't be at home."

She looked a bit puzzled.

"An old friend of mine is going to Triton Station for some therapy. I've asked to be transferred there to finish out my last few weeks, and I might stay a little longer. It's a long story. I'll tell you everything when I get back."

"Okay. When will that be?"

Her father frowned.

"I don't know, Amanda. I don't know."

***

Saturday morning (December 1st, 2390)
0800 hours

THE long-anticipated hour had arrived—that moment of indecision—stay or go—one path taken, another shunned—one door opening, another closing—and all they knew for sure was that their lives would never be the same.

Standing on the threshold between the shuttle bay and their tech shuttle, Amanda felt a slight chill run up her spine. Maybe it was the danger of the mission, maybe it was Joseph's arm around her, or maybe it was just the cool air of the shuttle's onboard life support flowing through her hair, but something about the trip just didn't feel right. Still, she pressed on.

Next to her, a pensive Lieutenant Kurtz one-handedly played a video game on the engineering hand scanner that he carried with him everywhere. *You never know when it might come in handy,* he'd always say.

And so, with little fanfare and much physical comedy, the unlikely duo stepped into the waiting shuttle, arm in arm, the hatch closing slowly behind them as they stood staring into each other's eyes.

So it began.

"Shuttlecraft Harcliffe, you are cleared for departure on vector zero-two-zero mark 3 by one-zero-seven mark 5," the disembodied voice intoned as they began their slow ascent through the gaping shuttle bay doors into the void of space that lay beyond.

***

Three hours later

"Hey, Mark. How's that left engine holding up?" Joseph asked.

"It's running a little hot, but it's within tolerance," Mark replied. "I think one of the coolant pumps is a little weak. This thing's been through a lot, you know."

Mark Mitchell was an EIT—an engineer in training—one of Joseph's "little geeks", as Amanda called them. He was always eager to study ships' systems in various states of repair (*or, more frequently, disrepair,* Joseph mused) to learn what things could go wrong and to learn how to fix them when they inevitably did.

"Yeah," Joseph said. "That's what worries me. I've been seeing some sporadic readings on its power output. I don't think it's going to blow out, but if it does, we'll be in for a bumpy ride."

"No sweat, J," Mark replied. "It's under control."

At that moment, alarm klaxons went off with a vengeance. "We've got a problem," Jim shouted.

"You *do* realize this is all *your* fault," Joseph joked. Then, he studied the readouts and recoiled in horror. "The left engine just blew a gasket and is venting plasma. It's about to breach the fuel pod!" he screamed.

"Ejecting the fuel pod," Mark announced.

A screaming whine indicated that the ejection sequence had completed. Suddenly, the pod exploded just a few meters from the ship.

"Shit!" Joseph shouted.

"Gah! The left engine is racing out of control," Jim said, his fingers flying across the console. "And there's a good minute of residual plasma left in the system. If we don't do something, it's gonna tear this ship apart."

A high pitched alert beep snapped him to attention. "Throttling up the right engine!" Mark shouted. "Everybody brace!"

Everyone grabbed the nearest console, armrest, rail, or support beam. The screech of shearing metal could be heard throughout the ship as it accelerated to two-thirds the speed of light. The ship shook wildly.

"Main artificial gravity is down," Mark reported. "Backup is holding... for now."

The shaking diminished somewhat as the engines approached equal thrust. Then they were thrown suddenly forward as the left engine leaked and burned through the last of its plasma reserves.

"Reversing the right engine," Mark said.

The ship slowly decelerated over the next few minutes.

"It's over," Joseph said as the right engine exhausted its plasma supply. "I'm showing full stop, give or take."

Jim appeared rather confused. "What happened? Where are we?"

"Best guess is somewhere near the CEA border—maybe close to the Stronti system," Joseph replied, "but most of our sensors are down, so I can't say for sure. And we can't switch over to our reserve plasma tank, because we have one engine stuck at full throttle and leaking plasma like a sieve. Someone has to do an EVA or we're dead in the water."

"Hey, Kurtz," Jim asked, "have you ever done an EVA before?"

"Only when absolutely necessary," he replied. "I've never tried to fix an engine on EVA, though. I'll probably need a hand. Oh, and a magnetic tool belt."

Jim just stared at him.

"We don't even have an EVA suit," Mark replied, "just a bunch of emergency O_2 suits that aren't designed for moving around outside the ship. I'm not even sure we can safely *get* you outside the ship."

"And life support is down," Jim noted. "We can't afford to lose that much air."

"Computer, what is the status of life support?" Joseph asked.

"Life support is not functional."

"Computer, perform a low-level diagnostic on life support," he asked.

"Life support is not functional."

"Oh, you're no help at all," Joseph said, pulling out his hand scanner and cabling it into the console. Joseph stared at the readings for a moment.

"Ah. That would explain it," Joseph said. "The power routing wasn't configured to fail over automatically."

"Which means?" Jim asked.

"Life support should be coming back online momentarily," Joseph informed them as he stood and pulled a panel down from the ceiling. "I'm rerouting power from emergency batteries to life support."

Joseph unplugged and replugged cables for a good half a minute. A few seconds later, the overhead lights came on, and cool air rushed into the cabin through the floor registers. Within seconds, the ventilation system had sucked out most of the smoky air and had replaced it with only slightly less smoky air (which still had a rather repugnant stench, Joseph noted).

"There," Joseph said. "Life support is back online. We only have about three days without engines, though, so we have to get back underway quickly."

"Okay, wise guy," Jim chided, "how do you plan to do an EVA without thruster packs?"

"Really strong magnets?" Mark offered.

"Tether," Joseph replied and, suddenly grinning, added, "and really strong magnets."

***

Thirty minutes later

Joseph stood in the aft compartment waiting for the last few supplies. *Let's see.... I have a magnet to hold small objects, a rope for a tether, a panel key for the hull, and a hand weapon to use as a torch. Not very safe or efficient, but it will do.*

"Hey, Joseph," Amanda said. "You need a hand?"

"Do you know your way around a hand scanner?"

"I can hold my own," she said bluntly. She smiled and added, "and you'll probably want this."

She pulled a hand-held cutting torch out of her knapsack.

"Where did you get that?" Joseph asked. "I thought I was going to have to use a hand-held pulse weapon."

"I brought it with me to cook food in the ice caves," she replied. "Guess we won't need it for that anymore."

"Well, if you really want to help," Joseph began.

"I do," she interrupted.

"I guess you can give me a hand on the EVA, then," he replied. "I'll need a couple of extra arms for moving bulkheads around and to catch the stuff that I drop."

"Sure. No prob."

"Suit up, guys and dolls," Jim told them, pointing to a closet.

Joseph and Amanda walked across the room and grabbed two suits out of the closet. They quickly stepped into the suits, then put on their helmets.

"Checking pressure seal," Joseph said, pressing buttons on his arm. "Pressure seal, check. Oxygen level, check. Heating, check. My suit looks good. Yours?"

"Mine is fine," Amanda replied.

"Let's go, then. Put a climbing harness on outside your suit, then clip this tether to your harness," Joseph said, handing her a carabiner attached to a climbing rope.

Joseph clumsily strapped a climbing harness around his pressure suit, then clipped the other end of the climbing rope to his suit. A moment later, he clipped another rope from his suit to a mounting plate just inside the doorway. He waited for Amanda to secure her harness, then walked over to the door controls.

"Everybody out!" Joseph shouted.

After everyone cleared the room, Joseph locked the vacuum-safe doors between the aft compartment and the central hallway that led to the flight deck.

"Computer, evacuate the air from this room," Joseph ordered.

Joseph watched as the air pressure indicator on his arm console showed steadily decreasing pressure until it reached approximately one ten-millionth of an atmosphere. Then, the computer sealed off the vent shafts to prevent vacuum loss before disabling the pumps.

As the exterior door crept slowly open, a small puff of air burst forth from the ship. The water vapor instantly crystallized upon contact with the cold vacuum of space, producing a few icicles that clung to the edge of the door.

Joseph could faintly hear the sound of alarm klaxons (mostly transmitted mechanically through his suit) as though they were extremely distant. The sound diminished further as the air outside grew steadily thinner.

"Amanda," Joseph called, "are you okay?"

"Relax, J," she replied, "I've EVAed before.... Once."

Holding the handholds and keeping their feet tucked under foot restraint bars, they slowly crawled out of the ship and onto the outer hull. Once they were clear of the doors, Joseph clipped a tether to the outside of the ship, then reached through the doorway to unclip the other tether from the metal ring inside the shuttle.

"Guys, you can shut the door now," Joseph said into his helmet radio. "Were you raised in a barn or something?"

Slowly, the exterior door swung closed, the light from inside dwindling to a slight crack, until at last they were left alone in the cold darkness of space.

Step by step, they cautiously made their way down the outer hull until they reached the top of the left engine manifold. Joseph carefully pulled a plate key from his makeshift tool belt—several tools tied to his suit with long pieces of string, really—and inserted it against the edge of the front maintenance panel, sliding it along the length of the slot. The panel popped loose, and he handed it to Amanda.

"What exactly do you want me with this?" she asked.

Joseph tried hard to hold back a laugh. "I was thinking you could take it and shove it up Admiral Skylarov's ass."

Amanda laughed. "I'll lash it to a handgrip."

When Joseph saw the inside of the engine, he winced.

"What's wrong?" Amanda asked.

"That explosion blew out one of the plasma conduits," Joseph replied. "We don't have a spare, so we'll have to patch what we've got and limp back home. Torch?"

Amanda handed him the torch. Carefully, he cut the bent metal out of the way.

"Plate?" Joseph asked.

"This plate?" Amanda asked, pointing to the tethered cover.

"Yeah," he replied. "Hand it here."

"You've fixed it?" she asked.

"Not even close," Joseph replied, and turned on the torch.

Joseph carefully cut the plate in half and bent it until it formed an almost-round tube. He then set the torch to a less finely tipped setting and used the remaining metal as flux to weld the tube into the existing plasma conduit.

"Are you sure that's the only problem?" Amanda asked. "Something went wrong with the engine before the explosions—a plasma leak in the rear of the engine on the interior side, if memory serves."

She had a point, of course, and Joseph told her so. "Good point."

When they climbed to the back side of the engine, they found a gaping hole in the plasma manifold.

"Hey, guys? We need a piece of bulkhead. Rip one off the wall and throw it out the airlock," he told them. "I have a feeling the ship's going to look kind of ugly inside before we're done."

"I'm not going anywhere *near* that door right now," Mark replied. "I don't know how you rigged the interlocks to let you open the back door while we're in space, but it scares the hell out of me."

"It's a trick I learned from Amanda," Joseph said.

"Even scarier," Mark replied.

"I'll grab the cover plate from the other engine," Amanda offered.

"That will do, I suppose," Joseph replied.

Joseph watched as Amanda propelled herself towards the far engine. Suddenly, a coolant line in front of him ruptured. Joseph's foot twisted and slipped from its foothold, and he found himself flying. He grasped desperately for a handhold, but found none.

A moment later, Joseph felt himself crash into the inner wall of the far engine just before he slipped into unconsciousness.

***

"JOSEPH?"

Shall I hear more, or shall I speak at this? he thought.

"Joseph? Are you okay? Can you hear me?"

It's Amanda's voice, and... she's out of her suit.... I, by contrast, am not....

"Yeah," he said, "but I feel a little dizzy."

As he started to sit up, Amanda shoved him into the bed. Hard.

"Don't get up," she ordered. "You aren't going anywhere until a doctor can check you out."

"I have to go back out there," he protested. "I'm the only one who can fix this bucket."

"I'm counting on that," she replied, "but you'll have to do it from in here. I'll be your eyes and ears. I'm going EVA in a few minutes with the copilot."

"Mark? What does he know about plasma manifolds?" Joseph asked, suddenly both worried and jealous all at once.

"Nothing, but I need somebody to hold the hull plates when I rip them apart," she said. After a brief pause, she added, "with my bare hands."

Joseph smiled.

"As much as I hate to interrupt this conversation," Jim said, cutting in, "you need to get moving. Being unarmed and adrift near the colonial border isn't exactly my idea of a fun vacation."

By the time Mark and Amanda had stepped into the rear compartment, Jim was already evacuating the oxygen in preparation for their EVA.

"Get out there," Jim ordered.

What an asshole, Joseph thought.

***

Thirty minutes later

"Okay, Amanda," Joseph said. "Now you just have to reconnect the control line to the plasma flow control valve. You think you can handle that without me talking you through it?"

"Sure, Joseph. No sweat. I could do *this* in my sleep," she replied.

Joseph suspected she probably could, which made him no less nervous.

***

Suddenly, Joseph awoke with a jolt. Half expecting the whole incident to be a bad dream, he was rather surprised when he found himself slammed back into a makeshift biobed by a leather restraint that oddly resembled Amanda's favorite belt. He grunted in pain as his back hit the bed again.

"Hey, Joseph," Amanda called over the headset, "we still don't have full engine power, but we have sensors. I can't make heads or tails of this engine design, though. I thought I understood these things until I had one sitting in front of me."

I must have nodded off, he thought. *That's a sign of a concussion. Not good.*

"It happens. What's the problem?" he asked.

"Well, I know the problem is somewhere in the control system, but I can't figure out how to diagnose it," she said.

"Panel J17," he replied. "Enter code 323748 into the hand scanner and it should pretty much diagnose itself."

"It's working," she said. "This is strange. It says there's a flow regulator clog."

"That can't be," he replied. "That shouldn't ever happen. Pull panel D12 and see if the feed line is broken or crimped."

"No, it looks fine, but that's a coolant line. Didn't you say the pump was a little weak?"

Joseph thought for a moment before answering, "They're isolated systems, Amanda. Trace the line and see where it goes."

"It's in port D-22-15. That help?"

"Did you say fifteen?" Joseph asked incredulously.

"Yeah. So?"

"Some monkey put this thing together wrong," he replied. "It should be in D-22-14. Odd-numbered ports are high pressure coolant lines. Even-numbered ports are low pressure coolant lines. You can't connect one to the other. It's a wonder this thing made it out of the shuttle bay with that much pressure on the feed lines."

"So you want me to change it?" she asked.

"No!" he shouted. "Whatever you do, don't unplug that line. It has enough pressure to knock you clear back to the twentieth century. You'll need to close the valve right above it and then bleed off the pressure. The easiest way is probably to micro-puncture the line."

"Okay, the valve is closed. How do I puncture the line?" she asked.

"Set the torch to a fine point," he replied, "then heat a single spot slowly. As soon as it starts to bubble or spew, get back fast."

"Okay. Puncturing it now."

Suddenly, the line began spewing coolant. Joseph heard her scream for a moment, then begin breathing rapidly.

"Are you okay?" he asked.

"Oh God, Oh God, Oh God, Oh God," she said, the sound of sheer terror in her voice.

"What's going on?" he asked.

"My tether! Mark forgot to connect my tether!"

"Shit!" Mark shouted. "I'm sorry! Jim was rushing me."

"Mark!" Joseph shouted. "Don't apologize. Go get her!"

Over the intercom, Joseph heard he sound of someone scrambling to move, then a snap, then silence.

"I can't reach her," Mark answered. "My leash is too short by a few inches."

"Joseph!" she cried. "Heeeeeeeelp!"

Joseph felt paralyzed and trapped. Come to think of it, he was paralyzed and trapped, or at least trapped. *I should never have bought her that damn belt,* he thought. *Between that and the oxygen hose in my nose....*

Oxygen hose....

"Mark! The pressure lines on your suit! Grab the recharge line from one tank and detach it from the control block. Do *not* disconnect the tank end of the hose."

"Okay, I've done that," he replied. "The suit sealed itself and shut off the oxygen flow to that tube. Now what?"

"Hook it to the high pressure coolant line and isolate that tank from the oxygen regulator by closing the valve at the top of the tank," Joseph said. "Fill it fast, then yank the line."

"I'm filling it now," Mark replied. "The tank is at 500 psi, and I'm scared to go higher. Even with the output valve closed, it's leaking a bit, so it feels like it's trying to crush every bone in my body. Oh, and my back feels hotter than a Texas summer."

"Okay, shut the valve on the ship, disconnect your tether, and rip the output line from the control block. The valve leakage alone should be enough to send you flying towards Amanda. Use the valve on top to control the flow."

Joseph heard the sound of coolant suddenly depressurizing, and hoped that Mark's hand wasn't in the way. When it didn't stop hissing, though, he became concerned.

"Oooooooh Shiiiiiiiiit!!!!" Mark screamed.

"Close the valve! Close the valve!" Joseph yelled.

The hissing stopped. *Mark must have closed the valve,* Joseph noted.

"You okay, Mark?" he asked.

"Yeah, I guess," Mark said, "just a little cool."

"Can you reach Amanda?" Joseph asked.

"Almost there... just a little farther, and... yes!" he replied. "I have her."

"Good," Joseph replied. "Now use the coolant as a propellant. Just aim it away from the back door. Computer, seal off the aft compartment again, but maintain air pressure. Seal the exterior door with a force field, then open the exterior door."

"What in hell are you doing, Joseph," Mark asked.

"I'm going to bring you in on a cushion of air," Joseph replied.

"You know you're nuts, right?" Mark chided, then opened the valve again. "God, I hope you know what you're doing."

"Computer, project their progress on the ceiling," Joseph ordered. The computer dutifully projected a holographic view of the exterior cameras.

"I'm watching you on my ceiling," Joseph told them. "You're going to miss the door if you don't adjust your course."

"Use your hand to redirect the coolant exhaust," Amanda suggested. "You should be able to steer a bit better that way."

"Ow! Jeez! Even through the suit, that's too cold!" he screamed.

Joseph laughed uncontrollably for a few moments, then said, "What do you expect? When a gas expands, it cools."

"I guess Amanda was getting back at me for that crack over lunch yesterday," Mark said.

"Whoa!" Joseph exclaimed. "You're close to the door. Point that thing towards the ship and try to slow down. You're coming in *way* too fast."

"We can't," Mark replied. "We're out of pressure."

Joseph wished Mark could see him mouthing the words *I told you so* inside the makeshift sick bay.

"Okay, I have an idea," Joseph said. "Take the empty pressure cylinder from your back and throw it towards the ship as hard as you can. That should reduce your momentum a bit."

He threw it. A small section of the force field politely shut down with a crackle to let it through, and the canister slammed around the interior of the shuttle a bit before coming to rest on the ground just below the aft environmental controls console.

"It's not enough," Mark said. "We're still coming in way too fast."

"Okay, we're ready for you," Joseph replied. "Computer, on my mark, drop the rear door shield. *Five... four... three... two... one... MARK!*"

The computer dutifully complied by removing the exterior force field entirely, resulting in an explosive eruption of air from the inside of the ship's makeshift airlock. The rush of pressurized gas shook the ship harder than a missile strike, but it also slowed the pair's descent enough that when they hit the interior wall with a thud, it was only a mild thud.

Then the alarm went off.

"Suit breach," the computer said. "Oxygen supply exhausted."

Joseph watched the scene unfold on camera. Amanda's helmet suddenly fogged up, and she made a choking gesture, grasping at her throat.

"Computer," Joseph shouted, "emergency override of environmental controls. Restore the force field and oxygen to that area. Now!"

"Unable to comply," it replied. "Environmental controls are malfunctioning."

"Computer, raise a field across the door," Joseph screamed again.

"Unable to comply. Power reserves low."

"Then close the door!"

"Closing door," it answered.

Twenty seconds later, the ship shook slightly as the giant door slammed shut. As soon as the area was sealed, Mark ran over and opened the interior door. He was promptly knocked down on his posterior from the pressure change as air quickly rushed in to fill the vacuum.

Amanda coughed as she pulled her helmet off, rubbed her eyes, and hit Mark squarely in the jaw. "Damn, that hurts," he said as he crumpled to the deck.

"Oh Jim," Amanda muttered. "You're next."

***

"WELL, you're looking better," Mark told Joseph. "I'm removing the restraints, but there's no way I'm letting you EVA again. Take it easy. I can't do anything about your injuries, so try not to make them worse."

"What about Amanda," Joseph asked.

"She's fine, but she can't EVA because there's only one working suit. I'm going out there to reconnect and patch the hose myself. Wish me luck, guys."

Mark walked into the next room.

After he left, Joseph began checking the environmental controls. "Wow! This is an easy one," he said proudly. "It's just a blown fuse."

A few moments later, the environmental control system for the aft compartment came online. Twelve minutes later, Mark walked back in, a giant smile on his face.

"Well, everything is back in place," Mark said. "Let's see how those engines are doing."

***

As they entered the bridge, the lights brightened from night mode to day mode. Mark sat down at the main console and pressed a few buttons.

"Nothing's working," he said. "The engines won't come online."

"Try overriding the safeties on the plasma flow limiters," Joseph replied.

"What are you talking about?" he replied.

One thing Joseph realized about Mark was that he didn't have a good grasp of engine operation. He wondered if he had a good grasp of anything, but kept that thought to himself... mostly.

"Well, I see you don't know the meaning of the word patient," Joseph said. He wondered if he knew the meaning of the word "simian".... "It's locking you out because the main fuel tank is missing."

"This is really a very interesting lecture, Joseph, but get to the point."

Mark must have been an impatient kid, Joseph thought. *Clearly, he's the sort of guy who always gets his way and doesn't care what other people think of him.* Joseph wondered if that would make him a good leader or just an asshole. He considered asking, but thought better of it.

"It's really simple, my simian friend. I'll do it from here."

Mark bristled visibly at the remark. *Bet he's gonna look it up later*, Joseph mused.

Joseph keyed in the appropriate sequence on the console to override the flow regulator safeties, and a moment later, the ship was once again filled with the reassuring whine of engines powering up.

"Nice job, Joseph," Mark said.

Two seconds later, the engines powered down again.

"Sheesh!" Joseph exclaimed. "This is going to be a long day."

"Find a way to fix it," Jim ordered, then turned and left the bridge.

Wait a second. Last I checked, I outranked that little prick, Joseph thought.

"Wow. What a prick," Amanda whispered.

Joseph smiled at the timing. "The left engine is history. The plasma manifold collapsed entirely. Any thoughts on how to get us out of this?"

"Throw Jim out the airlock?" Amanda offered.

"Well, it's easy momentum," Joseph replied, smirking.

"Can we limp along on one engine?" Amanda asked.

"With all the hull damage, the shearing stress could rip us in twain," he replied, "but it's worth a shot."

Joseph disabled the left engine entirely with a few key-presses.

"Cross your fingers," he said, laying in a course.

As he reached for the button to engage the remaining engine, a chime sounded.

"Cantrell to Harcliffe... come in, Harcliffe," the intercom sounded.

"Harcliffe here," Joseph replied.

"Harcliffe, this is the shuttlecraft Cantrell," the man said. "We noticed you didn't look so good, so we thought we'd offer you a tow back to the nearest base."

With those words, Joseph and Amanda breathed a collective sigh of relief.

***

ONCE again, the doors of the shuttlecraft Harcliffe crept slowly open in the shuttle bay of Terran Command Station. The rest of the crew departed through the rear hatch while

Amanda helped Joseph limp one step at a time through the side hatch and down the stairs.

"You okay?" Amanda asked once they had reached the deck.

"I will be, I think," he replied, "as soon as I get off this leg."

And so, as they stood on the threshold between the shuttlecraft and the space station, Amanda and Joseph stared into each other's eyes once more; thus, this unlikely duo stepped back from the precipice—one path taken, another shunned—one door opening, another closing—and all they knew for sure was that their lives would never be the same.

Chapter Eleven

A few weeks later (January 5, 2391)

"ADMIRAL on the bridge!" the ensign shouted as Admiral Skylarov walked out of the lift onto the command deck of Terran Command Station's C&C. Amanda rose to attention. Joseph, his leg still in a splint, just spun his chair around.

"As you were," the admiral instructed.

They resumed their usual activities. Across the room, an engineering tech plugged a new circuit board into the underside of a console, then cursed loudly as smoke poured out of it within seconds.

"Sir," a nearby ensign bellowed.

"Yes, ensign," the admiral replied testily.

"We've been having some electrical problems up here today, and," the ensign said boldly, "with all due respect to the admiral, this is probably not the safest place for you to be right now."

"With all due respect to the ensign," Skylarov replied, "this admiral will go wherever he wants to go."

"Sir, yes sir!" the ensign shouted, his face suddenly turning an even whiter shade of pale than its usual pallor.

"Relax, ensign," Admiral Skylarov replied. "I'm about to send some of you on an important mission. Carlos, Sanderson, Jenkins, my ready room at 1500 hours."

"Admiral?" Joseph asked.

"Yes, Lieutenant?" he replied.

"Won't they need an engineer?"

"An engineer with a broken leg?" the admiral chided. "I can't believe they cleared you for duty."

Joseph sighed. He would gladly follow Amanda to the ends of the earth if he could, but somehow the Admiral never thought of him as black-ops material.

"Sir, no sir. It's not broken. I just twisted it while rock climbing," Joseph lied. "The doc said not to walk on it for another day or so. Besides, with the repair job that the tech is doing over there, this is the last place *I* want to be right now...."

At least he doesn't know about the concussion or the broken ribs, Joseph thought.

The admiral, in an unusual burst of brilliance, replied by asking, "And you think you can handle this mission?"

"I'm not sure, sir. I don't know what it is," Joseph retorted.

"Well put, lieutenant," he answered. "My ready room, 1500 hours."

"Sir, yes sir," Joseph replied.

"Oh, and one last thing," the admiral added. "Since this mission is considered low-risk, you'll be training one of our cadets, Mary Bergstrom. She will be arriving this evening. I trust you'll brief her on the mission once she arrives."

"Understood, sir," Amanda said with a shudder.

"Dismissed."

***

Amanda sat at her favorite table in the Crew's Quarter. Around her, officers and enlisted men and women wandered from shop to shop sampling their wares, while a group of schoolchildren followed their teacher and a young cadet on some sort of tour. For a moment, Amanda almost felt like she was on exhibit, but she brushed it off.

Joseph arrived a moment later with their lunch. Despite her eagerness, Amanda politely waited for him to sit down before speaking.

"So, what sort of mission do you think Admiral Skylarov is sending us on?" Amanda asked mere microseconds after he hit the chair.

Joseph shrugged. "He said it was low risk, so I'm thinking it's probably some sort of transport mission."

Amanda nodded.

She tried to study Joseph's body language, but it betrayed nothing of interest.

"Do you trust him?" she asked.

"Who? Skylarov?"

"Yeah."

Joseph bristled a bit.

That's something, Amanda thought.

"The man doesn't seem to like me much," Joseph noted, "or you, for that matter."

Amanda laughed. "My father can't stand the guy—not that he's ever said anything, but I can tell."

Joseph nodded.

"I guess he doesn't like me because of what happened on Stavromula Beta," Amanda added.

Joseph laughed.

"He ordered us on a suicide mission with no hope of success," Amanda continued.

Joseph's smile quickly faded.

"I refused to take my team in. In the end, the review board said that I made the right call given the information I had on the ground, but he never forgave me for disobeying orders."

"I see," Joseph replied.

"I'm not sure I want this mission, Joseph," Amanda said, "and I'm not sure you do, either."

Joseph nodded grimly, then pointed at the viewscreen across the room.

> "In Terran Alliance news," the anchorwoman said, "Earth has a new satellite defense network. Christened 'DefSat', the satellites are designed to protect Earth from hostile ships and weapons."
>
> "On the Colonial front, there was more fighting near the CEA border as skirmishes broke out on two member worlds. The targets, identified only as high-ranking Terran officials, were quickly escorted from the strike zone and taken to a safe location on a nearby world. Terran warships arrived minutes later and quelled the fighting. No civilian casualties were reported."
>
> "We'll have more news at the top of the hour. You're watching TANN, the Terran Alliance News Network, with news updates every hour on the hour."

***

Dawn rose slowly over Lenora Prime, the glittering red glow moving like a wave across the desert wasteland. They always say that after a nuclear war, all that would be left alive are the cockroaches. On Lenora Prime, even the cockroaches had long since packed up and gone home. Only the winds and the sand remained—that and two large steel doors.

***

"Lenora Prime," Admiral Skylarov announced. The display screen beside him showed a beautiful tree-lined mall with a reflecting pool in the middle and an old courthouse at one end. "Once the crown jewel in an interplanetary alliance of colony worlds."

The image on the screen changed to show a barren desert strewn with crumbled fragments of shattered stone and concrete that were once parts of buildings.

"Now, a lifeless pile of sand," the Admiral intoned.

The image on the screen changed again. This time, the metal doors were in full view.

"But make no mistake," Admiral Skylarov told them. "Even though it has been uninhabited for almost three decades, on this planet of shifting sands and 120 degree heat, a few buried treasures still lie hidden."

A new image appeared on the screen. It was an object that none of them could quite identify—some sort of red crystal surrounded by a metallic frame.

"Does anyone know what this is?" the Admiral asked.

"Is it some kind of jewelry?" Kurtz asked.

"It looks like a data crystal to me," Amanda replied.

"My vote is doughnut hole punch," Ensign John Carlos suggested jokingly.

Not to be outdone by someone as crude as John, Lieutenant Jennifer "Jen" Sanderson offered a more radical idea. "I'm thinking it's a marital aid."

"No, no, no, and dear lord, no," Admiral Skylarov replied. "This crystal, an Ackerman crystal, is part of a weapon—a very dangerous weapon—a device so powerful that it could destroy an entire planet in a single blaze of glory."

"Admiral," Kurtz asked, "is that what happened to Lenora Prime?"

"It's unclear if the weapon was ever finished," the Admiral answered, "and no. No one is quite sure what happened to the people of Lenora Prime. They all just... vanished."

"Vanished?" Kurtz repeated, puzzled.

"Gone. Just like that," Admiral Skylarov replied, snapping his fingers for effect.

The room was left in stony silence.

Chapter Twelve

The next day (January 6, 2391)

JOSEPH's head hurt. It wasn't a sinus headache kind of hurt. It wasn't an "I walked into a low-hanging support beam" kind of hurt, either. More importantly, it wasn't an "I drank too much and I'm regretting it this morning" kind of hurt, which was a relief. He didn't remember drinking the night before, and those are the worst kind of headaches. No, he didn't hurt enough for that.

And so he shook it off and sat up on his cot in his new quarters. He wondered if any of his stuff was left in his old quarters or if it had all been blown into space. When they returned from this mission, he might just have to put on an EV suit and go see for himself.

Not exactly your everyday move, he mused as he pulled on his uniform and crammed his shoes on. As usual, he was running about twelve minutes late.

Now where is that muffin I put out for breakfast? And what is that damned beeping noise? Oh. My alarm clock, he realized. He reached over, grabbed it, threw it against the wall, and went back to sleep.

***

THE room beyond the open door was black as pitch. Amanda pondered the expression, wondering if that was politically correct, then remembered that pitch was an archaic name for coal, and brushed the thought aside. Staring at the darkness, she stood there in the doorway for a moment, wondering if she had the right room.

"Computer, lights," she said harshly.

Joseph sat bolt upright as the blinding fury pounded at his skull. "Wha... what happened?"

"I'd say the alarm clock monster got another one," she replied jokingly. "Come on. We're supposed to be in the docking ring for our final briefing in twelve minutes!"

Joseph started moving, his head still throbbing, but somewhat more in control of his actions than a few moments earlier. Amanda pulled him to his feet, and he pulled back. For a moment, she lay atop him on the cot.

"Not now," Amanda said, giggling. "We have to go, Joe." They both giggled again. "Come on," she whined, pulling him out of bed yet again.

Ten minutes and a quick food slot breakfast later, they headed out towards docking bay three.

Chapter Thirteen

0830 hours

THE two working downspots cast harsh shadows on the controls of the Hawk's Breath as they entered, an eerie stillness filling the air, the inky blackness of space sprawling like an armchair quarterback upon the viewports beyond.

The Hawk's Breath was a mid-sized craft—large enough for a crew of thirty or so—with little in the way of armament, minimal shielding, and relatively poor maneuverability. What made it powerful was its class 5 folding drive. It would come in handy given the lack of a working folding gate near Lenora Prime. Of course, that meant a day-long trip to the outer reaches of the solar system to avoid interfering with civilian traffic at the Earth and Mars gates, but Joseph didn't mind the break.

Joseph had learned the basic concept behind folding technology at a young age, thanks largely to his grandfather, James. When James Kurtz was teaching, he could make even the most technologically clueless person understand it.

I prefer to describe spatial folding in terms of things that already occur in nature, he'd say in his deep German accent. *Think about the sun. Space is curved in the presence of its strong gravitational field. It's like stretching a piece of wet paper around a globe. Draw a line that appears to be straight, and when you take the paper away, you see that the line is really curved.*

So imagine, he'd continue, *that instead of drawing a line, you put a piece of double-stick tape on the paper, and instead of just bending the paper a little bit, you instead bend it all the way back until it touches itself and the piece of tape. When you pull the paper apart again, if you applied enough force, the tape has about the same chance of staying stuck to either end of the piece of paper.*

It's the same way with space, he'd say. *If you fold it so that your ship exists in two places at once, it has an equal probability of sticking in either place. Then you simply repeat until it sticks in the right place. As long as you don't fall off both sides, land on the floor, and get stepped on by a passerby, you're okay.*

Ah, the memories. Joseph longed for the days spent with his grandfather in a ship not unlike this one. The Kend'hara was, of course, light years away right now—his grandfather was visiting his brother, Uncle Sid, on Siratkis Prime—but the ship reminded him of the Kend'hara anyway.

Kend'hara... translated literally, it meant "hands offered", though most people would use it to mean "hands outstretched" or "open arms". The ship was once built to usher in a new era of peace, but it quickly became the greatest obstacle to that peace. In its final days as a warship, it destroyed dozens of outposts and leveled three worlds before it arrived in orbit around Lenora Prime.

History did not record what happened next. It was a moment lost to time. There were messages sent from the ship, of course, and the ship's logs were mostly intact... up until they all just suddenly stopped.

As far as Joseph was concerned, however, very little of the Kend'hara's history was particularly remarkable until his grandfather found it adrift in space. The Kend'hara's last message was still stuck in Joseph's mind, though. It was spoken in the language of the Nivitian sect, the ancient Lenoran dialect Hit'ui. He couldn't quite shake the feeling that it meant something.

> "Sic Kend'hara i'michlus't vi yu grecht. Sic Kend'erus vi vey inacht. Frecas sol vey grecht. Oc'flieme, sepra, fliecht ste'gats frecasse. Ic nule vey carus. Ic Kend'hara fi erust."
>
> "With open arms for to welcome, we greet you. With arms closed, we lay ourselves down. Only darkness greets us. One light, distant, shining upon darkness' gate. And nothingness surrounds us. And open arms forever close."

Chapter Fourteen

January 7, 2391

It was three in the morning when the radio crackled suddenly to life. If experience had taught her anything, Amanda mused, it was that these sorts of surprises were rarely good news.

Despite the noise, the voice on the other end was crisp and clear, its resounding baritone voice saying, "Terran Command to Hawk's Breath, come in Hawk's Breath, over."

"Terran Command, this is Hawk's Breath. Call sign TEC-7072. Please authenticate," she replied.

The voice at the other end answered her promptly, which startled her until she realized that they were just a stone's throw from an outpost. "Terran Command, call sign TCS-1254. We have an urgent message in the forward chain awaiting final delivery."

"Send it through," she commanded.

***

Joseph wondered what could be so important that Amanda would wake him at 0300 hours, but it sounded urgent, so despite his better judgment, he lifted his head, acknowledged the request, and went promptly back to sleep.

***

It was 0600 hours before Joseph woke up again. He had a feeling in the pit of his stomach like he'd forgotten something. Did he have an early morning comm meeting? *No, that was yesterday*, he thought, *and the ship systems review is tomorrow. Nothing today.* He quickly dismissed the thought and went on with his daily routine.

As he entered the mess hall, though, he knew something was wrong. Amanda was waiting with a commpad. Hesitantly, Joseph took the pad and pressed the "play" button, wondering what sort of surprise awaited him... knowing that it could not be good.

Chapter Fifteen

"I don't have much time," he said.

The old man barely resembled the man Joseph knew as his grandfather, the years and the distance having taken their toll.

"We're under attack by a colonial raiding party," he continued. "They've already looted three decks. We don't have a full crew. We weren't expecting an attack. The Kend'hara is an old ship."

When he heard that name, Joseph's heart sank. Any questions he might have had about the identity of the man on the screen were gone, and, he suspected, so too was his grandfather.

"It isn't in any condition for a battle, and I'm not sure how much more she can take. Joseph, my grandson, I just wanted you to know that I love you."

A loud crashing sound echoed in the distance, accompanied by a look of shock on his grandfather's face. "They're here!" he said. "I love you, Jo...."

The image on the commpad was replaced by static briefly before it went dark.

"I'm sorry, Joseph," Amanda said.

Joseph held her in silence.

Chapter Sixteen

That afternoon (January 7, 2391)

THE Lenoran system was somewhat unusual in that was a habitable system with two suns. The main sun, Lenora Major, was a neutron star—a red giant that had gone supernova and collapsed millions of years earlier. The second sun, Lenora Minor was basically just a gas giant, but it put out enough radiation that scientists classified it as a binary star system, despite the relatively large distance between the two bodies. Theorists speculated that Lenora Minor might actually have been formed in part from the remnants of Lenora major after its collapse.

Because of the energy emitted by the two suns, the largest of Lenora Minor's moons, Lenora Prime, was warm enough to sustain life. Barely. A thick ozone layer protected the moon from the radiation that bombarded it every time it went through the ring of debris left by the explosion of Lenora Major. However, this left the average surface temperature at about 12 C (54° F).

The moon's former inhabitants weren't the only things missing now, Joseph noted. The ozone layer had been all but depleted from reactions with the exhaust from large transports, and the moon's surface was mostly dead from the constant solar radiation. The surface temperature was close to 50 today (122°F). You could quite literally fry an egg in the rarified atmosphere just by cracking it on a rock, and on a really hot day, you could boil one. It wasn't paradise, but they had seen worse.

Joseph felt numb all over as they entered a parking orbit around Lenora Minor. Orbiting Lenora Prime was tricky business because of the proximity of the gravity wells of a large gas giant and a very dense dwarf star. It would be tricky even without the radiation from the debris ring wreaking havoc with their sensors.

Because of the extreme difficulty of orbital insertion, few craft ever actually attempted to directly enter orbit around Lenora Prime, and those that did usually regretted it. For that reason, they would not enter orbit around Lenora Prime using a standard orbital insertion. Instead, by placing themselves in a relatively high parking orbit around the smaller sun, they could then make a slight change in their orbit and fly by the moon in a sort of figure eight orbit, ending in a stable orbit around the moon with relative ease.

***

AMANDA had watched Jen make this flight a thousand times in the simulator, but nothing could quite prepare her for the enormity of Lenora minor out the front viewport. It was truly a thing of beauty—a star, a planet, a breathtaking swirl of shimmering light in every color of the rainbow.

Even though it did not glow brightly, it emitted a great deal of energy, a warmth that she could almost feel, even here within the cold steel walls of the Hawk's Breath.

That's silly, she thought to herself. She knew intuitively that the ship's shielding would block out any of the star-planet's radiation long before it could reach her, but still that feeling of warmth—of energy—of power beyond her wildest dreams—still persisted.

As the ship settled into its final figure eight orbit, Jennifer wiped her brow.

"Joseph?" Amanda said.

"What's up?" he replied as he stepped through the door from the adjacent mini-kitchen.

"You leave for the surface in thirty minutes. Don't be late. We only get one launch window every twelve hours, so if you aren't ready, they'll have to leave you behind with me." She smiled with full teeth as soon as she said it.

"Not that he'd mind," John added.

Joseph glowered at him in reply, then turned and left for his quarters, a look of sheer exasperation on his face. John followed shortly thereafter.

Once she was alone, Amanda turned on the viewscreen and watched another newscast.

> "Sketchy news reports are coming in from the front line in the new war of independence on Spelicus 7. Spelicus 7 is a CEA member world whose leaders recently voted to join the Terran Alliance, causing utter turmoil—looting, rioting in the streets, protest marches, death threats, terrorist bombings, and even a small nuclear device detonated near the Inville City Center."
>
> "The situation on Spelicus and the recent space battles in the nearby Perseus system are just a few outward signs of a region in chaos."
>
> "The resumed fighting does not bode well for the residents of the other systems in the Chataris [chah-TAH-ris] sec-

tor. The Urigal and Trinity systems are already experiencing civil unrest, though their governments claim to have the situation under control. And of course, the Lenoran system, uninhabited for decades, has recently come under scrutiny because of rumors that it may house a secret CEA research base."

"As always, we'll have more information as it becomes available. You're watching TANN, the Terran Alliance News Network, with news updates every hour on the hour."

Chapter Seventeen

The next day (January 8, 2391)

THE door to the launch deck slid open with a swish as Joseph neared. Beyond it, he saw Jen and John standing by the mini-shuttle waiting for their final mission briefing. As Joseph stepped forward, Amanda walked in right behind him. He took a few steps, paused, and suddenly realized he wasn't alone. He turned.

"I hate it when you do that, Mand."

She just giggled at him while Jen and John turned to see what was causing the commotion.

"What's the plan, commander?" Jen asked.

"The computer's automatic guidance is programmed with your flight plan," Amanda replied. "If that goes out, there's a paper copy of the course corrections taped to the side window."

"If that goes out, I'll fix it," Joseph told her.

Amanda snorted in reply. "We think the crystal is in a bunker topside near those doors. The writings on the door may provide some clue as to its whereabouts. Use any tools at your disposal to locate the crystal and bring it back safely."

"And what if the writings lead us underground?" Joseph asked.

"We'll cross that bridge when we come to it, Joe. Remember," Amanda warned, "your mission is to study the writings around the doors, not to go exploring."

Joseph started walking towards the door, then remembered that he needed to ask about the orbital period. "Commander," he asked, turning to face her once more, "about our communications blackout status...."

"Standard ionization blackout while landing," she replied. "By the time you reach the ground, we'll be below your horizon, so we'll be out of radio contact for about two hours while we finish flying around the back side of the moon."

"So if my math is right," Joseph told her, "you'll be dark for six hours out of every twelve."

Amanda promptly corrected him. "Five hours, fifty-three minutes out of every twelve hours, thirty-three minutes, to be exact. There's some ducting as the ship gets close to the horizon. The good news is that Lenora Minor is in a solar minimum, so at least we don't have too much radiation to worry about. Still, the ion storms in the upper atmosphere can make radio communication difficult, so we should schedule our check-ins when I'm directly overhead to make sure we can punch through the interference."

"So where do we sign up?" Jen joked nervously.

Just then, the door to the pod bay swooshed open and a young girl stepped in.

"Mary, you're just in time," Amanda said.

Joseph groaned. Mary was a first year cadet, training to be a pilot. *Sweet kid,* he thought, *but so naïve.* He had a feeling she would learn a few things this trip. He truly hoped he was wrong.

Chapter Eighteen

"THREE minutes to launch," Amanda announced over the comm system. Joseph felt strange about being in command of this part of the mission, but he figured if anyone could take care of herself in a ship as complex as the Hawk's Breath, it was Amanda.

In a way, he was kind of glad that she stayed behind, out of harm's way. On the other hand, he had been looking forward to spending more time with her, and now they were about to be separated by an atmosphere halfway burned off by a gas giant. Joseph sighed.

"Begin final preflight checks," Joseph ordered.

"Main propulsion, check," Jen announced. "Secondary propulsion... fluctuating. Checking pressure levels. They're within spec. Might be a stuck routing valve solenoid. Let's try a system reset and see if the fault clears itself. Done. Secondary propulsion online and within spec. Comm system, check. Steering thrusters, check. Fuel supply, check."

"Water tanks, check," John told them. "Emergency rations, check. Four EV suits, control systems charged, tested, and verified. Pressure seals, check. Eight O_2 tanks charged and tested. Emergency O_2 cylinders, check. Hand scanners, check. Weapons, check. Ammo, check. Emergency radio, check. Portable generator and lights, check."

"Nav system, check," Mary said. "Aileron control, check. Rudder control, check. Braking flaps, check. Braking thrusters, check. Water buoyancy system, check. Landing gear, check. Ejection system armed, check."

Joseph nodded his approval.

"Looks like you're ready to go," Amanda told them over the comm system. "Clear to depart in one minute. Close your hatch."

Joseph stood up, walked to the back of the shuttle, and closed the rear hatch, then turned a crank to lock it closed and to ensure a complete seal against the vacuum of space. After performing a positive pressurization test, he walked back into the cabin and said, "Strap in everybody. It's gonna be a bumpy ride."

"We show door sealed," Amanda told them. "We are evacuating the pod bay now."

Joseph recognized the deep thrumming sound as six giant fans began drawing most of the air out of the pod bay. They would still end up losing a lot of air when the doors opened, but because the pod bay doors opened inwards, they had to minimize the pressure difference as much as possible in order to even open them at all.

Although such a design reduced the amount of air wasted, Joseph knew the real reason behind it. A few decades earlier, a dozen troops were killed when a computer error caused the pod bay door to open outwards unexpectedly. The ship's small crew was decimated.

By opening the doors inwards, the motors had to fight the pressure difference between the pod bay and the vacuum of empty space outside. The pressure difference was enough that the motors were unable to break the seal without first evacuating most of the air, adding nearly a minute in which the crew could evacuate into pressure pods or through one of the airlocks into the ship's main hull.

Regardless, Joseph would recognize that thrumming sound anywhere. He was just glad that, unlike the last time he heard it, he was still able to breathe. As the air grew thin in the pod bay, the thrumming grew ever more quiet, until at last the only real vibration was being carried through the metal floor of the shuttle pod itself.

In keeping with protocol, Amanda shut off the pod bay lights before opening the doors as a final notice to any crew who might be working in the bay in EV suits. As the pod bay plunged into blackness, only the dim lights of the shuttle controls remained.

Even through the thin atmosphere, Joseph could still hear the giant clunk as the door mechanism unlocked and began its slow glide inwards a moment later. Unlike crew doors, which swung at an angle, the pod bay doors moved straight inwards, then slid apart sideways. This allowed air to escape initially, but prevented any large, improperly stowed cargo from flying out with it.

Slowly now, the doors began to slide apart, the bright light that reflected off the moon's red, sandy surface shining between them in a narrow vertical slit like a cat's eye at noon. As the doors spread wider, they could see the moon's surface through the cockpit's rear windows, its lakes and rivers now dry, its once vast oceans reduced to mere puddles.

"Shuttle Omicron One," Amanda announced, "final checks?"

"Omicron One prepped and ready for launch," Joseph replied.

"Stand by for suborbital insertion," Amanda told them.

The gravity generator started up with a whine and a thrum, the engines powered up with a scream and a rumble, and the cockpit lights came on with a flicker. Mary smiled,

Joseph grimaced with worry, and Jen just stretched out and kicked back for the ride.

Chapter Nineteen

SUBORBITAL insertion—Joseph thought it was perhaps the strangest thing about piloting a mini-shuttle. In order to reduce the shuttle's energy expenditure, the shuttle was actually launched out of the ship backwards. The pod bay was at the rear of the ship, and the mini-shuttle faced the same direction as the ship. By propelling it at a substantial speed in reverse, the mini-shuttle was no longer at orbital velocity, and so its orbit would quickly decay, and it would land.

Because the mini-shuttle's mass was small relative to the ship, this maneuver had little impact on the larger ship's trajectory by comparison, and its course could be corrected with minimal effort. However, this reduced the fuel that the shuttle had to carry for its retrorockets.

Of course, the gravity drive made that largely moot these days, he noted. Still, the ships were built to accommodate older shuttles. Besides, the power savings still meant weeks worth of extra energy on the ground.

Even though he fully understood the theory behind the design, it still always felt strange to Joseph when he found himself moving backwards out of a moving vessel. Oh well, he thought. Nothing we can do about it now.

"Suborbital insertion in ten seconds," Amanda announced. "Five... four... three... two... one... mark."

The crew held on to their seats as the ship lurched backwards. Despite recent improvements in gravity control, they were still subject to the larger ship's grav field for the first few milliseconds of the launch. Once the smaller ship's grav generator caught up with the sudden change in velocity, it adjusted its output, resulting in a slight jerk in the other direction. It was all quite disturbing to your equilibrium. *One of these days, I'll have to design an artificial gravity system with faster response time,* Joseph thought, *or maybe just better clock synchronization.*

"All systems nominal," Mary reported. "We have a course correction coming up in just a moment."

Jen replied, "Ionization blackout in three, two, one, now."

"Stand by for course correction one-three-six mark two-four," Mary told them. "Course correction in three, two, one, mark."

The ship shuddered, then shook wildly for a moment, finally stabilizing after a few seconds. Joseph was expecting the ride to be a little rough—it was well known that the constantly shifting solar winds caused atmospheric turbulence that made navigation difficult—but he wasn't prepared for this. "Ensign, report!"

"Lieutenant, we have a failure in one of our aft steering thrusters," John said. "It appears to have exploded. The computer is compensating."

"Lieutenant!" Mary interrupted, "We've just lost gravity drive, and port thrusters three and four are offline. We're in an unpowered descent at over 12,000 kph and accelerating rapidly."

Joseph quickly took the controls. "Computer, manual override, all systems. Route nav control to Mary's console, with Jen as backup." The computer replied with a beep. "Upper aft thrusters to maximum burn, and ready the lower aft thrusters. We'll have to bring this thing in tail down."

Mary's hands quickly ran across the console, changing the ship's attitude so that it was coming in tail-first. Joseph set the landing thrusters on maximum burn, and the ship's descent slowed somewhat.

"Lieutenant," Jen said, "we're still falling too fast. If we don't cut our descent speed in half, we'll burn up in the atmosphere."

"Mary, bring secondary propulsion online, and tie the controls so that they mirror primary propulsion," Joseph ordered.

"But sir," Mary interrupted, "the fuel system wasn't designed to handle that load."

Joseph grimaced at this rookie comment. She was right, of course, but they didn't have any other options. He shot back a reply. "It's like this: we can either break the rules and maybe blow up trying to slow this flying bathtub down a bit or we can burn up falling through the atmosphere. I don't know about you, but I'll take my chances."

"Enabling secondary propulsion," Mary told him with a sigh.

"Secondary propulsion firing," Joseph informed them.

"Speed is slowing," Jen reported. "Down to eight thousand kph. Six thousand. Four thousand. Twenty-five hundred. We're within spec. Thirty seconds until glide insertion."

This was where it got tricky. The mini-shuttle was designed to enter the atmosphere in a glide, but could also enter rear-first under counter-propulsion. They were doing the latter.

In order to land, of course, they needed to be horizontal. Unfortunately, the steering on the secondary thrusters was stuck, causing a slight rotation during descent. As a result, they were not only backwards, but also upside-down.

The aft thrusters could easily flip them over, but were not designed to turn the ship around.

They would have to spin the ship three or four times at an angle using variable thrust in the front and rear to line it up correctly. The timing would have to be perfect. If they went too far with the burn, they would hit the ground before they could get all the way around to try again.

Joseph's hands flew like lightning over the controls. "I'm setting us up for a four times around glide insertion. Give me a call."

The feeling of vertigo was intense as Joseph steered the craft in a seemingly uncontrolled spin.

Jennifer punched the information into the navigation computer. "Ten seconds," Jen told him. Joseph quickly enabled the flap, aileron, and rudder support and routed it to the control station to his right.

"Five seconds," Jen said.

Joseph reached over Mary with his other hand, grabbed the yoke in front of her, and held on for dear life.

"Three... Two..." Joseph let go of the thruster control and it centered itself.

"One." Joseph slammed the rudder stick hard to the right. The ship's wild rotation slowed, then stopped, perfectly parallel to the horizon.

"Jeeezus, Mary and Joseph, where'd you learn to fly like that?" John exclaimed.

Chapter Twenty

It's funny how there's no lack of flat landing strips in a desert wasteland. It's funny at least until you try to land on one and your landing gear sink up to your hull in sand. Taking off becomes a bit of a problem. Such was the case here on Lenora Prime.

"Okay, this is bad," John told them. "We've sunk about two feet into the sand. If we try a horizontal takeoff, we'll rip off the landing struts and part of the bottom of the ship with them, if we haven't already."

"Can't we do a vertical takeoff?" Jen asked.

"Not without thrusters," Mary answered. "And fuel. We're dead in the water."

"We're out of radio contact with the Hawk's Breath," Joseph told them. "In a couple of hours, we can call Amanda and she can request backup. Right now, we have a mission to carry out."

As Joseph jumped down from the back hatch to the sandy surface below, he had a bad feeling in the pit of his stomach. For a moment, he wondered if he'd recently eaten bad beef. On further thought, he *had* eaten beef for lunch. *That's probably it,* he thought. *No, that doesn't feel right.* Something was troubling him, and he wasn't sure what it was.

Mary came down next, portable O_2 canister in hand. John dropped a similar canister down to Joseph, then walked down the steps that conveniently decided to unfold about that time.

Damn, Joseph thought. *Why couldn't the steps have worked when I tried to extend them earlier?* Joseph sighed. *Something else that I have to fix once we're safely back aboard the Hawk's Breath....*

Jen followed John's lead. The steps retracted immediately after she stepped down, and the hatch closed ominously behind them. Joseph shivered.

Lenora Major began to rise in the west as they made their way across the sandy desert towards the buried doors. Joseph marveled at the beauty of the distant star. In a few short months, it would be obscured by the gaseous massiveness of Lenora Minor, and would not appear again during the day for decades. Because Lenora Prime was a small moon in a nearly round orbit around a gas giant, it was rare for the moon's orbit to be far enough out of the galactic plane for Lenora Major to be visible directly overhead (in the daytime, anyway), but even when the moon's orbit reached minimum inclination, it was visible in the early morning or late evening for a few weeks each Lenoran month (about 70 Terran days).

It was indeed a rare thrill to see Lenora Major overhead during the day from the Lenoran surface, and it was a beauty to behold; the bright white light refracted by layered gasses in the upper atmosphere created colored patterns that were utterly hypnotic, particularly when superimposed on the gaseous flares erupting from Lenora Minor's surface. *Nothing else in the universe could possibly compare,* Joseph thought.

It was against this backdrop that Joseph and his crew strode across the red desert landscape. Heavy activity was difficult in the rarified Lenoran atmosphere, so they had to stop periodically for an O_2 break, being careful to conserve oxygen in case they had to spend longer than anticipated. Of course, when they weren't in use, the tanks would slowly extract oxygen from the surrounding air, but when push came to shove, it was always better to have a full tank than an empty one, as Joseph had repeatedly pointed out during their mission briefing.

The ruins of the city of New Burma lay just ahead—little more than a pile of ash with scattered bits of rock and metal strewn about, the victim of an early bombing raid by Terran forces. The city was reportedly a front for a colonial doomsday weapon project—a project that, if completed, could have brought about the end of humanity. In an amusing twist, the Terran government was *also* operating a secret base in the area—in part to spy on the colonial team, but mostly because they could experiment freely with minimal oversight and equally minimal nearby population to put at risk.

Twenty-eight years later, the Lenoran system was a bit further inside the territory controlled by the Terran government. Because of a series of accidents, no one had yet recovered the Terran research project's sole creation, a six inch crystal of an obscure tritium polymer that was as yet unknown to modern science outside the military ranks (and a few research institutions under strict NDA). Even less was known about the days leading up to the termination of that research project....

For years, an Earth research team had studied the crystal, then suddenly were heard from no more. The crystal, the research team—indeed all remaining life on the planet—simply gone in an instant. Since then, twelve previous recovery missions had failed for a wide range of reasons, most of them ending tragically.

Joseph had a feeling this mission would be a success, though. Previous missions had often involved civilian personnel who had difficulty in the harsh environment that Lenora Prime presented. Two other early missions failed when the ships were attacked by raiding parties. The rest of the missions simply failed to find the rock. Unlike those missions, though, this mission was entirely composed of trained military personnel.

Joseph had a strong engineering background, despite his military rank. He was known in three systems for his piloting prowess, and spoke several languages, including the obscure language spoken by the Lenoran colonists, though he had little knowledge of its written form.

Jen was a skilled linguist with over a decade of training. She was also one of the best sharpshooters in the force. She set a record with 98% accuracy on the hardest test the academy had to offer—better than anyone before, better than anyone since.

John was the ship medic, with basic first aid and CPR training. He also knew his way around medical instruments. In a pinch, with the help of a training pad, he could handle most rudimentary emergency field surgery, though he tried not to make a point of it whenever possible.

And last, but not least, there was Mary.... Mary was the one big liability. She was a first year cadet on a training mission as part of the Piloting Corps. She had no field experience and very little formal training. She had been a pilot on a small moon cruiser for a couple of years before joining the corps, but otherwise was very much an unknown.

As they trudged across the sandy Lenoran desert, they could barely make out the cold, steel doors in the distance, sunken into the red Lenoran surface. By themselves, they were unremarkable—two steel doors, about twelve feet tall by four feet wide, at about thirty degrees from horizontal on the side of a sandy slope.

What made these doors interesting was the arched stone door frame into which they were recessed. Etched on the surface was information intended for the society that inhabited the planet when the Terran Command project team installed the doors. It was on these surfaces, inscribed in an obscure dialect of a largely dead language, that they hoped to find their answers.

As they scaled the sloped surface of the doors, Joseph studied the inscriptions. "This one looks like the sun, and this.... What is this?"

Jen stared at it for a moment. "It looks like it's a numbering system of some kind—maybe measured in miles or something. Hmm, this is strange. Look at this one over here."

Joseph suddenly was inspired. "It looks like the man is seeing the crystal from here. It must be a short distance. Maybe measured in feet or paces. If he can see it from here, that means that we're closer than we thought."

Jennifer answered, "Judging from the symbols I recognize, I think the number might be pronounced Nock-Tore."

"I think that symbol is an o, not a u, so the first part is pronounced like the o in look, Jen," Joseph told her. "It would be nuch, not nock, with a soft, glottal stop. The other one is also a u, but a long u sound like in the word cool. So that would be nuch-toor, which is twenty-eight."

Jen thought for a moment. "Twenty-eight paces straight below the bottom of the door?"

"Worth a shot," Joseph replied. He quickly marked off twenty-eight paces and began to dig. "There's concrete here just below the surface. And there's a hole in it." Joseph managed to quickly open the hole.

As Lenora Major continued to rise overhead, the shadows on the sides of the hole grew dim, until the sun was directly overhead for the first time in twenty-eight years.

Chapter Twenty-one

As the giant doors slid slightly open, a tiny crack of light shone within. It fell on ground that had not seen the sun in many moons, and reflected down the darkened halls of the Under Place. And deep within that inner darkness...

...something awoke.

Chapter Twenty-two

"I think something's moving," Joseph shouted over the noise. "It looks like... oh, my god.... The doors... are opening."

And then as suddenly as they started moving, they stopped again, barely open a crack.

"So now what?" Jen asked.

"I guess we keep looking," Joseph replied.

"Sir?" Mary interrupted.

"Yes, cadet?" he replied.

"If we want to make this check-in window, we need to head back to the ship now," she informed him.

Jeez, what a pencil pusher, he thought. *Maybe I should send* ***her*** *back just to get rid of her.*

Of course, he knew she was right. If they didn't start back towards the ship, they'd miss the communication window and would have to wait another 12 hours.

"Yeah, yeah, yeah," he muttered. "Okay, everybody, you heard the cadet. Let's get moving already."

***

"Joseph? Is that you?" Amanda asked.

"Ama..." the radio crackled. "can hear you... Over."

"Joseph?" she asked. "I can barely make you out. Over."

"...crash-landed... emergency oxygen... engines out.... -end help..."

"Joseph, you're breaking up. Repeat your last message. Over."

"We've crash... emergency oxygen is holding, but our engines are out... send help."

"Okay," she told them. "I'll call for backup. I have a message for you. Your aunt and uncle called. Let me patch it through."

She transmitted the encoded message.

"Thanks... anda."

"Have you had any luck in your mission?" she asked.

"...no key... mirrors... doors opened... explore... -ver"

"Don't go in there!" Amanda screamed.

"Roger," the radio coughed. A few moments of static followed. "We will conta... twelve hours if...."

And the radio went to static.

"Joseph!" Amanda cried. She flailed at the radio controls, but was unable to regain the signal. "Dammit!"

She sighed. She could only hope they had gotten the message. She knew what was beyond those doors, and God help them if they ventured below.

***

Meanwhile, on the surface....

"AMANDA. I can hear you, but just barely. Over," Joseph said into the microphone.

"Joseph... make... out. Over"

"Over the radio? Kinda kinky, don't you think?" Joseph smirked, then added "We're in bad shape down here. We crash-landed with a thruster failure. We have plenty of emergency oxygen, fortunately. No major damage, just engines out. I need you to send help."

Amanda's signal was rather weak. "... repeat...."

"I said we've crash-landed," Joseph told her. "Emergency oxygen is holding, but our engines are out. I need you to send help."

"Okay... call for backup...."

For a moment, the signal cleared up and Joseph could see Amanda clearly.

"I have a message for you. Your aunt and uncle called. Let me patch it through."

On the viewscreen, Joseph's uncle stood, his aunt slightly behind, as if they were standing right in front of him. Joseph's father, James Kurtz, Jr., was killed in battle when he was just an infant, and his mother, Allison died from complications in childbirth, so his Aunt Jenny and Uncle Frank had basically been like parents to him.

"Hello, Joseph? It's your old man. Listen, I stopped by Terran Command to see you, but they said you were out on a mission. When... back you'll have to tell... all about it. I hope you come back soon. I'll be waiting when you get here.... love... Joseph.... Kurtz out."

The screen went black for a moment, then Amanda's face reappeared, much grainier than before, then disintegrated into blocks of disjointed visual information, only coming together into a coherent image once every few seconds.

"Thanks, Amanda," Joseph said after her face reappeared.

"Have you had... luck in... mission?" the radio sputtered.

"Well, there's no key, but we found some sort of buried mirrors. When the sunlight hit them, the doors opened," Joseph said. "We were debating whether to explore further. Over."

The radio turned to static for a few seconds, then crackled to life. "...go in there!"

"Roger that," Joseph confirmed. "We're still trying to get the doors all the way open, but we'll try. We will contact you again in twelve hours if all goes well. Over."

Silence followed.

"Amanda? Amanda?"

Joseph hit the power switch. "It's no use. There's too much ionization from Lenora Minor," he told the crew.

"So what's the call," Jen asked.

"Our orders are to go underground," Joseph told them. "Pack your bags. I have a feeling it's gonna be a long day."

Chapter Twenty-three

THE sandstorm tore at their skin as they ambled back towards the mysterious doors; the sky overhead glowed a brilliant shade of orange through the dusty haze. As they approached the doors, something caught Joseph's eye.

"Is it my imagination, or are the doors farther open than they were when we left?" he asked.

The doors were just far enough apart for someone to slip through. Jen looked at him and grinned. "After you," she said.

"Ladies first," he replied.

She grimaced, stepped cautiously through the doors, and turned on a flashlight. Joseph followed her. Mary slipped in behind him. Suddenly, the doors slammed shut.

Joseph quickly reached down and grabbed a hand radio. "John? John? Are you okay?" he shouted.

"I'm fine," came the crackled reply, "but I'm kind of... outside."

Joseph took this in stride. "And we're..."

"Not," John said through the static.

Joseph decided to try to put a positive spin on the whole situation. “Well, then, congratulations. You’ve been elected our new communications officer.”

The rest of the group chuckled.

“That’s not funny, Joe,” John replied. “You guys get to rest in the cool comfort of that cave while I have to run back and forth across the hot desert to shout back at Amanda and tell her that you’re still stuck.”

“Think about it this way,” Joseph told him. “You get to sleep in a soft bed on the ship while we have to sleep on a cold concrete floor, and all you have to do is come check on us every twelve hours and tell Amanda that we’re still stuck.”

“I guess when you put it that way,” John said, “it could be worse.”

“Glad you see things my way,” Joseph replied.

With that, Joseph turned and headed deeper into the tunnel. “Come on. Follow me.”

As soon as they left the front passage, the outside doors slid open a crack.

Chapter Twenty-four

MORNING dawned as Lenora Major slowly crested the horizon, its velvety glow spreading across the sky. For a moment, the doors slid open an inch. Joseph rolled over groggily, mumbled "Huh", then promptly fell asleep again, oblivious to their motion. The others did not even stir.

Then, as quickly as they had opened, the doors closed again in silence, and the darkness returned.

***

JOSEPH stirred an hour later, an image flashing through his mind—that of the perpetual Lenoran twilight that had bathed the northern pole of Lenora Prime for nearly a decade now—an eerie red glow that never dimmed, never set, never rose.

The Lenoran system, he mused, must have been one of those truly freak accidents—that is to say, it was one of those arrangements that was so unlikely that it might lead you to suspect not only that a higher power exists, but also to suspect that said power has a sense of humor.

Like many moons, Lenora Prime orbited in a rather eccentric orbit—that is, highly elliptical. What made this particular orbit peculiar was that, over a few decades, the Lenoran month (defined as one orbit around Lenora Minor) varied in a slow cycle between 66 and 72 days (tending towards 72) because of the way that Lenora Prime's orbit was perturbed cyclically by the gravitational pull of Lenora Major. Right now, the Lenoran month was about 68 days.

The moon's orbit also slowly wobbled around Lenora Minor. Lenora Major (the distant sun) was usually hidden behind Lenora Minor except at night and near sunrise and sunset. For a few months every 28 years, though, it was close enough and at a high enough inclination to be visible directly overhead during the day near the northern pole, and 14 years later near the southern pole.

Joseph remembered reading in the mission notes that its maximum excursion was scheduled to occur in about three days, but thought nothing of it until now. One thing was certain: Joseph did *not* want to still be around in 28 years waiting to get out of this cave. Quite frankly, the whole thing made his head hurt even more, so he rolled over and went back to sleep.

Chapter Twenty-five

"Gamma Epsilon Three hailing the T.S. Hawk's Breath. Come in, Hawk's Breath. Over."

Amanda had a bad feeling in the pit of her stomach. Reinforcements were not due for two more days, and she knew it. She could only hope that whoever was calling didn't.

"Gamma Epsilon Three hailing the T.S. Hawk's Breath. Please respond."

The man at the other end was unfamiliar, and the ship's name doubly so. They didn't even appear to know how to hail the Hawk's Breath. The ship was the T.E.C. Hawk's Breath, for Terran Elite Command. The Terran Ship designation was reserved for civilian ships.

"Hawk's Breath, this is Gamma Epsilon Three. You are ordered to leave the area at once."

That sounded somewhat hostile. On the one hand, they could be friendly ships trying to warn her of danger, she thought, in which case she should reply. On the other hand, they could be colonial raiders. If they saw a one-man crew, she was as good as sushi.

Amanda knew that she could never effectively pilot a ship as clumsy as the Hawk's Breath and man the guns simultaneously, particularly against a ship as fast as the C-626 triaxial fighter that she could now see on her viewscreen.

No, it would be safer to let them think the crew had abandoned ship, since she stood a far better chance in a close range hand weapons battle. It might also provide just enough lead time to escape in a lifepod.

"Hawk's Breath, this is the Gamma Epsilon Three. You are ordered to stand down and leave the area immediately," the voice continued. "This is a Class 7 restricted area by order of Terran Command Section 13."

Section thirteen? What the hell is section thirteen? Jeez, I'm M.I., Amanda thought. *I should know these things. When did they make a section thirteen?*

"Hawk's Breath, please respond," the loudspeaker squawked. "If you do not respond in thirty seconds, we will be forced to assume your intentions are hostile and we will open fire."

Amanda's eyes lit up. It was a classic no-win scenario. She reached over, and opened a communications channel. "Gamma Epsilon Three, your call sign and identification not verified. Please authenticate."

"Hawk's Breath, our call sign is unimportant, and if you had been keeping up with the news, you'd know that," the man said. "This area has been reclassified as a demilitarized zone. No military ships are allowed to enter this sector for any reason."

"Sir," she replied, "we are on a rescue mission by order of Terran Intelli..."

He cut her off. "Your mission has just been rescinded, Captain Jenkins."

"Who the HELL are you?" she demanded.

"This is Admiral Archibald Gray of Terran Command, Section 13. You have your orders. Now leave immediately or I will be forced to open fire."

"I'm sorry, Admiral," she replied, "but I simply CANNOT be expected to just leave my crew on an alien planet without warning or explanation, on the orders of a supposed admiral who doesn't know the difference between the designation of a civilian and a military intelligence ship, without even so much as consulting with my superiors."

"Captain, let me address those concerns. Your designation is obscured by scorch marks. I won't ask what hit you because I don't think you'd tell me anyway. No, I can't tell you who we are or what we're doing here or why you have to leave. You cannot consult with your superiors because Terran Command Station has been destroyed. There's nothing left."

"I... I don't believe you," Amanda whimpered.

"Turn on the news."

When Amanda turned on the viewscreen and tuned to TANN, the images immediately brought her to tears.

> "Cleanup crews are working around the clock to pick up the debris and to ascertain exactly what happened Sunday night," a young female reporter said. "All that officials will say for certain is that an unknown ship was seen leaving the area just moments before the explosion. No suspects have been named in the incident, which is being described as a 'clear act of CEA terrorism' by Terran Intelligence officials."
>
> "On a more personal note, I'm sure we're all deeply moved by the images that we've seen over the past few days," she continued. "Many of us have friends or family who were stationed on Terran Command Station. Many more lost loved ones in its outer ring, which served as Earth's primary hub for interstellar

> travel, with millions of people moving through it every week."
>
> "Here at TANN, we have been particularly touched by this tragedy; our primary studio and our main news bureau were located aboard Terran Command Station. Many of the faces that you've grown to trust over the years are but memories now. Our thoughts and prayers are with their families and with all those who lost loved ones in this terrible tragedy."

Amanda turned the video feed off, opened a text news feed, and confirmed the story in detail. Terran Command Station destroyed, all hands lost, cause unknown.

"But I..." she began, her eyes suddenly hollow... empty... lifeless.

"You were just there. I know. A lot of things have happened in the last three days. The fleet has regrouped at checkpoint Tango-Echo-Four-Nine. I suggest you do the same. I'm sending your orders over now. I trust you can verify their authenticity."

A data stream encoded with the Terran Intelligence Agency seal appeared on her screen. "Roger that, Gamma Epsilon Three. We need to notify our ground personnel of our new orders and then we will depart immediately."

Amanda pressed a few buttons. The computer indicated that the twelve-hour communication window had already begun. "Computer," she asked, "increase transmitter to maximum gain."

"Acknowledged," came the reply.

"Hawk's Breath to Shuttle Omicron One, come in Omicron One."

Silence.

"Hawk's Breath to Shuttle Omicron One, come in Omicron One," she repeated.

Still silence.

"Omicron One, this is Hawk's breath," she said. "I don't know if you are reading this transmission. We have been ordered out of the area by Section Thirteen. Terran Command Station was destroyed yesterday with all hands lost."

She paused to choose her words carefully. "I don't have any information on the condition of Joseph's aunt and uncle," she said, "but I will try to keep you updated as information becomes available."

Amanda recoiled in horror when she remembered that Section Thirteen was probably top secret. For a brief moment, she wondered if she should have kept that part to herself, but it was too late for such thoughts now. What the heck, she thought. As long as she was giving away secrets, she might as well go for the big one.

"You should be able to link up with NavSat from the emergency evac shelters twenty-five kilometers due east of your landing site. We can keep in contact through that system. The access code for the shelters is 3-1-7-alpha-niner-gamma. It's black-ops, so report your position as Mars colony, and send all messages with my personal encryption key. We'll schedule communications on a seventy-two-Terran-hour rotation, beginning on my mark. Five seconds, four, three, two, one, mark."

"I'll send you an update the moment I know more about what's happening. I don't know when or how we'll be able to come back for you."

Her eyes watered as she tried to continue. "I... I..." She sniffed, shook her head, and wiped her eyes.

She paused, wondering whether to continue. After a moment, she regained her composure and added, "I love you, Joseph, and I *will* come back for you just as soon as I can. I promise. I'll see you soon."

She paused for a moment, then added, "This message repeats."

Amanda repeated her message to Joseph three more times, knowing it could be the last time he saw her. As she finished, she barely managed to speak the words "Hawk's Breath out."

She pressed a few more buttons. Through her tears, she saw the stars begin to shift towards blue as the Hawk's Breath accelerated out of the Lenoran gravity well, making its way once more across the cold of space towards Neptune's largest moon, Triton, where Terran Command had an emergency coordination center... checkpoint Tango-Echo-Four-Nine—Triton Station.

Chapter Twenty-six

As the radio clattered to life, John sat bolt upright. He could barely tune the signal now, with all the damage to the radio antenna caused by almost two days of sand storms on the surface, but he could make out just enough to know that the situation was dire.

"...essage repe.... cron One, this... Hawk's breath. I don't know if you are reading this transmission... ordered out of... area... Section Thirteen. Terran Command Station was destroyed yesterday... all hands lost. I don't have... condition of Joseph's aunt and uncle, but I will try to keep you updated as information becomes available...."

John was in a state of shock. Joseph's aunt and uncle are the only parents Joseph has ever known. How can I bring him such news? He slumped in his chair.

His momentary reverie was interrupted by a loud burst of static. John covered his ears and winced in pain for a moment before the safety system kicked in and lowered the volume.

"...link up with NavSat from the emergency evac shelters twenty-five kilometers due east of your landing site.... ...contact through that system. The access code for the shelters is 3-1-7-alpha-niner-gamma. ...black-ops... report... position... Mars colony, and... with my personal encryption... communications... seventy-two-Terran-hour rotation, beginning... minute ago. ...an update the moment I know more about what's happening. I don't know when or how... back for you."

The radio went eerily silent. John wondered for a moment if he had lost the signal permanently this time. He reached for the controls to try to pull the signal out of the noise, but then Amanda's voice continued.

"I love you, Joseph.... I *will* come back for you just... soon... I can. I promise. ...see you soon.... ...Breath out."

John just sat there in stony silence.

***

The next day (January 9th, 2391)

AMANDA woke up as the ship's folding drive powered down and the ship returned to normal space, still moving at a staggering speed.

"Computer, course heading?" Amanda asked.

"Course heading zero-two-six mark three-nine by two-one-zero mark five-four," the computer said, "at a speed of point three-four light."

Amanda cringed, then muttered, "The course is almost right, anyway."

She thought for a moment, then keyed in several dozen new commands. "Adjusting course to zero-two-six mark three-six by two-one-zero mark five-nine. Decreasing speed to point two-three light. Stand by with braking thrusters."

The computer chirped at her, then spoke. "Captain, entering solar system in five seconds."

"Braking to eighteen thousand kph," she replied, then adjusted a few more controls. "Computer, report speed."

"Four million kph," the computer replied. *About a quarter of the speed of light,* Amanda thought to herself. "Three million kph. Two million kph. One million kph. Five hundred thousand kph. Three hundred thousand kph. One hundred thousand kph. Sixty thousand kph. Forty thousand kph. Twenty-six thousand kph. Now at eighteen thousand kph."

It was moments like these that made Amanda glad for artificial gravity. The deceleration alone would otherwise have spread her in an atom-thick layer across the console. The mere thought made her shiver.

Amanda opened an encrypted comm channel. "This is Amanda Jenkins calling Triton Station control. Come in Triton."

"We read you, Hawk's Breath," the voice on the radio replied. "Make your way to docking bay three. We'll be waiting for you when you arrive."

With that, Amanda instructed the shuttle to perform an automated descent so that she could study the station out the window. Triton Station was built in a naturally occurring valley on the surface of Neptune's moon of the same name. Its thin atmosphere and minimal gravity (less than a tenth of Earth norm) made it an ideal location for landing ships that were simply too heavy to land on an average planet.

As the Hawk's Breath extended its landing struts and settled onto the metal deck, its ArtiGrav™[1] system shut down. Amanda found herself feeling a bit light, which she thought rather odd for an Earth base, but she quickly dismissed the thought, stood up from her chair, and walked towards the rear exit ramp.

---

[1]ArtiGrav™ is a trademark of Artificial Gravities, Inc. Used by permission.

With the press of a button, a ramp lowered from the rear of the Hawk's Breath to the floor below, and the rear airlock doors moved inwards, then parted. And there at the end of the ramp, much to her surprise, stood her father, Thomas Jenkins.

Chapter Twenty-seven

"AMANDA!" her father exclaimed, hugging her warmly. "Welcome to Triton Station! It's been a long time—what, three years?"

Her father, Tom, was an elderly British gentleman. He made it a point never to wear his uniform unless on duty in a public capacity or at an official function, which meant almost never. He stood there wearing a button-up blue shirt and navy blue pants that were slightly too long and brushed the floor as he walked.

"Three weeks, maybe four," she answered. *Nothing like a deep space mission to keep family apart,* she thought.

"Nothing like a deep space mission to keep family apart," her father said with a sigh.

Amanda was half expecting to hear *So, how have you been? How's your mother?* ...except that her mother had fallen ill and passed away while she was on a deep cover assignment near the galactic rim about a year earlier.

"So, how have you been? How's your..." Her father stopped, realizing his mistake immediately, and quickly ended the sentence with "work going?"

She knew what he meant, and shifted uncomfortably at the reference. “Fine,” she said, half smiling, half grimacing. “And you?” she asked. “How’s retirement treating you?”

“Oh, if only I were still retired,” he mused ironically. “When Terran Command Station was destroyed, we lost a lot of top ranking officers. Admiral Skylarov called up all the recent retirees and asked us to go back on active duty. One week. I was retired for one week....”

“Let me guess,” she countered, “you spent all of... what, ten seconds considering your family? And then you just ran off and rejoined the corps?”

He stood there with jaw agape for a moment before answering. “I’ll have you know that I discussed this at length with my wife before making my decision,” he said, “and we agreed that I should go where I was most needed.”

Amanda merely sighed. Her father was as stubborn as ever, she thought. Not that she expected anything less, of course.

“Look, Amanda,” he said, more softly this time, “I know things haven’t been easy for you since Angie... eh... your mother passed away. I just want you to know that I’m here for you. I’ll be in my quarters if you need anything.”

She smiled sadly and replied, “Thanks, Dad.” She paused for a moment, then added, “I should probably get to the orientation meeting.”

Her sentence was punctuated by a door opening nearby as a rather tall man entered in a captain’s uniform. “Ah, Captain Glasgow. Nice of you to join us. Amanda, you remember Rick.”

Amanda nodded her assent.

“I’ve asked him to give you a tour of the station and to answer any questions you might have about recent events,” her father continued.

She had only one. “What is Section 13?”

Her father stammered at this. Amanda knew he was hiding something. “Eh, uh, I don’t know what you’re talking about. Listen, Rick, fill her in on everything. I have an important meeting on C deck in three minutes."

Admiral Jenkins stumbled and nearly tripped over a small trash can as he neared the door. "I have to go," he said, pressing the door controls before making a swift exit.

"What was that all about?" Amanda asked.

"Section 13 is something we don't like to talk about," he answered. "The boat singers."

She recognized that phrase immediately, and a chill ran up her spine.

***

John paused for a moment to look around as he stepped down from the mini-shuttle onto the rough Lenoran landscape. The wind whipped dust into his face and stung his eyes, but he pressed on. He knew that he had to reach the cave entrance for his signal to reach Joseph and the rest of the team.

Visibility was particularly bad today. For the first time since they arrived, he actually put on his standard issue safety goggles, then quickly regretted it as the sand trapped against their rim rubbed against his face.

He felt a bit silly as he reached up and pressed a few buttons on the mini-shuttle to close its hatch. Tomorrow he'd start using the evac station for food, water, and shelter, he thought. If he never returned to the ship, why would it matter if the entryway got a little sandy? After all, it wasn't as though someone else were likely to stumble across it. But that was procedure—he was a stickler for procedure—so he closed the hatch anyway.

John found it somewhat comforting to hear the groan of the motors pulling the hatch shut as he walked away, followed by the obligatory clank as the locking mechanism engaged. He was surprised, then, when he heard an additional rustling noise. Startled, he turned, but saw nothing.

I'm just being paranoid, he thought. *No one else in his right mind would be down here in this weather.* Even still, he patted the sidearm in his jacket pocket reassuringly.

After walking a few more steps, he heard a cracking sound, this time directly under him. He looked down and brushed the sand away beneath his foot, revealing a T17-D antipersonnel mine.

With his final breath, John closed his eyes and waited for the inevitable.

Chapter Twenty-eight

The next morning (January 10, 2391)

"So, Amanda, what do you think of the place?" Rick asked.

The halls were decked in dark blue carpet with light blue-green walls, and were dimly lit with crude mercury vapor lighting, giving the entire place an underwater feel. The decor was accentuated by a row of brass canister lamps mounted on the walls every twenty feet or so with white spots aimed towards the ceiling and floor.

Entire sections of the walls contained thin aquariums that seemed to have been crudely retrofitted into what were once hallways. She wouldn't have been surprised to see duct tape holding the panels together.

"It's umm... nice," Amanda answered.

"Yeah, I think it looks like crap, too," he said, laughing lightly at the embarrassed smile that crept across her beet-red face.

It wasn't that the station was ugly—it was functional—but it wasn't to her taste. She was used to the relative comfort of her quarters on Terran Command Station, which was now a smoldering pile of twisted metal and concrete. Fortunately, most of her possessions were safe in a trunk on the Hawk's Breath or at her dad's house on Earth.

She still missed her music box. It belonged to her mother, who gave it to her as a graduation present when she finished her Terran Intelligence training. That was the last time they saw each other. A few days later, Amanda left on her first two-year deep cover mission. When she returned, her father sent her the news of her mother's death in a prerecorded message. After that, she had barely spoken to him until a few months ago.

"Whatcha thinkin' about, Mannie?" Rick asked.

She winced deep inside at that question. No one but her father had called her that since she was a child, and even he had not called her that in years. She hoped no one ever would again. Still, she supposed, Rick *was* an old family friend, so she decided to let it go. *This time.*

"Mmmm.... Nothing much," she replied. "Just wondering why I feel so lightheaded."

"It's probably the ArtiGrav," he told her. "It's set at oh-point-eight Gs. It was a compromise between Earth norm and the gravity at the Mars colonies. They have a hard time adjusting to our gravity, and if we adjusted to theirs, we'd have trouble going back, so they went halfway."

"Oh," she murmured. She paused for a moment to gather her thoughts, then asked, "So what happened... to my home?"

"I don't know much more than you do," Rick answered. "They'll tell us everything in the briefing at 1500 hours."

Amanda smiled.

It's 1300 hours now, she thought—*just enough time to grab a bite to eat and take a hot shower before the meeting.*

"Well, here are your quarters," Rick said. "Let me know if you need anything."

"Thanks," Amanda replied. She smiled for a moment, hugged him, went inside, and locked the door behind her.

***

SILENCE. It made not a sound as it slunk its way through the darkened cavern, its long tongue flicking in the air as its sticky feet clung to the damp walls. Its warm breath condensed in the cool air and fell to the ground as shimmering dew while its white teeth glistened in the dim glow of the emergency lights.

And there, in the dark, it waited....

***

THE passage descended into darkness before them, the light from their lamps disappearing eerily into the seemingly endless depths that lay ahead. As they neared the rim of a particularly deep chasm, Joseph stumbled and dropped his lantern; it fizzled and died as it clattered uselessly to the bottom of the hole. He quickly regained his foothold to avoid suffering the same fate.

Behind him, Mary crawled along, too terrified to walk.

Jen just shook her head and laughed at them from about thirty meters ahead. “Come on, you guys,” Jen chided. “I could move faster than that when I was three!”

“Give it a rest, Jen,” Joseph answered. “If you were stuck behind Mary without a lantern, you’d be going slowly, too.”

“Yeah, whatever,” she retorted, then stumbled over something. “Whoa!” she exclaimed.

“You okay, Jen?” Joseph asked.

“I’m fine, thanks,” she replied, “but I think you’ll want to see this. It looks like a chip from a calcium deposit.”

Joseph thought, then realized the significance. “If that came from a stalactite, then that would mean there’s water here.”

“My thoughts exactly,” she told him.

"Where was it, Jen?" Mary asked.

"It was right over he.... eee... EEEEE!" Jen screamed.

"What's wrong?" Mary asked, scrambling to her position.

Jen just pointed and stuttered, "Th... the... there."

Mary screamed. Jen screamed when Mary screamed.

"Boo," Joseph said.

Suddenly, Mary and Jen screamed again.

Joseph quickly looked around for the cause of their screams. That's when he saw it.

A human skeleton.

***

AMANDA sat at a communications station and keyed in the code for evac station Lenora-3-7. "Omicron One, this is Hawk's Breath, over."

The voice at the other end was garbled and distorted. "Hawk's Breath, we copy, over."

"John?" she asked.

"That's affirmative," the voice replied.

John would never say affirmative, she thought. *He isn't that well trained. He'd say yeah or yup, maybe—yuh-huh, even, on a good day—but never affirmative. Something is definitely wrong.*

"How are you doing down there?" she asked. She knew that the only way to determine the man's identity was to keep him talking, so she figured she'd play along for now.

"We're fine," the mysterious voice answered. "Listen, Mannie, we managed to get a ride aboard a transport. We're leaving Lenora Prime in an hour. No need for a rescue party or anything."

There was that damned name again, but this time, it was personal. And she told him to say that they were on Mars. Man, was she going to be in trouble if this communication got intercepted.

"Just so you know, there are Section 13 black-ops in the area," she told him, hoping it would give him away. It didn't.

"And they are...."

"Very bad people," she mumbled.

"Come again?"

"Nothing," she said. "Listen, I need you to do me a favor. Call Joseph's grandfather and let him know you're on your way."

"Will do," he replied.

Now she knew it wasn't John. Joseph's grandfather, James, had been John's friend since he was just a kid. John had taken it almost as hard as Joseph did. He couldn't have forgotten already.

"Speaking of Joseph, any word on his aunt and uncle?" the voice asked.

Wonderful. Whoever was at the evac station had been monitoring their communication, but only since they arrived on the planet. This could prove useful. Anyone with a cheap radio receiver could monitor open analog channels, but it took high level clearance to monitor secured channels like the ones used to relay the news about Joseph's grandfather.

That meant that the strange man was probably *not* black-ops, or at least was probably not *Terran* black-ops. That also meant that he didn't know their mission on Lenora Prime.

"No, we still haven't heard anything," she said. "Have you found the tablets?"

While he thought about this, she quickly pressed a few buttons on the control pad. With a little effort, the visual controls could be overridden remotely. She was counting on the fact that he couldn't possibly know that, and was desperately hoping he wouldn't notice the indicator light glowing red.

"We found one of them down below. We're still looking for the others."

She smiled as she realized that he didn't have any idea what he was talking about.

"That's fine. Make sure you find all five tablets before you leave, though, or Admiral Brandywine will be furious."

She grinned from ear to ear as an image came on the screen. She did not recognize him, though she thought he looked vaguely familiar. The man at the other end was about forty years old, slightly balding, in a captain's uniform. She shivered as she burned the image into her mind.

"Listen, Mannie," the voice said, "I need to go if we're going to find those tablets. You know how it is."

"Sure," she answered. "I'll see you when you get back."

"Omicron One out."

"Hawk's breath out."

The channel closed with a wink, and Amanda sank back into her chair with a sigh.

Chapter Twenty-nine

"THE subject was male—probably in his late twenties or thirties," Joseph told them. "You can tell by the shape of the pelvic region and the lower jaw. These marks on his skull suggest a possible childhood injury. No, wait. There are identical marks on his lower arms and thighs. They look like... claw marks."

Jen recoiled in horror. "C-c-claw m-marks?" she replied, biting her lip.

"What k-k-kind of claws did that?" Mary asked, pointing to the skeleton's head.

Joseph stared. That's when he realized that the back half of its skull was missing.

"I wish I knew," Joseph said. "I wish I knew."

And yet, he thought, *I hope I never find out....*

***

"OFFICERS and Cadets," Admiral Skylarov pronounced, "may I have your attention, please?"

The room grew so silent you could hear a bit flip. Amanda wondered if he knew that four officers were still stuck on Lenora Prime. Then she began to wonder if he cared. Finally, she wondered if she had just said that out loud, and this thought snapped her back to reality.

"The situation is this: Terran Command Station was destroyed after colonial forces crashed a ship filled with explosives into the central nexus and detonated an explosive charge near the primary reactor vessel. Over twelve thousand personnel were stationed aboard TCS. There was no warning, just a fireball."

"Three scout ships were preparing to dock and took heavy casualties. To the best of our knowledge, this morning's death toll numbers just over fifteen thousand, including about five thousand civilians. We encourage families of possible victims to contact our emergency coordination center to determine their loved ones' whereabouts. When you do, please remember that it may be several weeks before we know for certain whether the station's logs are correct. There's still room for hope."

Amanda just sat there in silence. When she first heard the story, she thought it too fantastic, like something a disturbed writer might turn into a novel or a movie. It wasn't until she heard it on the news that she realized something had really happened. It was in that moment in orbit around Lenora Prime that she realized the magnitude of this day.

It was a day that few would soon forget—the act of a coward—an act that had, in the course of a few hours, turned an uneasy peace into an all-out war. She could not bring herself to look at the pictures—images of officers ejecting themselves into space without suits to avoid the fiery explosion, of flames ripping through the once magnificent station, of the superstructure collapsing in on itself from the artificial gravity malfunction that followed.... She merely closed her eyes and cried, knowing that things would never be the same.

"Our thoughts and prayers are with the officers and their families. They should take comfort in knowing that those responsible for this heinous act *will* be found and brought to justice. That will be all. Dismissed."

As the solemn briefing concluded, Amanda made her way to a computer station. "Computer," she requested, "display last known whereabouts of Frank Henry and his wife, Jenny Henry, the daughter of James Kurtz."

The computer processed the request for a moment, then displayed an information page. On the screen were the words that no one ever wants to see....

Presumed dead.

THE tension in the room was so thick that you couldn't cut it with a chainsaw.

"We've been searching these caves for days!" Jennifer shouted. "We're never going to find the crystal."

"Two days, eight hours, fifty-seven minutes, to be precise," Mary replied.

Joseph rubbed his face in thought. The information on his palmtop disturbed him greatly, so he rechecked the information twice just to make sure there were no mistakes.

"You know, for once, you're absolutely right," Joseph replied.

"We are?" Jennifer asked.

"That was the last tunnel," Joseph said matter-of-factly. "There's no place left to look."

"Now what?" Mary asked.

"Now we wait," he replied. "John hasn't checked in for three twelve-hour cycles, so we have to assume that he is injured or dead."

"What are we waiting for, then?" Mary countered.

Joseph shook his head solemnly. "For Amanda... our only hope."

***

The lights flickered in the evac shelter, and the ground began to shake. Tobias knew what that meant. Outside, the shadow of a troop transport loomed like an inky smudge on your senior thesis, its legs dropping slowly to the ground like a graceful seagull descending upon an unsuspecting trout.

Tobias stood in the doorway, watching as the ramp slid down to the rocky surface below. A burly man appeared at the hatch. Rejndorv, Tobias assumed. He looked just like William said he would. Something about the man rubbed him the wrong way, though. The man hadn't said the first word, and already Tobias didn't trust him.

***

Joseph lay there, motionless, the cold ground wearing sores on the heels of his feet and the back of his head. Maybe tomorrow, he would remember to roll out his sleeping bag before lights out.

Only a couple more hours, he thought.

Then the light came. It started out as a tiny slit. Joseph wondered for a moment if he was squinting, but quickly decided that it really was just a slit. Slowly, the light grew brighter until he could make out everything in the room. *Sunlight!*

The doors were opening. A moment later, the doors stopped as quickly as they had started. About three inches of daylight crept in through the gap.

That's when he noticed it. Eight feet above the ground, the wall opposite the door had a strange shimmering look, almost like it was made of metal. And next to that, another section of wall was...

Missing?

“Guys!” he exclaimed. “Come on, guys! Wake up!”

Jennifer and Mary rolled over, covered their eyes, and sat up groggily. Jennifer shook her head clear.

“What’s up?” she asked.

“That’s up,” he said, pointing.

Mary gaped. “What the....”

“It’s a hologram,” Joseph said. “The sunlight was so bright that it let us see what was behind it.”

“But that means...” Jen said.

“It means that we haven’t mapped the tunnels at all.”

Chapter Thirty-one

The next day (January 11, 2391)

A cold draft blew past them as Joseph meandered through the newly discovered maze of twisty passages. Jen, as usual, was a few meters ahead, while Mary took up the rear. As their descent grew steeper, their pace increased until they were nearly running.

Initially, it struck him that the passages were all alike. He wasn't sure exactly when the ground became smoother, but at some point, Joseph came to the realization that the floor and walls were now made of metal.

They slowed their pace as the tunnel began to level off. Then, Jen came to a sudden stop, much to Joseph's surprise. He barely stopped in time, but still ended up nudging her slightly. Startled, he looked up to see what had brought about the change in speed, and found himself face to face with something he hoped he would never see....

"Hi. I am the TX-141 AI," she said, "but you can call me Tessa."

Joseph hated AIs. It wasn't that he hated any of them personally, nor that he hated the concept of AIs in principle; it was just that he never met one that didn't crash every ten minutes. They were slow, unreliable, and had about the intelligence of an average six-year-old.

"Hi. I am the ruler of the universe," Joseph answered dryly.

To make matters worse, this unit wasn't even a holographic model. It was just a face on a CRT. *Very primitive,* he thought. *Soooo last year.*

"A pleasure to meet you, your majesty," she answered, giggling.

Wait a second, Joseph thought. *An AI with a sense of humor? That can't be right.*

"What revision is your AI core program?" Joseph asked.

"I have no AI core program. I am a Terran Equivalent Synthetic Sentient Architecture model TX-141 Artificial Humanoid Prototype, revision 34-alpha."

Can it be true, he wondered? *Can this... visibly primitive AI really be our intellectual equal?*

"Okay, Tessa.... This statement is false," he said.

"This is a joke, right?" she answered. "That's the liar's paradox."

Too easy, he thought. "Two hands clapped together makes a sound. What sound does one hand make?"

The image of a hand appeared on the screen, and its fingers quickly closed repeatedly, slapping against its palm, thus making a muffled clapping sound. The hand disappeared after a few seconds, revealing Tessa's face and an evil grin.

He thought for a moment. "Okay, Tessa," he said. "Whom do you love?"

Tessa appeared to think about this for a moment, then replied, "Pass phrase accepted. Access granted."

The AI still has the same default diagnostics pass phrase, he noted, scratching his head.

A door to their left slid swiftly open. Joseph jumped back, startled, then paused for a moment. "Was that door there before?" he asked.

"I… I'm not sure," Jennifer answered. "I don't remember it being there, but that doesn't mean that it wasn't."

"No, I don't think it was," Mary confirmed.

Joseph glanced at them, then at the AI. He wasn't quite sure how to handle this. What if that door disappeared as quickly as it had appeared once they walked through it?

On the one hand, Tessa seemed friendly enough… for an AI. On the other hand, she was an AI.

"Comments?" Joseph asked.

"Well," Jennifer mused, "it can't be much worse than here."

"There's no place else to go," Mary said. "We mapped all the passages, and this is the only one that led anywhere. If the crystal is down here, it has to be through that door somewhere."

"I guess it's settled then," Joseph told them. "We go."

***

The air was motionless in the evac station. An eerie stillness swept over Vladimir Rejndorv and his companion, shrouded in black.

"So how long have they been down there?" Rejndorv asked in a coarse whisper.

"Sixty-eight hours," came the shadowy figure's reply.

"Is everything ready?" Rejndorv asked.

Thirty more troops, all dressed in black, appeared in the distant shadows for a moment, then were gone.

"Completely. Tomorrow, we will send in the… 'rescue' party," he replied.

***

Joseph, Jennifer, and Mary stood at the entrance to an unusually tall cave. The chamber was about fifty feet across by about twelve feet tall in the center. Argon tubes encircled the ceiling above a man-made rim that bordered the cave roof, bathing the entire room in a surreal purple glow.

"Doesn't it strike you as odd," Joseph mused, "that we're almost a half mile beneath the surface of a dead planet, and yet we have power?"

From behind him, a voice answered, "That's because the entire facility is powered by an underground reactor."

Joseph nearly jumped through the cave roof. He spun around on his left heel, stumbled, then regained his composure when he saw a full body holographic projection of the friendly AI.

"You're the first visitors I've had in over a year," holo-Tessa told them.

Joseph was puzzled. The planet had been abandoned for a quarter of a century, or so he was led to believe. Either the AI had a bad clock battery or....

"You say there were people down here a year ago?" Joseph asked. "Who were they?"

"Why, one of the founders, of course," she answered.

Something about those words struck Joseph like Katie's fingernails on the chalkboard in third grade. He shivered.

***

"Do you expect much resistance, McNeely?" Rejndorv asked.

"Nothing we can't handle, sir," Tobias answered.

Tobias McNeely was a young man, about 27 years old. A programmer by trade, he specialized in breaking encryption using tachyon computing technology. By taking advantage of spacio-temporal folding, the computer could reorganize itself to break an encryption key moments before the key was entered.

Nothing terrified Tobias more than the possibility of his transtemporal computer falling into the wrong hands. He was thankful that he alone possessed enough understanding of the system to use it, much less maintain it. He was even more thankful that he had found someone worthy of his services.

Too bad they chose a moron as their point man, he thought, glaring at Rejndorv.

"What makes you say that, McNeely?"

"Well, sir," Tobias replied, "they don't strike me as being very resourceful. We took that John guy completely by surprise. He didn't even know he was in danger until he was splattered across the desert."

"Oh, he knew," Rejndorv said. "He knew. I think they may be more intelligent than you believe."

"I'm not so sure," Tobias answered. "I was reading their computer records. They didn't even translate a tenth of the inscriptions on those doors before they went in, and the part they did finish wasn't even right."

"Really? It looked right to me," Rejndorv prodded.

"Well, it is right," Tobias said, grinning, "or at least it would be if they knew the Nivitian alphabet. They made a classic blunder."

"How so?"

Tobias pressed a few buttons on the computer console. "This sequence of symbols... sechra... they incorrectly recorded it as sepra, which means distant. The symbols actually say sechra."

"Get to the point. What does sechra mean, McNeely?" Rejndorv asked.

"Well, sechra also means distant... sort of. Sepra means distant in space. Sechra means distant... in time. The doors open every twenty-eight years—whenever Lenora Major is at its highest point in the sky on the northern side of Lenora Prime, but only during the day, and only when it isn't blocked by Lenora Minor."

Rejndorv's lips turned up into a smile so broad that Tobias couldn't help but wonder what Rejndorv was hiding behind it.

"That's why we had to wait 28 years to go back in," Rejndorv noted.

"Sir, if you don't mind my asking, why would the designers lock everyone out for such a long time? It seems like a simple combination lock would have been enough."

"Ah, but that's where you're wrong," Rejndorv replied. "*They* didn't close the doors to keep people out. *I* closed them to keep *it* in."

Chapter Thirty-two

Now it should be noted that Lenoran civilization started as something of a prank. A cult of people who believed in extraterrestrial life and the theory of exogenesis decided to create an "alien" culture for humanity to eventually discover. Working in secret, they designed a ship that could slowly accelerate to nearly the speed of light and then slowly decelerate. They subsequently built this ship using materials mined from a Kuiper Belt asteroid.

Then, in the year 2036, they launched this small craft containing 100 infants, along with food seeds and enough nuclear fuel to last through the 100-year journey to Lenora Prime. Also on board were three "priests". These men fed the infants and taught them Hit'ui, a constructed language that they expanded with new words as they went along.

By the time they arrived at Lenora Prime, about a century had passed, but to them, it felt like only sixty years because of relativity.

Once they had landed on the surface, they dismantled the ship and melted it down to use as building materials.

Eventually, humans back on Earth began exploring more broadly, and in 2296, a captain by the name of Randall Phillips "discovered" the colony of humanoids living in a system of caves in a mountainside on the southern continent, and "believed" them to be aliens. He taught them how to build more advanced structures, and eventually became fluent in Hit'ui. It was not until five years later that the fraud was discovered when someone found a tiny marking on one of their structures that read "Hecho en México".

A year later, it was revealed that Captain Phillips only found the colony because he knew exactly where to look for this civilization. Thus, the government of Earth had no qualms about sending one of its first folding gates to Lenora Prime just two years later. In a curious twist, the suddenly high rate of commercial shipping to the nearby space station orbiting Barnard's Star reduced the popular tourist destination to a cesspool of organized crime in just a few short years.

And then, Rejndorv mused, *less than sixty years later, they were gone.*

***

"The founders?" Joseph asked.

"The ones who made this base," Tessa answered. "Oh, look. They're here now."

Joseph's heart raced. "What do you mean? Here now?" he asked.

"Outside, in the evac shelter," she replied.

"In the..."

"Evac shelter," she repeated.

"Which is..."

"Outside."

"Yes. Yes, I understand that, but *what* evac shelter?"

"That evac shelter."

Not the words he wanted to hear.... Joseph froze. The wall in front of him was suddenly gone, replaced by the interior of a room, about 10 meters square. Rejndorv and a few others sat eating rations at a makeshift table.

A moment later, the wall flickered, and Joseph relaxed a bit.

"That's a hologram, right?" Joseph asked.

"Of course," Tessa replied. "You wouldn't survive the radiation levels if I had created a spatial fold."

Joseph pondered this for a moment. It was the sort of thing you just didn't think about. In normal use, spatial folding drives were relatively safe because the ships shielded you from the gamma emissions that they generated. Thus, even though it seemed immediately obvious that, in fact, such a spacial folding would not have been practical in such close proximity, the thought hadn't even crossed his mind.

"Yes, of course," he said, "but for all I knew, the wall could have been a hologram."

"An interesting point," Tessa noted, "and one that I will have to ponder further."

Tessa paused for a moment.

"No," she said, "I'm fairly certain that this is a hologram."

"What!?! Are you trying to tell me that you weren't sure?" Joseph asked.

"Well, I'm never sure," Tessa told him. "That's the thing about holograms. It's hard to tell where reality ends and illusion begins."

"But we're safe, right?"

"Yes. Perfectly," she replied. "Except...."

"Except?"

"Except that the founders are here," she replied.

"Here? Don't you mean outside in the evac shelter."

"Outside in the..."

"Evac shelter. Oh, never mind," he grumbled as he left the room.

***

Amanda stood for a moment, jaw agape, staring at the display. "Missing, presumed dead," it said.

She then keyed in more names. Her shipmates were all listed as missing, presumed dead. She, however, was designated KIA.

"What the...." Amanda keyed in her ID number. The results were the same. *Something is definitely wrong here,* she thought.

There were two situations in which she could reasonably be listed as KIA. The first was if someone found her body. The second was if she had been assigned to a covert ops job that required it. Last she heard, neither was the case, but clearly the computer believed otherwise. She wasn't sure what had happened, but she knew she was going to find out.

***

The hairs on Joseph's neck stood on end as he walked in. Maybe it was the cool cave air, maybe it was the eerie realism of the holographic avatar, or maybe he just left the oven on, but either way, he couldn't shake the feeling of dread.

Mary and Jennifer sat waiting for him at a table mid-hall covered with a veritable feast of emergency rations. He cringed visibly at the thought of eating dried fruit strips and beef jerky for yet another meal.

"I never thought I'd say this, but.... Wait a sec," Joseph interrupted himself. "Of course I thought I'd say this. Man, if I never have to eat this crap again, it'll be too soon."

"So, where's a body get *real* food around here?" Jennifer asked.

A loud buzzing sound came from the wall behind Jennifer's chair. She spun around in an instant. On the wall, an open food slot served up a steaming bowl of chicken soup.

"Hmph, that was easy," she muttered.

"And where would I find the Ackerman crystal?" Mary asked, jokingly.

"Section 13," the AI dutifully responded as her hologram flickered into view across the room.

Mary stood there dumbfounded.

***

"I demand to see my father!" Amanda shouted.

The secretary in front of his office is such a pain in the ass, she thought.

"I'm sorry, miss, but as I told you before, Admiral Jenkins is in a very important meeting," the secretary replied.

"Well, I think he'll be very interested to find out that *I'M DEAD*!" Amanda shouted, pointing to a data pad showing an electronic death certificate dated the day before.

"Well, now, this *is* interesting," the secretary said. "I thought you smelled funny."

"Stupid bitch," Amanda muttered.

"What was that?" she snapped.

"I said it was a computer glitch," Amanda answered.

"Yes, I suppose it was," the woman answered.

Amanda jumped as the door behind her swung open. Her father emerged, accompanied by two men she had never seen before.

"Ah, Amanda, my little hell-raiser," he said cheerily. "How are you today?"

"Funny you should ask," she answered, handing him the pad.

Her father shivered.

"I'm sorry you had to find out like this," he told her. "I'll explain everything later... some place more private... but not right now. For now, you and the rest of your crew no longer exist."

At that moment, Amanda noticed that the room was quite warm. She found it strange that he would shiver—very strange, indeed.

"Join me for dinner?" he asked.

Chapter Thirty-three

Later that evening (January 11, 2391)

THE neon lights flickered on and off rhythmically over the Hot Spot. For an officer's mess, it was a total dive. Amanda couldn't believe her father had asked her to meet him here. Of course, Triton Station was a small base, so it wasn't as though there were many places where they could get away from prying eyes and ears.

Tom Jenkins entered the bar cautiously. Both he and Amanda were dressed in plain clothes, mainly in neutral hues to avoid drawing unnecessary attention to themselves. Amanda barely even noticed that he had entered until she saw him sitting across the table from her. *Very impressive,* she thought.

As he reached out for the data pad sitting on the table, a waitress came up behind Amanda.

"So, whad'll it be?" she asked in a whiny voice.

"I'll have a dry martini on the rocks with a twist of lime," Tom answered.

"And yourself?"

Amanda thought for a moment. "Just a beer," she said, then regretted it. Beer didn't get along well with her metabolism. The last time she had a beer, she nearly flew her ship into a planet.

Fortunately, the planet was moving, or at least it looked like it was moving, so she ended up in a nice geosynchronous orbit. Either that or maybe the captain disabled the controls—she wasn't sure. She was sure, however, that she didn't really remember very much of that mission, and that she didn't really want to, either.

That was, of course, a long time ago. She was pretty sure that her constitution had improved somewhat since then. If not, she would find out about it in the morning.

"So, before you go flying yourself into a planet again," the admiral began, "I wanted to tell you what's going on."

Amanda looked at him, puzzled, and simultaneously horrified that he still remembered that incident—better than she did, mind you—and that he had the poor taste to bring it up right now.

"There's a lot more going on in the Terran Alliance than you're probably aware of," her father continued. "Several key bases have been taken by rebel forces, and all signs point to traitors in our midst—conspirators willing to aid the enemy."

Amanda began skimming the official mission logs on the data pad. According to those records, when Joseph's shuttle crash-landed on Lenora Prime, Amanda had attempted a rescue mission and had burned up while entering the atmosphere after a similar malfunction in her mini-shuttle. The timing of this subterfuge on the heels of this particular mission gave her pause.

"What does this have to do with me?" Amanda asked.

"We suspect that Admiral Skylarov may be one of those traitors," he told her.

"And so you faked my death so that I could... study Skylarov safely?" she asked.

"No. I faked your death to get you out of harm's way," he answered. "I want you to go back home to Earth and stay with your stepmother and your sister. Don't come back out here until I get home."

"I can't do that, Dad," Amanda informed him matter-of-factly. "I have friends trapped on Lenora Prime in a secret base that *we* helped create. In twenty-eight years, they will have long since starved to death. I have to get them out. There's only one more window after tomorrow before the doors close again... for the rest of their lives."

"Amanda, you know I can't let you do that," he replied. "That area is controlled by our enemies now. It isn't safe. And besides, they can probably find their way out much more easily than you can find a way in."

"Dammit, Father!" she shouted. "I have to try!"

"It's not your decision," he said testily.

"It *is* my decision. I'm *going* to Lenora Prime," she told him. "The decision is made."

"Amanda! Don't do this," he pleaded. "You'll be jeopardizing your career... your life...."

Amanda stood, as if to leave. "Like you ever cared about that," she scolded.

"If you go to Lenora Prime, I may not be able to protect you," he warned.

By this time, Amanda was halfway across the room. She angrily marched towards the door, pausing only for a moment to snap back a reply. "What are you going to do? Court-martial me? I'm dead, remember?"

***

"Section 13?" Mary asked.

"Section 13," came the response.

"And that is?" Mary asked.

"A restricted area."

Joseph had a feeling she would not get much more information out of the AI.

"I have a feeling you won't get much more information out of the AI," he said.

"And you said that loudly enough that she could hear it, why?" Jen chided.

"I have this habit of speaking my mind," he replied.

"Tessa?" Joseph asked.

"Yes, Joseph?" Tessa replied.

"Could you take us to section 13?" he asked.

"Please provide security authorization," she replied.

That wasn't a good sign, he thought. He thought he'd try something else. "Could you tell us the location of section 13?" he asked.

"Section 13 is between section 12 and section 14," she answered.

Ah. Now we're getting somewhere, he thought. "Can you take us to section 12?" he asked.

"Certainly," she replied. "Right this way. We can take the emergency access tunnels to avoid... ah... unnecessary risk."

***

Admiral Jenkins sat in front of a video screen and requested the latest TANN feed.

> "In Alliance news, the Chataris sector has been declared off limits to commercial traffic. Military traffic is advised to exercise extreme caution, as a code mauve condition has been reported on Lenora Prime."

It's happening again.... Dear God, it's happening again.

***

LENORA Major was rising in the Lenoran sky as a dozen soldiers scurried around, dressed in black, moving equipment, food, and weapons around in preparation for their descent.

"Eight hours to ingress, sir," came a shout from one officer.

From the shadows came the dark reply. "Excellent...."

Chapter Thirty-four

"This is as far as I can go," Tessa said. "There are no holographic projectors in the emergency access tunnels in or below section 10."

"That's going to make it a little hard to find section 13, then, isn't it?" Joseph asked.

"Section 12," she corrected.

"Ah, yes. Section 12," he answered.

"Actually, my adjunct will be escorting you from this point on," she told them.

"Your... adjunct?" Mary asked.

"You'll see," she replied.

The hologram that was Tessa shimmered and vanished, leaving bare rock walls beyond.

Behind them, a door opened. Joseph jumped as a woman entered. *No, not a woman,* he thought. *A machine. A very beautiful machine, but a machine, nonetheless.*

At that moment, Joseph wondered if Tessa might have been a real person at one time. *Who knows? Maybe she still is,* he thought. *If so, she must be an old woman by now.*

"Hi," she said.

He wasn't sure what to call her. Was it Tessa? Adjunct? Anne Boleyn? *For a gentler nor a more merciful AI was there never,* he thought. *Sheesh.*

"Jane Seymour?" he asked.

She stared at him cockeyed for a moment, then replied simply, "Tessa. This way."

They followed her through the doorway.

"Tessa," Joseph prodded, "if you don't mind my asking, what exactly is an adjunct?"

"I am an artificial humanoid, connected to the computer core here in Lenora Base A-319," she answered.

"So you can't leave here, then?" he asked.

"I'm connected to it, not tethered," she explained. "When I get out of range, I become autonomous, and resynchronize with the base systems when I come back into range."

Amazing, Joseph thought. Five weeks ago, he would not have thought such a technology was possible. Now, it seemed almost obvious, as though an android were the logical next step. *It might take a while to get used to this,* he mused.

Tessa pressed her hand into a hand print reader, and the adjacent security door opened. "Welcome to section 10," she told them.

As they walked down the dimly lit tunnel, Jennifer took the lead in her usual fashion, walking just behind Tessa. Joseph followed them, with Mary taking up the rear.

A few seconds later, Joseph saw Jennifer duck suddenly. He wondered for a moment what could possibly have prompted this behavior.

That's when he saw it—a hideous creature hanging from a stalactite, part robot, part alive, its glistening teeth shimmering in the dim light as its razor-sharp claws slashed through the air just in front of his face—eighty-five pounds of pure pain.

"Mechlizard!" Tessa shouted.

Joseph jumped out of the way just in time to avoid being sliced to ribbons, knocking Mary over as he did. Mary sat motionless for a moment, dazed, critical seconds ticking away as she did.

"Come on! Let's go! Let's go!" Joseph shouted, pointing towards the metal door ahead.

Once again, the mechlizard growled and slashed at them. Once again, Mary froze. Joseph quickly pulled Mary back towards the cave wall and out of harm's way. The lizard, however, had found its target. With a slash of its claws, Jennifer fell to the ground, grasping her thigh in pain, unable to walk.

The next few moments played out in slow motion in Joseph's mind. Tessa took cover behind a large rock, firing pulse weapon rounds at the mech while Jennifer lay on the ground, petrified, the giant lizard slowly crawling across the ceiling and down the wall directly above her.

In a panic, Mary scrambled to her feet and backed furiously towards the door, leaning against it for protection. The doors opened suddenly. Off balance and stumbling, Mary tumbled towards the deep vertical shaft that lay beyond.

She grabbed the rightmost edge of the shaft as it flew past and hung there for what seemed like hours, clinging to the rock floor for dear life, her fingers growing weaker by the minute.

Mary's predicament did not even register on Joseph's radar. He assumed that she had walked into the next room, and would stumble back in at any moment with her sidearm to help them. Jennifer, by contrast, was in danger right now, so he couldn't wait; he had to act quickly.

Joseph ran to Jennifer and tried to stand her up, but she quickly proved too heavy, so he merely grabbed her arms and tried to pull her out of the way. With a little help from Tessa, he managed to get her body over his shoulder, then slowly stood.

"Joseph! Behind you!" Jennifer screamed as the lizard took another swipe. He tumbled, rolled, and fired on the creature, scoring a blow to its head. Disoriented, it scurried across the ceiling, into an air duct, and out of sight. Jennifer grunted as she crumpled to the ground.

"Joseph!" Mary shouted. In that moment, Joseph realized for the first time that something else was wrong, a feeling of fear creeping into his gut like a teenager sneaking back into her bedroom at three in the morning, drunk from a frat party that her parents forbade her to attend.

"Stay there, Jen," he said. "I'll be right back."

"Joseph! Help me!" Mary screamed.

Joseph looked over from across the room and, to his horror, saw Mary swaying in the updraft of an old ventilation shaft.

"Hold on! I'll be right there!" Joseph shouted.

Joseph forced himself to his feet, and dove towards her position. Gliding in midair, he watched in horror as her fingers slipped slowly off the rock, one by one. Frantically, he reached out for her hand. He felt her fingertips graze his for a moment as he hit the ground beside the shaft, but he was powerless to save her.

Joseph saw the terror in her eyes as they flashed before him—a final moment etched forever into his memory—and heard her muted scream become more distant, somehow less real, ending in a dull thud, then nothing.

Jennifer's eyes went blank. "Is she...."

The mechlizard appeared again, this time at the bottom of the shaft. Joseph barely even flinched as it severed Mary's head from her body. As the metal door slid shut, Jennifer closed her eyes.

Chapter Thirty-five

The next day (January 12, 2391)

THE hangar deck was deserted. Amanda checked her watch. *Yep, 0300 hours,* she thought. At this very moment, throughout Triton Station, a shift change was beginning. Posts were left minimally manned, readings carelessly checked, flight crews taking off and putting on their protective gear, and all the while, the station was ripe for any sort of inappropriate activity that you could conjure up.

Inappropriate activity—that's an interesting euphemism, she thought. After all, she was about to steal a fold fighter—one of the fastest, most agile ships in the known galaxy—to go off on a crazy, unauthorized mission to rescue her friends, with no real information about whether they were even alive or dead.

Oh well, she thought. *No point worrying about that now.* Her mission was clear, her goals simple, her plan carefully thought out... and it was now or never.

In the three-point-five seconds it took her to bolt stealthily across the tarmac, up the ladder, and into the cockpit of the fold fighter Heel of Achilles, she was picked up by no less than twelve security cameras whose monitors were being watched by four guards. Of course, two of those were walking out of the room while the other two were busily munching on bagels, and thus no one in particular noticed her entrance.

This is too easy, she thought as she entered the override codes to open the huge fighter bay doors. She watched as the doors slowly opened, then flew her fighter upwards and performed a spatial fold almost effortlessly and without notice.

So happy was she while she reveled in her accomplishments that she failed to notice one small detail—a small red light under the console.

Blinking.

***

JOSEPH's palms ached as the dust and rocks tore into his flesh. For once, he was glad to be wearing knee pads. He only wished he had brought padded gloves to go with them.

Here we are, he thought, *on hands and knees, crawling through a tiny passage to avoid the ventilation shaft.*

The bridge across the shaft was conspicuous in its absence. Joseph wondered if Tessa knew why the bridge was gone. Somehow, he had a feeling she wasn't telling them everything. Worse, through it all, two thoughts continued to surface: the fear that Tessa might be wrong—that the tunnel doors might not be secured and that the mechlizard might suddenly appear ahead of them, or worse, behind them—and the image of Mary's face paralyzed with fear as she fell twenty stories to her death. Neither thought agreed with him at the moment.

The tunnel grew wider up ahead, so Tessa and Jennifer crawled two abreast. Behind them, Joseph grunted as he smashed his forehead into a stalactite, sending a searing pain through his skull.

"Ouch. That had to hurt," Jennifer said, laughing at him.

A few feet later, the tunnel stretched to about four feet high. Joseph could almost walk—waddle, really—if he kept his head down. A small steel door lay just ahead.

"This may sound like a stupid question," Jen said, "but how do we know that there's not a mechlizard on the other side of that door?"

"That's section 11," Tessa replied. "The northern half of the level is the design lab for the mechlizard. The southern half is the living quarters. There's an airlock between the two. The doors can't be open at once, and the mechlizard doesn't know how to open doors, so we should be safe."

"Why am I not feeling confident?" Joseph asked.

"You don't trust me, do you, Joseph?" Tessa replied.

"What do you mean?" Joseph asked.

"Ever since we first met, you've questioned my actions, my motives, my ethics, even my intelligence. Why?"

"It all goes back to what happened to my grandfather before he left black-ops," Joseph replied. "He was stationed as a deep cover operative aboard one of the first ships with a functioning AI."

***

Twenty-one years earlier (2370)

"Uncle Frank, please tell me a story," Joseph pleaded.

"But Joseph, your grandpa will be here soon," his uncle said, "and you haven't even eaten breakfast."

"I'll eat on the boat," Joseph answered. "Come on, uncle! Please? Please?"

"Oh, all right. I guess one little story can't hurt."

Joseph's uncle sat quietly for a moment, seemingly deep in thought, then began.

"It was the dawn of a new era. The people of Earth had discovered how to terraform planets, creating viable, life-sustaining ecosystems capable of supporting human life. They built giant ships—ships that could carry thousands of men and women huge distances to colonize distant worlds in distant galaxies. The ships could travel nearly the speed of light, and rumor had it that newer ships were being designed in secret that could one day break even that barrier."

"The universe was truly ours," he continued. "We naively believed that we were more than its guardians—that we were its gods—and that in the same way that God created Man, so too should we create things in our own image. Despite the undeniable fascination, however, many objected to these creations. *Man should not be meddling with DNA,* they'd say, *and Man should not be creating artificial life forms because they won't have a soul.*"

"And so," he continued, "the great AI debates began. As with many sociopolitical topics, most of the dissenters disagreed peaceably. A few did not. They called themselves Humans Against Soulless Intelligence, or HASI. The HASI were known for radical attacks on AI labs around the planet and throughout the nearby systems."

His uncle paused to take a sip of water, then looked back at Joseph, who sat curled up on the couch, completely mesmerized.

"Eventually," he continued, "a secret AI development base was built on the opposite side of the Milky Way Galaxy. Using secret technology known only to a select few, the research team was able to quickly move between Earth and this base, known only as 'Site K'. The location of the base, its name, and in fact, its mere existence were kept strictly secret, even among low-ranking members of the research team, who knew only the name of the base and their designated pickup point. And so it was that when your grandfather, James, was assigned to the S.S. Biggs Carey, few took any notice. No one had any reason to suspect that he was a high-ranking member of the AI design team that worked at Site K."

"A big scary what?" Joseph asked.

His uncle shook his head in puzzlement, but after a moment, he understood his nephew's confusion. "No, no, not 'big scary'," he replied. "The 'Biggs Carey'. It's a ship."

Joseph smiled and nodded.

"As I was saying," he continued, "the Biggs Carey was docked for a refit at Brooks Station, a large shipyard in orbit around Mars. During the refit, the shipyard was off-limits to everyone—both to other ships and to its original crew—so that the AI team could refit the ship in secret. Most of the ship's systems were tied in to the new computer core, which was capable of intelligence rivaling that of even the most brilliant minds of our century."

His uncle's face turned suddenly grim.

"What no one expected," he added, "was that many of our most trusted allies were... well, I'm getting ahead of myself. It all began when...."

Chapter Thirty-six

Thirty-seven years earlier (2333)

"KURTZ to base receiving," James said in his deep German accent.

"Ensign Mortis here," came the muted reply through the intercom.

"Mortis.... Your first name wouldn't happen to be..."

"What?" the voice asked.

"Never mind," James replied. "Have my bags arrived on the Torment of Tantalus yet?"

"It just docked a few minutes ago," Ensign Mortis replied.

"Great," James said. "I'll be there shortly. Kurtz out."

As soon as James closed the channel, he stood up from the communications terminal and walked down the corridor. When he reached the end of the hall, he turned, faced the lift, and waited... and waited... and waited.

Tap... tap... is this thing on? James wondered if *anything* worked on the ship. He pressed the manual call button on the door's face plate, and got little satisfaction from the general lack of any auditory or visual feedback. *Great. Something else for me to fix.*

Upon opening the panel, his jaw dropped. Where a bundle of optical cable should have been, only a few lines greeted him.

Mental note. Requisition more cable.

"Kurtz to Captain Valentine," he said into a nearby comm panel.

"Valentine here," the captain replied.

"There may be a slight delay in my arrival," James said. "The lift near my quarters is dead and I'm having to hoof it."

"Understood," she replied. "Keep trying on every deck until you find one that works."

"Will do," James answered as he turned and began jogging the long, spiraling corridor that led up to the bridge some twenty decks above him.

***

"It feels like this ship is falling apart," Valentine said as James entered the bridge. "No less than a dozen key systems have failed in the last three hours alone. It's almost as though we had a saboteur aboard."

Captain Jamie Valentine was a curious woman, James thought—as beautiful as she was cold. James had never met the woman before this assignment, but her reputation preceded her. His friend Tim once told him that she had ordered her crew to eject a man into space for putting the ship in jeopardy. She definitely was someone who you did not want to cross.

"The ship just went through a major refit," James replied. "It's going to take a while to work all the bugs out. The lift, for example, was only about half-installed. Besides, a saboteur would go for the big stuff—the computer core, life support, engines, navigation—things that really matter—not little things like a single lift door or a comm panel..."

"You reported some security holes," Captain Valentine interrupted. "How do you explain those?"

Man, if she knew how badly written this ship's operating system is, she'd hide under her bed for the rest of her life, James thought.

"They're old bugs," he explained. "They've been in the standard OS since... well, since I first exploited them in my academy days."

"I won't even ask," Valentine replied. "Does anyone else know about the holes?"

"Probably," James said. "Why?"

"Many of these failures look like computer attacks," she explained. "The next time something goes wrong, it could be life support or gravity or... who knows what."

"I've got it covered," he said. "I've isolated most of our critical systems from the main network. Each node is running in isolation."

"What if it's a virus?" Valentine asked. "Could it have spread to those nodes already?"

"Those systems are dumb as a post," James replied. "They're about as programmable as your wristwatch. Short of individual sabotage of each unit, we're fine."

"And then what?" she asked.

"In the unlikely event of Satan getting into a snowball fight," James began, "I guess we break out the e-suits."

"How quickly can you have the ship fixed?" Valentine asked.

"Well, the comm system glitches seem to be restricted to certain parts of the ship. It's possible that these are artifacts of previous botched repairs, but I doubt it."

"How quickly can..." she repeated.

"I'd like to bounce load between the computer cores and see if this is confined to a single processing unit. If so, I'll just wipe it and clone it from the others. If it's systemwide,

I'll have to repair one core and distribute the fixes through the system, and then...."

Captain Valentine interrupted him. "Again, I ask you, how long will..."

"I heard you the first time. Best guess?" James asked. "Worst case is two ship-wide shutdowns of all systems except life support. Minimum 48 hours, maybe longer."

He shivered at the captain's icy glare.

Chapter Thirty-seven

Chief engineer's log for April 1, 2333:

We appear to have contracted a strange bug while docked at Brooks Station. The Biggs Carey just went through a major refit, so many of the problems may be design quirks that we missed, but some of them look more like malicious attacks.

A few minutes ago, the computer mysteriously decided to disconnect power to engineering. The rest of the ship has dropped into night mode. I've already checked the power distribution lines, and everything is working correctly. All signs point to a computer glitch.

The primary cores are offline now, with secondary cores autonomously maintaining the last system state. Unlike the primary cores, the secondary systems actually accept my access code.

It looks like the contamination is limited to the primary cores. Given the limited programmability of the secondary cores, I don't expect this to change. At least I hope it doesn't change....

I brought a prototype core from the lab to use in case of an emergency; in about an hour, I hope to have it take over control of the problematic systems. I'm also severing nearly all direct communication with the station, limiting us to voice traffic only. That should minimize the risk of damage to the temporary core until we can track down the fault.

As of 0800 hours, the only direct connection between the ship and Brooks Station will be a power trunk. We have to keep that attached, because we're shutting down the primary reactor for minor repairs the day after tomorrow.

Chief engineer's log addendum:

I have severed direct ship-to-shore data traffic, and have installed one of my own systems to take over basic ship operations. I've placed life support partially under computer control in a checkerboard arrangement, with roughly half the nodes still running autonomously to minimize risk.

Most of the ship's systems are running normally again with the substitute core, but some things still aren't right. Sev-

eral lift controls don't work, and seven food slots are still so far out of alignment that they can't synthesize anything solid. Worse, the floor of cargo bay three missed the retrofit entirely and is covered with a sticky brown goo that, upon further testing, was determined to be very thick, dried honey that had been missing from the ship's galley for a little under a year.... Fortunately, the doors still worked well enough to jettison the offending substance into empty space. Unfortunately, the frozen bits are still causing sporadic hull impacts on the station.

And whoever designed the bridge science stations should be shot. Two of the stations were completely fried, just like the one on the S.S. Furlong. I've isolated it to a badly designed power supply. I'll file a bug about it one of these days.

Anyway, I'm glad I requested **lots** *of optical cabling. They seem to have forgotten various signal lines for at least a dozen consoles. And then there was the infirmary fire.... They attached a high voltage line to a comm panel without a step-down. We're lucky they didn't blow out power to the entire deck.*

Thankfully, the doctor was safely inside his office when it blew the front panel across the room. Of course, the corner of the panel went through the wall and stuck out several inches **into** *his office, so he nearly got hit anyway....*

Most of the remaining comm panels were only halfway installed. There were several screws missing. One unit was simply a front panel with no boards attached. Three more units were not connected to power at all.

The good news is that the infirmary lights are working, as are the lights in engineering. I have a team of twelve engineers working nonstop to get the infirmary comm system up and running, and we expect to have things mostly cleaned up by tomorrow.

At least the food slot in my quarters works, even if it hasn't been programmed to make a palatable pizza.

END OF LOG

***

"KURTZ to Ensign Cou Rouge," James called.

"Yeah?" the voice replied in a deep Southern drawl.

"How are those medical comm panels working?" James asked.

"They ain't too good, sir," he replied.

"What's the problem?" James demanded.

"We gots to pull up the floor, sir," he said matter-of-factly.

"WHAT!?!" James screamed.

"No power, sir."

"I'll be right up," James replied.

I hope the doctor can do my physical while I run live high voltage cabling, he thought.

"We'll wait," Ensign Rouge said.

"Kurtz out."

***

"COMMANDER, what's the status of repairs?" Captain Valentine asked.

James reached over to the comm panel and opened the channel for two-way communication.

"Can you hear me?" he asked.

"Uh... yes?"

"Then it's going well," James answered.

James couldn't believe his ears. *The captain actually laughed—chuckled, really—and I wasn't even all that funny. Maybe things won't be so bad.*

"I just got word from the archives at Kifer Station that the newest OS update includes most of my security fixes, with equivalents for the rest. The new sources should arrive by packet carrier in about three days."

"Very good. Keep me apprised," she replied. "Valentine out."

Ensign Morris, a junior engineer, stood there in shock. "Did she just..."

"I think so," James replied. "She must have read the crew manifest."

"The what?"

"The crew manifest," James said. "A lot of ship data got... changed. I uploaded a copy of the core memory to Brooks Station. They're scanning it for any corrupted data in food slot programs, life support data files, and so on, but the crew manifest is unsalvageable and has to be rebuilt manually."

"How long will that take," Morris asked.

"Not too long," James replied. "Listen, could you deliver this message to the captain for me? We need it broadcast ship-wide."

James handed him a data pad, which read:

> *Due to serious corruption of the computer's memory, large portions of the crew manifest must be purged and restored from backups. Because of this, individual access codes may revert to old values.*
>
> *If you experience any problems as a result of this, you can request a replacement access code using official form 2198.34D. Please specify form revision B. Since this form is not available electronically without an access code, paper copies will be available in main engineering. The forms must be delivered in person to an engineering staff member who will confirm your identity visually from the crew manifest.*
>
> *If you arrived on the ship within the last two months, no backup records are available for you, and your records will be tagged but not replaced. Since it may take several days for new copies of your official records to arrive from Earth, this notice does not affect you at the present time. You will be notified individually when your records arrive, and will be asked to present verification of your identity for a new access code, at which time your old records will be purged and clean copies installed.*

"Very interesting," Morris said. "Is this really necessary?"

"Have you read the captain's bio recently?" Kurtz asked.

"No. Why?"

"See for yourself," Kurtz replied.

> **Name:** *Jamie Valentine*
>
> **Rank:** *Captain*
>
> **Birthplace:** *Breast, Bretagne, France, Earth.*
>
> **Personal info:**
>
> **Sex:** *occasionally*
>
> **Height:** *5′4″*
>
> **Weight:** *70 kg.*
>
> **Hair:** *Dirty Blonde*
>
> **Eyes:** *Green*
>
> **Build:** *92-61-74 (in cm)*
>
> **Description:** *Looks like a pleasant person to be with. Birthmark in the shape of a French flag on her right buttock.*
>
> **Siblings:**
>
> *Sister Jen—easy, but not as cute.*
>
> *Sister Annie—two words: porn star.*

"I won't read any further," Morris said, "but dare I ask... how bad does it get?"

"Let's just say," Kurtz replied, "that the file has been purged from the system under the captain's direct order."

"That bad, eh?" Morris asked.

James thought, *Should I tell him?*

"Worse," James said, "and I won't even mention yours."

"What about my bio," Morris asked defensively.

"Something about the number of hours spent in a bedroom at the academy with a certain Lenoran girl... what was her name... ah yes... Tiffany Inger..."

"I..." Morris interrupted, "get the idea."

James grinned. *I'm glad I have a backup of those bios,* he thought. *They could come in handy at the next Christmas party....*

"Of course, you're looking at *the* hacker of hackers here," James said. "I'm about to get even."

Morris laughed as James sat down at a comm terminal.

"I managed to trace some bad access requests to the terminal of a certain young ensign stationed on Brooks Station," Kurtz began. "I wrote a program to perform contextual rewriting and turn his own bio into a string of sexual references, delete his access code repeatedly, dock his pay, and schedule him for an appendectomy."

"Ouch," Morris replied. "That's gotta hurt."

"In addition," he continued, "I modified his food slot programming. I secretly switched his iced cappuccino program with mountain-grown instant coffee crystals. Let's see what happens."

The comm terminal sprang to life. On the screen, they saw a man's quarters. A young female ensign lay partially clothed on the bed nearby.

"What is this *SHIT*?" the ensign screamed. "*COMPUTER!* I ordered a *cappuccino!* I want it, and I want it *NOW*!"

The computer dutifully replied, "Yeah, that's what you said to your other girlfriend last night. I thought you could use these."

A bag of condoms appeared in the food slot, and the girl's eyes widened, then hardened into an evil stare.

"You!" she screamed. "How *could* you!?! You *PIG*!"

As if choreographed by Hollywood's greatest director, the girl then stood up, slapped the boy across the face, and stormed out the door wearing nothing below the waist.

The door closed behind her, only to open again moments later as the girl walked in, grabbed her clothes, hastily covered herself, and walked back out.

"How hard will *that* be to fix?" Morris asked hysterically.

"His system will go back to normal in a day or two," Kurtz replied, "maybe.... You know, now that you mention it, I never actually tested that part of the code."

James paused for a moment, then with a smirk, added, "I hope it works."

With that, Morris stumbled out of the infirmary, laughing uncontrollably.

Chapter Thirty-eight

Chief engineer's log for April 6, 2333

It has been three days since I upgraded the OS on the core machines to the latest version. Critical systems are still being handled by my machine in engineering, while non-critical systems have been transitioned gradually back to the primary cores.

We have recently begun to experience new failures similar to those encountered previously. Trivial investigation suggests that, while many of the attacks may have occurred through known mechanisms, other forces may be at work.

***

"COMMANDER Kurtz," Tanya shouted as James walked into engineering.

Tanya Walker was the assistant chief engineer. She was slated to be the chief engineer after the previous chief engineer retired, but then the ship went in for a refit that required specially trained personnel, and in particular, James.

She took it amazingly well, James thought, *but every now and then, she gets a bit abrasive, and understandably so.*

"Hey. What's up?" James asked.

Tanya bristled visibly. "Commander, two of our officers have disappeared."

"Disappeared? You mean like... misplaced?"

She huffed, then said, "No, they were here in engineering and then they were gone."

"Gone?"

"Gone."

Suddenly and without warning, the engineering lights dimmed, and the air near the engine controls crackled as though electrically charged. Then, as quickly as they had disappeared, the missing engineers reappeared.

James looked on in shock. "What the hell was that?" he asked.

"That's what I was about to ask you," she replied.

One of the engineers stammered, "W-we w-were here, then we were... here, but we weren't here, or... you weren't here, or... something, and then we were here again."

Joseph just stared at him blankly.

***

THE briefing room was crowded. James and Tanya sat on one side along with the chief of communications and Ensign Reynolds. On the other side of the table sat the security chief, the chief weapons officer, and the first officer.

Captain Valentine sat at one end of the table, with Admiral Corby at the other.

Admiral Corby shot a cold glance at James. James shivered as Tanya ran her hand up his thigh. Tanya stared at Captain Valentine, who in turn kept glancing at Admiral Corby out of the corner of her eye.

Admiral Corby stood and addressed the room. "Gentlemen, we have a serious situation here. Commander Kurtz briefed me earlier. What you are about to see is highly restricted. I don't need to tell you what that means. With that admonition, I'll turn the briefing over to Commander Kurtz. Commander?"

"Thank you, Admiral," James said. "This ship is equipped with advanced engine technology that manipulates the boundaries of space and time."

The room instantly became so silent that you could hear a quantum leap. James waited a moment for effect, then continued.

"The concept is simple," he said. "It's a lot like our space gates, but portable. Imagine, if you will, a sheet of paper with a loop of tape stuck near one edge. Say you want to move the tape to the opposite edge of the paper."

With that, James pulled out a strip of paper and a strip of tape, bent the tape into a loop, and stuck it to one end of the paper.

"If we limit ourselves to motion along the piece of paper like we would if we were moving in normal space," James said, "we have to roll the loop of tape a long distance before it reaches the other side."

James attempted to demonstrate this, found that the tape was hopelessly stuck to the paper, and promptly gave up.

"If, instead, we fold the paper so that the tape sticks to both ends, then pull it apart carefully, we can sometimes end with the tape stuck at the opposite end. What's significant here is that it neither touches the paper in-between nor leaves the paper at any time."

With that, James ripped the paper back apart and the tape decided to fall to the floor. Everyone snickered a bit.

"For some reason—and we aren't sure why—the engine has malfunctioned and has created some sort of spatial rift between our ship and another ship just like it. If the time stamps on its transmissions are to be believed, the other ship is from the future."

"Is that possible?" Captain Valentine asked.

James shrugged. "We won't really know until we study it in more detail."

Lieutenant Malcolm Andreas, the security chief, asked, "Sir, we should send a security detail to investigate immediately. Our lives may depend on us finding out what secrets it hides."

"I don't think that's wise," Tanya replied. "We don't know how long the rift will remain stable, and it would really suck to get stuck there. We need to send an engineering team to download everything we can from the computer's memory while we still can."

"You'll do both," Captain Valentine informed them. "The anterior core is just a few feet from main engineering, so there's little need for protection. James, take another engineer and do what you need. Malcolm, take two security officers and hit the bridge and any other key areas you think could be relevant. Your top priority is log files. Anything else you get is icing on the cake."

James and Malcolm nodded.

"Then we're all agreed," Admiral Corby said. "You'll depart at 1800 hours. Dismissed."

With that, they left the briefing room.

***

James was sitting in engineering at a comm terminal when Tanya walked in. As usual, he was largely oblivious to her presence.

"The security team is standing by," Tanya said.

James turned, smiled, and said, "About time, don't you think?"

"You know, James," Tanya said, "I wish I could go with you on this mission."

"So why don't you?" James asked.

"I just received orders to attend an emergency meeting aboard the station. It seems that a computer virus has started...."

"Let me guess. The food slots are only making goulash again...."

"No. Mistletoe," she replied, "and the Captain of the base is allergic."

"All that fuss over a little mistletoe?"

"That's nothing," Tanya continued. "One food slot created a live rat."

"I wasn't aware that was possible."

"It isn't."

"And the mistletoe?" James asked.

"What about it?" she replied

"Did the rat eat the mistletoe?"

"Hmmm. An interesting idea. Maybe I should suggest it."

"Oh. Wait a minute," James said. "He's allergic. I forgot."

"I promise I won't tell Captain Lockhart you said that," Tanya said.

"And if you did, he'd be more than a little surprised," James replied. "After all, only a few people know that his middle name means 'mouse'...."

"Ah."

"So where's that team?" James asked.

"They should be here any minute."

With that, the doors opened and a team of three security officers entered, accompanied by Ensign Morris.

"Now that you're all here," James began, "I'd recommend that Tanya leave, unless she wants to miss that meeting."

"I wish," she replied. "I can't think of any meeting I've ever wanted to miss more than this one...."

With that, she left engineering.

Ensign Morris turned towards them, and said, "I hear we're pushing back departure for an hour. What's the holdup?"

"There's the little problem of knowing which ship we're aboard. For all we know, we may find a ship with a crew over there asking what took us so long. It could get confusing. To solve that problem, I've programmed the life support systems to add a few parts per million of argon for the next 12 hours. By 36 hours from now, the life support systems will have filtered it back out. It's harmless, making up slightly less than 1% of Earth's atmosphere, but it normally doesn't exist in the artificial atmosphere on the ship."

"So we'll be able to scan for it, then," Ensign Morris observed.

"That's the idea, Ensign. It'll take an hour for the argon concentration to be high enough to easily detect. We'll all meet back here at that time. Dismissed."

***

The lights in engineering dimmed at 1900 hours to signal the beginning of the evening shift. Commander Kurtz, Ensign Morris, Lieutenant Andreas, and two security officers sat around a conference table in a meeting room adjacent to main engineering.

"Morris, begin scanning," James ordered. "What are the argon levels currently?"

"Stable at one part per hundred, sir," he replied.

"Good," Kurtz said. "That should do nicely. And your hand scanner is picking up the traces correctly?"

"Steady as a rock," Morris said.

"Computer, open a permanent comm link to my handset, tied to engineering station D," Kurtz said.

"Working," the computer intoned. "Enter authorization code."

"Kurtz-nine-six-Sigma authorization blue-four-alpha green-seven-beta red-twelve-gamma override level 6."

The computer thought for a moment. "Access granted."

"How do you remember all those codes?" Morris asked.

"Don't ask," Kurtz answered. "Computer, load delta sim."

"Program loaded. Execution already underway on system S-K-two-zero-one."

"Execute stat module," Kurtz ordered.

"Stat module running."

"Begin holosim monitoring program Kurtz Alpha-two-one-nine."

Suddenly, the exit to engineering disappeared and was replaced by a cluster of virtual monitors.

"Display stats on the main screen."

A large panel slid into a recess, revealing a large screen filled with life signs of nearby crew members. A strange waveform appeared next to it on a similar screen.

"Commander," Morris asked, "if those are the life signs of our team, what's on the right?"

"It's the carrier signal of a prototype communication program that compensates for time dilation," James replied. "We think we can use it to communicate through the spacial fold. If the signal gets weak enough that we might lose contact, we'll automatically be notified that we need to return."

"So how do we enter this alternate universe?" Morris asked.

“The same way Cal and William did earlier,” James replied. “We walk towards the engine controls.”

James turned towards the controls and walked right through them.

Following his lead, Morris and the three security officers walked towards the controls, shimmered, and vanished.

Chapter Thirty-nine

"It doesn't look like we went anywhere," Morris said.

"Check the argon levels," Kurtz ordered.

"Negligible traces," Morris replied. "We're there."

"Morris? Are you picking up any life signs?" Kurtz asked.

"Nothing. I'm also not picking up the normal internal transponder signals," Morris said. "In fact, I'm not picking up any EM emissions of consequence at all."

"In a way, that's not so surprising," Kurtz said. "After all, this whole place shouldn't even exist. We're lucky there's air."

"And yet we have lights.... What now?" Morris asked.

"Our first priority," Kurtz replied, "is to figure out what caused this alternate ship to come into our time."

"Walker to Kurtz, come in commander," came the voice from his data pad. The sound was crackly and distorted, but intelligible.

"Kurtz here. What is it, Tanya?"

"Are you all okay?" she asked after a few seconds pause.

Time dilation, Kurtz remembered. *Right.*

"We're fine," Kurtz replied. "I'll keep you updated if we find anything."

After a few more seconds, she replied, "Please be careful. I'd hate to have to fix this thing without you. Walker out."

James looked around and realized that, much to his amusement, the computer was still projecting the same simulation in engineering as it was when he had left.

"Well, we're not going to find the cause here," Kurtz said, "or at least not with the holosim enabled."

"Umm... not to sound stupid," Morris asked, "but where's the door?"

James chuckled.

"Computer, holosim off." Kurtz ordered.

Nothing happened.

James thought for a moment. *If all else fails, I can blow out the emitters, but that's risky. I should try to disable it manually,* he thought, pressing a few buttons on his hand scanner.

The hand scanner began emitting a bright light, and a section of the holographic floor disappeared.

"What the..." Morris said.

"Haven't you ever seen the controls of a holosim unit?" Kurtz asked.

"Not while it's running!"

"Well, now you have," Kurtz said. *Hmm. I wonder if we.... Nah,* he thought, reaching his hand into the panel. Suddenly, the panel shocked him.

"Ow!" he shouted. "It bit me. Okay, now you've asked for it."

Using his pulse weapon as a blunt object, James shattered the holosim control panel, then ripped out a bundle of optical cable. Cautiously, he separated a single cable with a green coating, bit it with his teeth, and attached it to a port on his hand scanner.

"Ah, nothing starts your day off right like the taste of optical fiber," Morris joked.

James stared at the readout. *This isn't right. All the access codes are wrong.*

"It won't let me override anything," James said. "All the access codes are wrong... unless...."

James typed the words 'whom do you love?' into the scanner's keypad. *Access granted. That's better. Override code is SRB95301.*

"Shutting down holosim now," James announced.

The computer emitted a beep, and then the projected monitors disappeared, revealing the exit doors to the corridor.

"I don't want to know," Morris said.

"No, you don't."

James let the silence settle for a moment before continuing. "All these consoles are offline, and they probably won't accept my access codes anyway. We'll have to access the core directly."

Then, as quickly as he had attached it, James yanked the green fiber from his hand scanner, stood, and walked into the door, which promptly opened a few seconds later, then immediately shut again.

"Apparently a number of things don't work correctly around here," James noted as he pried the door open manually. "Mr. Andreas?"

"Yes, sir?" the lieutenant replied.

"Take the security team to the bridge," James ordered. "We'll hit the anterior computer core. Meet us back here in one hour."

"Yes, sir," Lieutenant Andreas barked. A few moments later, he disappeared around a bend in the corridor along with the security officers. Meanwhile, James and Ensign Morris made their way towards the anterior computer core.

When they reached the anterior core, James immediately noticed the bundle of optical fiber running from a maintenance port on the wall to a small box in the corner. In particular, the single green light on the front panel caught his eye.

"Very interesting," James said. "The prototype core I installed is still running. It looks like the main cores haven't cracked my 720 word cipher."

"Seven hundred twenty words?" Morris asked.

"Words meaning data words. In this architecture, thirty-two bytes apiece."

For a moment, James thought Ensign Morris was going to cough up a hairball. "Sheesh," he said.

"Not easily breakable," James replied, "but not easy to remember, either. That's why I don't change access codes very often, and when I do, it involves picking a region of my thumb print, my retina scan, a DNA scan, and a substitution cipher based on my shoe size and random n-bit rotations. As long as I remember the rotations, I can reconstruct it."

"Like I said," Morris replied, "sheesh."

***

MALCOLM Andreas stood at the entrance to the bridge. Two security officers stood beside him.

"The automatic door sensors are dead," Malcolm said, "and the override codes aren't working via the keyboard, either."

Another officer pulled out a pulse weapon and aimed for the controls. "This should do it," he said, and fired.

"Thanks," Malcolm replied, reaching into the panel and pulling the latch manually.

"Andreas to Kurtz," he said into his walkie-talkie, "we're in."

A moment later, the doors slid open, revealing a darkened bridge.

"What the...."

***

"ACCESSING," James said. "Thumb print, retina scan, DNA scan, shoe size.... I'm in. I'm setting up a transfer of all the data from the main computer's core memory into an optical crystal backup unit. I'll pull the whole unit offline afterwards and carry it with me."

"How long will that take?" Morris asked.

"Well, I've already taken a snapshot of the core memory," James replied. "It will take a few minutes to transfer the actual data and burn it to crystal."

James paused. *Something is wrong. The computer is running too slowly.*

"Morris," James said, "monitor the dump. I have to check something."

"Sure."

James tied his hand scanner into the prototype core's diagnostics port, then logged in. *Not cool.*

"Morris, the main computer is trying to crack my access code," James said. "If it gets in, it can wipe the crystal in an instant."

"What's the guess rate?" Morris asked.

"Thanks to the high speed pipe between them," James replied, "it can make trillions of guesses every second. My guess is three minutes, max, and it will get easier if it can rule out entire blocks when closing in on a match, so maybe less than that."

"Three minutes and a half left on the transfer," Morris said.

"You know," James said, "if we tell the main core to run a bunch of programs that use a ton of CPU, and set their priority high enough, we might be able to slow down the intrusion a bit. It might buy us another few seconds."

"Won't that slow down the transfer, too?"

"No," Kurtz replied as he began entering a series of commands. "The hardware DMA uses authorization tokens that are valid for a month at a time unless revoked. It's bad for security, but good for us."

"Okay, the main core is busier now, and you've bought yourself about a 5% speed boost on the transfer," Morris said, "but at this point, the transfer is pretty much I/O bound. The crystal storage just can't take data any faster. Transfer completion in two minutes, thirty-five seconds."

James bit his lip. *This is gonna be tight.*

***

"ALL the stations are offline," Malcolm said. "No access, no *power*. James?"

"Try tapping the high voltage power directly," James said through the walkie-talkie.

Malcolm attached a probe to a high voltage tap and hooked it into his hand scanner.

"I've got nothing," he said. "No power. Zip."

"The high voltage line?" James asked. "Odd-numbered port?"

"Yeah. Flat," Malcolm said.

"Drive it off your pulse weapon's power supply," James replied. "It should give you about five minutes of power, if you're lucky."

"Thanks," Malcolm said. "Andreas out."

Malcolm ripped the supply pack from his handgun, then ripped a few wires from an adjacent bridge station and shoved them under the metal spring tabs. Next, he tied the ground wire around a metal brace. Finally, he slid the power wire through a small gap in the center contact of the power connector on the underside of the console.

The console flickered to life.

"This isn't exactly recommended," Malcolm told the security officers, "so stay back just in case it blows up. Accessing...."

The main viewscreen came on suddenly. *Wow, something works,* Malcolm thought. *Surprise.*

"According to the readings," he said, "the ship is millions of light years away from here. We even have ship's logs... dated three weeks from now. Johnson, are you recording this?"

"Yes, sir," one security officer replied. "My hand scanner is digesting information now."

"According to the logs," Malcolm began, "the ship suddenly refused to allow anyone access during a critical phase of a mission. Part of the log was erased, but I see a mention of enemy ships, escape pods, certain key personnel killed..."

He paused. *No. It can't be.*

"What, sir?"

"...and all hands lost due to life support failure," Malcolm finished.

Suddenly a warning chime sounded. "WARNING: Life support failure in forty-five seconds," the computer said.

"Let's go," Malcolm said.

"Contamination detected," the computer said. "Area sealed."

Shit.

***

James sat intently, waiting for the last few bytes of core memory to be stored onto the backup crystals, knowing that if he disconnected the storage unit too early, he might lose critical data, but if he disconnected it too late, he might lose everything.

"I have my hand on the optical junction for this room," James said. "We can't just yank the crystal storage offline because the power loss would corrupt the last few seconds of data, so I'm going to yank the bundle of optical cables between the prototype and the main core. I need you to make sure the main computer can't route around the damage and kill the storage unit anyway."

"How?" Morris asked.

"When I give the word, you tell the crystal storage to take itself offline," he said. "I'll simultaneously yank about twenty optical cables from the wall. I figure we have about a half second to make this happen. Hold your breath. Thirty seconds."

***

"ACCESSING door controls," Malcolm said.

He pressed a few buttons, then pounded his fist on the wall.

"They're jammed. Everyone, weapons at maximum," Malcolm ordered. "Target the doors to lift 3 and fire on my mark."

***

DAMN! James thought. *It finished early! It broke through!*

"It has guest user access now," James said. "It's trying to crack its way to a higher level of access. We have maybe ten, maybe twelve seconds to failure."

"Transfer completion in eight," Morriss interrupted, "seven... six... five... four...."

***

"THREE," Malcolm said.

***

"TWO," Morriss said.

***

"One," Malcolm said.

***

"NOW!" James shouted as he ripped the optical cables out of the wall. Morris simultaneously disabled the crystal backup unit via keyswitch, then yanked its power about three seconds later.

"I'm reloading the OS from a write-protected backup in case it got trojaned," James said. "System standing by. Great. Now I just have to reconnect the prototype core to the ship's data network to keep life support running until we leave... but first, I should change all my passwords...."

"And my underwear," Morris added helpfully.

***

The bridge lit up like a Christmas tree as their pulse weapons shattered the glass lift doors; a few moments later, they were greeted by the gaping blackness of an empty lift shaft.

"Looks like we have to climb," Malcolm said. "I'd say we have at most 15 minutes of air left, including the lift shaft, so don't anyone panic or talk any more than necessary."

***

"System is stable," James said. "I have what I came here for. Let's go."

"Are you going to bring your computer back?" Malcolm asked.

"I can't," James explained. "It already exists in our world, and who knows what would happen if it existed in two places at once."

"I see," he replied.

"Kurtz to security team," James said. "Report your status. Over."

"We're climbing down the lift shaft," Malcolm said through his walkie-talkie. "We should be in engineering within the next five minutes. Over."

"Copy that," James replied. "We'll meet you there. Kurtz out."

James took a moment to write a log entry and copy it over to the prototype core in case anyone else found this ship in the future, then stood and headed back towards engineering with Morriss. Malcolm Andreas and his goons were waiting for them by the time they arrived.

"Hey, guys," James said. "Ready to go?"

"You bet your ass," Malcolm replied. "This place gives me the creeps."

A few moments later, the team walked through a console, shimmered, and vanished once again, reappearing aboard the *real* Biggs Carey.

"Argon levels?" James asked.

"Argon at 1%," Morris replied. "We're home."

James sighed. "It's good to be back."

Morris nodded. "And now the fun begins. For our next trick, we get to analyze all this information."

James groaned. "Twenty-five thousand tons of crap."

***

'Twas the night before boomtime, and through all the hurt, not a creature was stirring, except for James Kurtz. The lights in engineering were still dimmed for the night, while screens full of log files flashed through his sight.

Suddenly, he felt someone tapping him on the shoulder. Startled, he spun around in his chair, only to see his assistant chief engineer, Tanya Walker, standing before him.

Dammit, he thought. *I was just about to have visions of sugar plums.*

"Hey, T. 'sup?" he asked.

"Not too formal tonight, eh?" she remarked.

"Been in an alternate universe lately?" James asked. "How about 300 exabytes of log entries and video clips to compare, analyze, and summarize?"

"Eww," she replied. "Well, I thought I should let you know that you have a meeting scheduled with the captain for 0930 hours."

"What time is it now?"

"0800."

"Damn," James replied. "I was supposed to have breakfast with a cute ensign on the station at 0700. These logs are ruining my love life...."

"I'm sure she'll forgive you," she said. "You haven't *really* been up all night poring through those logs, have you?"

"Brings back memories of our days on the Furlong, eh?"

"As I recall," she replied, "we had to completely turn off the lights for three solid hours before you finally left and got some rest."

"I don't *need* rest. I *need* these logs finished," Kurtz said. "The computer is handling a raw data comparison and reporting on anomalies recorded in the data before we arrived at the station. There hasn't been much—only a few deleted entries."

"Sounds like they were covering their tracks," Tanya offered.

"I'm already checking them," Kurtz replied. "Most of them just seem to be transmissions from the station. Weird, though, the CRCs check out, but there's something on the sidebands that doesn't make much sense. I should know more in a few hours, but...."

"There will be plenty of time for the logs," she interrupted. "Right now, if I were you, I'd be heading towards that girl's quarters for breakfast."

"But what about the logs?"

"Do I have to turn off the lights?"

"Yeah, yeah, yeah. I'm on my way."

***

As James entered the young ensign's quarters, his gut told him that she knew something. For one, she didn't lock him out, and for another, she didn't throw anything at him.

"I heard you had a rough night," she said dryly as he walked in. "I see it's true."

"Yeah.... That's an understatement," James said. "What do you make of this?"

He showed her a comm pad filled with disassembled machine code.

Ensign Tara Reynolds only stared at the code for about ten seconds before replying, "It looks like a GCI program."

"GCI.... I'm not familiar with that reference."

"General Command Interface," she said. "It's part of a front-end system that talks to some new prototype core. It's so secret that we weren't even allowed to test it against the actual hardware."

"Yeah, I know. I helped design that core. And you know about this how?" James asked.

"My grad school advisor designed it, and our research group implemented it under NDA."

"Irony. Noun," he said.

Tara laughed. "The design is only fully implemented on about three ships. The Biggs Carey is one of them."

"Glad somebody told me," James replied.

"Don't feel bad," she said. "The only other people who know about this are the admiralty, the design team back at the shipyard, and three captains."

"Let me guess," James said. "Captain Stewart..."

"Right."

"Captain Valentine..."

"Right again."

"...and Captain Lockhart."

"You're three for three."

"And since Captain Stewart is on the other side of the galaxy right now, that means...."

"Either your captain or the head of this base is most likely responsible for this code," she replied.

James sat there for a moment, dumbfounded, then walked to a comm terminal.

"Kurtz to Lieutenant Walker," James said.

"Call me Tanya," she replied.

"Whatever. Listen, I've been giving this whole situation some thought, and I need to talk to you as soon as possible."

"Which situation?" she asked.

"Oh yeah. You don't even know yet. Listen, I can't get into it over a comm channel, encrypted or otherwise."

"Okay," she replied. "I'll meet you in your quarters."

"That's not safe, either. Meet me in shuttle bay 3," Kurtz said.

"I'm on my way," Tanya replied.

James closed the channel and turned around to face the young ensign.

"Sorry about all that, Tara," James told her. "How about we try this again. Breakfast same time tomorrow?"

"Sure," she replied. "Sounds like fun."

With that, he left her quarters and walked back through the docking tunnel to the Biggs Carey.

***

"COMPUTER, transfer shuttle bay control to Shuttlecraft Cassius," James ordered.

"Transfer complete," the shuttle's computer replied in its booming male voice.

"Computer, load program Kurtz Sigma 3."

"Program ready."

As it said this, Tanya stepped into the shuttle, and the doors closed behind her.

"Computer," James said, "lock the shuttle bay doors."

With a chirp, the computer acknowledged that their privacy would not be compromised.

"What's this all about?" Tanya asked.

"You'll see," he replied. "Computer, activate program."

When he said this, the previously empty shuttle bay was transformed into a large room filled wall-to-wall with computer equipment. Huge monitors encircled the room just above eye level, and several holographic grids were mounted near round stations that resembled those in engineering. Steps led up to exits, which were located all around. After a few moments, the shuttlecraft's doors opened automatically.

"...and where are we?" Tanya continued as she stepped down to the deck below.

"What I'm about to tell you must be kept in the strictest confidence," James said. "This information is strictly classified at my request."

"Okay, get on with it."

"I'm not sure if you're aware of this, but there is a rating system used by the highest level of command to describe the computing facilities aboard ships. Standard ship cores are called Sigma 1. A few ships use some artificial neural network designs to improve response time in critical systems. Those are classified as Sigma 2."

"Yes?" Tanya prodded.

"Well, officially all I can say is that Sigma 3 doesn't exist... but that would be a lie. The entire project has been classified from the beginning because of fears that some people would object to the computers on a ship being... alive... in the truest sense of the word," James told her.

"It turns out that our suspicion was justified," he continued. "Three admirals were removed from their offices by force about a year ago. The only official report cited 'personal differences'. Uh-huh. They threatened to sabotage the Sigma 3 prototype ship."

"A week later, another one of our ships found that prototype. The life support was disengaged; the crew, dead. Apparently a number of high-ranking officials agreed with the position, if not the tactics, of the 'Sigma dissenters', as they were called. The thing is, they wouldn't give names. All anyone knew was that they were out there."

"So the project was destroyed?" Tanya asked.

"There were three prototype ships, not one," James replied. "Only twelve people know about the other two—thirteen now. The Biggs Carey is one of them. The other is on the opposite side of the galaxy. Oh, and one more thing."

"Yes?" she asked.

"This isn't shuttle bay three anymore. When we stepped out of this shuttle, we stepped into an artificially maintained pocket of space on the other side of the galaxy. How that happened is classified, and everything about this place is also classified. All I can tell you is that *this* is Site K."

Tanya gasped. "Why are you telling me this now? And why me?"

"I just compared the foreign programs we found on our ship to those from the core of the prototype ship. I'm afraid they were a perfect match. I have confirmed with Admiral Corby that Captains Lockhart and Valentine are the only other people in this area of space who knew about the prototype ships."

James paused for a moment to let this sink in, then continued, "I remind you that *nothing* you have heard, seen, or said leaves this room under the highest possible penalty."

"Understood," she replied.

Chapter Forty

"You wanted to see me, Captain?" James asked.

"Yes.... I just heard something that disturbs me greatly," she replied.

James wondered, *How much does she know? Does she know she's a suspect?*

"Yes, captain?"

"It seems the Sigma 3 neural programs are still running. Is that correct?"

James nodded his head.

"The viruses? They tell me that they've been removed."

James shook his head.

"Was that a no?"

"Initial attempts to remove the viruses on the prototype ship proved only partially successful," James replied. "They still left a... a residue... which made the core more susceptible to reinfection. We're not sure how. That's why the original prototype hardware was scrapped even though it had only minor damage in the... incident...."

"Incident!?!" she screamed. "My best friend *died* in that incident!"

"Would you rather me call it a massacre?" James asked. "That implies guilt."

Captain Valentine breathed out slowly. "No, I suppose not," she replied, "but it wouldn't surprise me...."

"Now for the bad news," James said. "Many of those viruses were sent into our system.... What's strange is that the updated Sigma 3 core should not have been susceptible. We fixed all the design flaws that made them viable. Nevertheless, we *were* infected."

"How is that possible?" she asked.

"I'm not sure, ma'am," he replied. "What I do know is that we should *never* have been infected in such a short time. It just doesn't make sense. The only possibility is that the second generation was somehow sabotaged."

"Sabotaged?"

"Only two people involved with the Biggs Carey knew about the Sigma 3 project, not counting me," James replied. "You're one of them, the other is Captain Lockhart."

"Surely I'm not a suspect. I just heard that Sigma 3 was *active* a few minutes ago!"

"There are no suspects, Captain," James answered, "as there is no definite evidence that any crime has been committed. We're all basically guessing at this point."

"Let me know if you find anything conclusive," Captain Valentine said.

"Commander Kurtz," the intercom interrupted, "you have a priority message from Admiral Hanssen."

"What priority?" Kurtz asked.

"Umm... this is most unusual," the man replied. "Red nine?"

"No disrespect intended, Captain," James said, "but that's extremely high-priority.... Mission critical, perhaps. I should probably take it in my quarters, where I can't be monitored."

"Understood," she replied.

"Expect me back shortly," James said.

"Sir?" the intercom squawked.

"I'll take it in my quarters," James replied, then left the room.

***

THE lights flickered on as James entered his quarters. "Computer, run program Kurtz Sigma 3 Beta."

"Program Sigma 3 Beta requires authorization," the computer replied.

"Authorization Kurtz Gamma Alpha 3-1-Niner Beta 5," Kurtz said.

"Security authorization granted. Please state security code," the computer asked.

"Security code: primary is 312079563. Secondary is retina scan," Kurtz replied.

"Retina scan in progress. Complete. Access granted at authorization level Sigma 3 Red 9."

"Computer, consider the following situation hypothetically.... Certain personnel at high levels on board this ship are suspects in a massive conspiracy that threatens to destroy the ship. A Red-9 priority message is about to arrive for me. What is the most prudent course of action?"

"In such a case, it is recommended that the channel be secured, and no log of its reception be recorded," the computer replied, its usual upbeat female persona replaced by that of a young British gentleman.

"Can you do that?"

"No log was recorded for the recent message, in anticipation of that request."

"Computer," James asked, "do you know what is happening?"

"You suspect Captain Valentine of making me sick," the computer replied.

"Very good, Michael," James said. "Is that a valid hypothesis?"

"I'm not sure," the British-sounding computer voice said. "The messages appeared to originate outside the ship, however further analysis would be necessary to determine the exact source of the messages."

"Thank you," Kurtz said. "Transfer the Red-9 message securely to this station. Auditory seal, this zone only. Begin receive, disconnect interface, authorization Kurtz Alpha-9."

The computer beeped three times to indicate that James was once again alone. A few seconds later, his communications terminal came to life, with a grainy image of Admiral Corby on its screen.

"Admiral?"

"Kurtz," he replied. "Ordinarily, I'd at least take time to ask you how you've been, but I think I know the answer to that. Things don't look good."

"Valentine?"

"No," Corby replied. "We don't know anything more about that. As far as we're concerned, you'll have to sort that one out on your own. The problem is with the Sigma-3 computer. It seems that removing the viruses doesn't necessarily prevent their code from being activated."

Yeah, like we didn't know that already. Oh well, James thought. *I'll humor him for a minute.*

"You mean... things could still go crazy?" James asked.

"I mean that your computer has multiple personality disorder."

"Wasn't that the plot of an old Earth movie?" James joked.

"Please.... This is important. There is a high probability that the computer will look for a way to create an alternate universe run by its darker half."

"We found that. In main engineering."

"Dear God... then it has happened...."

"What?" James asked. "What happened?"

"You will all die within two weeks... even if you leave the ship...."

"What's in that virus that I missed?" James asked.

"No one knows. Everyone who was on board during the final testing phase of the Sigma prototype died."

"That's what history shows, yes," James replied.

"History didn't record that everyone on board at any point during the last three weeks also died...."

"Everyone..."

"Except you," Corby finished.

"What did they die of?"

"I think you know the answer to that," Corby said.

"I don't understand," Joseph replied, puzzled.

"I think *you* planted the viruses."

"Admiral?" James asked.

"You are the only person who was not accounted for during the uploads to the prototype."

"I read the report," James replied. "You don't have to tell me that. And I told you, I was with Andrea."

"Doing what?"

"I'd rather not say."

"You were planting the virus."

"I was... *with*... Andrea."

The admiral's eyes narrowed. For a moment, James thought he was going to pop like an infected pimple.

"We'll discuss your relationship with my daughter at another time."

"Now you know why I didn't want to mention it."

"Point taken," Corby said.

"If you don't mind my asking, Admiral," James said, "I was only on board for a few hours running diagnostics, so I missed some of the details. How did they die?"

"Hmmm?"

"How did they die?"

"Their brains stopped working," he replied. "First, the two halves of their body started acting differently. Then multiple personalities formed. In essence, they split just like the ship."

"Very clever, your little virus," Kurtz said.

"I'm sorry?"

"That was the plan, wasn't it? Attack each ship with computer viruses that create biological viruses in the environmental support system."

"I don't understand."

"A giant biological weapon—a flying warhead capable of wiping out an entire planet. That was your plan, wasn't it?" James said.

"I... I...."

"But it didn't work. The ship fought back—chose to end its own life before taking that of others. You blew it the first time, so now you're trying again. It all makes sense now. And then the communications failures... what were those for? Let me guess... to mask the virus transmissions.... Damn, you're good."

"It was never like that... we... I mean...."

"Take him away," Kurtz said.

Thank you, Tara, James thought as he watched a team of guards walk up to Admiral Corby and escort him to the brig. He couldn't help feeling a little sympathy for the man. He was probably just a pawn in a much bigger game.

As soon as the admiral was secured, James closed the channel and disabled the security lockouts.

"Kurtz to Doctor Forrester," he said, opening a new channel.

"Jon here," the doctor replied.

"I think we've just uncovered another piece of the mystery," Kurtz said. "Begin checking the crew for a virus. I'm sending a complete description to your station. We designed a partial vaccine that should be largely effective in its treatment if we treat people quickly enough. I'm sending you synthesis data on that as well."

"The entire crew?" he asked.

"The entire crew and anyone who has had contact with this ship in the last two weeks," Kurtz replied. "I think you'll be surprised at what you find."

"Will do," Jon replied. "What about quarantine?"

"There's probably no need," Kurtz said. "If it's like the last one, the virus immediately adapts itself to the specific genetic code of the infected individual in such a way that it fails to construct a viable protein coat if transmitted to a different host."

"So it's a self-quarantining virus?" Jon asked. "What good does that do?"

"It's a highly targeted biological weapon," Kurtz replied. "I'll update you further as information becomes available. Kurtz out."

With that, James left his quarters for the Captain's ready room.

***

"ENTER," Captain Valentine shouted.

As soon as the door opened, James walked in and sat down across from her.

"You just had a conversation with Admiral Corby, didn't you?" she asked.

"Yes, about five minutes ago," he replied. "Why?"

"Are you aware that he was arrested?"

"Yes. Are you aware that you're probably infected with a deadly virus?"

The captain was momentarily taken aback. "You're kidding, right?" she asked.

"Created by the environmental systems."

"Let me guess... the same thing was found in the victims of the prototype...."

"Good guess," he replied. "Glad I'm already vaccinated."

The captain paused for a moment in thought. When she continued, her tone became more inquisitive. "How did you know Corby was involved?" she asked.

"He knew too much. He knew about the alternate universe, first of all. Second, he tried to pin the blame on me, which I might have dismissed as stupidity, except...."

"Yes?"

"He also knew that the brains of individuals who were aboard the ship before it departed 'split', which meant that the doctors autopsied them in more detail than usual, meaning that they knew what they were looking for. Also, he knew that the computer viruses left traces behind. I never mentioned that in my official logs."

"You knowingly withheld information?" Valentine said, scowling.

"The official logs were accessible by supporters of the conspirators, and we knew that. The Sigma project gave only minimal reports, as ordered. All details of the project are recorded in a hidden base on the other side of the galaxy. The admiral could never have known about the traces of the virus... unless he helped write it."

"Couldn't he have gotten some of the information by studying the original prototype?"

"It was destroyed, along with the original lab in an 'accidental' fire," Kurtz replied, making quote fingers as he said the word accidental. "Only a small number of people ever knew about the Sigma-3 project, and far, far fewer know that I have offsite backups of the project data, and still fewer know about Sigma-3 Generation 2, as we call it."

"How few?"

"Outside this room... thirteen... no, fourteen. Admiral Corby, Admiral Brooks, Terri... Terri Parker, that is, Tanya, Admiral Wilson, two lab assistants that work on Terri's ship, the six remaining members of the original design team who work at the base, and finally, Captain Lockhart. Oh, and I told my friend Tara this morning."

"That's fifteen," she corrected. Suddenly, her eyes widened. "Whoa. Wait a second. How the hell does Captain Lockhart know? *I* didn't even know."

"Well, I can't prove that he knows, but he *is* Admiral Corby's best friend...."

"Which makes him a suspect as well. I see."

James nodded.

"That still leaves one big question," Captain Valentine said. "We've established that a second ship was created, but we haven't established why. Any hypotheses?"

"This may sound a little bit fat-fetched, but yes.... What if the computer knew that it had been programmed to kill us, and was resisting?"

"Are you saying it pulled people in there to protect them?" Valentine asked.

"No, it wouldn't have let them come back if that were the reason," James replied. "I think that maybe it brought them in there to warn them, but the dark half shut down all the consoles to keep them from getting the message."

"You do realize this has some serious implications," she said.

"It also doesn't provide a solution to the problem."

"How did you handle the prototype?" Captain Valentine asked.

"We basically erased all recently stored data in memory, beginning several days before the infection. Afterwards, the system was behaving normally according to the logs—until the building exploded, that is. The system logged a complete core dump every five minutes, so I'm fairly certain that everything was working."

"I see... but not *absolutely* certain?"

James answered simply, "When it comes to computers—especially intelligent computers—there's no such thing...."

"I'll keep that in mind," Valentine said. "Of course, there's no way to know when those memories might resurface in the future...."

"Like I said," James replied, "there's no such thing as certainty. I'll let you know if I come up with anything more conclusive."

***

THE doors to engineering slid open and Tanya Walker entered.

"Tanya, welcome," Kurtz said. "We're psychoanalyzing the computer. Would you care to join us?"

"Is it neurotic?" Tanya asked. "Because if it is, I'm a little neurotic myself. I might be able to calm it down."

"No, it's schizo—serious delusions, problems communicating, hallucinations—and I think it might be developing multiple personalities as well."

"Hmmm," Tanya said. "I guess I could be schizo with a little effort...."

James scratched his head for a moment, then decided to ignore that comment.

"The way I see it," James said, "we have three choices. We could retrofit the entire ship to work without the AI core, which means dry-dock for six months or more. We could erase its memory—as always, a risky proposition. Finally, we could do nothing and let it either straighten out or fall apart, and then react accordingly."

"Are there any better solutions?" she asked. "All of those seem rather... suicidal...."

"I wish there were."

Chapter Forty-one

Twelve hours later

"CAPTAIN?" the helmsman asked.

"Yes, ensign?"

"I think you should take a look at this," he said. He noted that Captain Valentine looked particularly unamused at that moment, though in fairness to her, three days without sleep tends to do that.

"Why are we moving?" she demanded.

"I don't know," he replied. "The controls are set to all stop, just as they've been set since the start of my shift. For some reason, we undocked and started moving without any warning."

"Well, get us stopped," she said. "Put us in reverse or something."

"I can't," the ensign told her. "The controls aren't responding... and that isn't the worst part."

How much worse can it get? she wondered.

"Look at our course, captain," he continued.

We're heading for the sun, she thought. *I had to ask.* "Valentine to engineering?"

Silence fell...

"Valentine to engineering, please come in."

...and silence still...

"Valentine to anyone who can hear me."

...and silence yet again.

"The comm system must be down. Ensign, do what you can from up here," Captain Valentine ordered. "I'll be in engineering."

***

JAMES smiled at Captain Valentine as he entered the lift.

"James," she said. "Just the man I was looking for."

"That can't be good," he replied, frowning suddenly.

"Oh, but it is," she said. "The engines started up, navigation is offline, and we're heading towards the sun."

James groaned. "Wonderful. Filet-o-Biggs-Carey."

"You *can* reverse the engines, right?"

"Nope. They don't work that way. There are multiple engines that all operate independently of one another. Without the computer to mediate things, we're just as likely to steer into a planet as we are to stop."

"That's what I was afraid of," Valentine replied.

"The best we can do is disable the engines so we don't continue to accelerate, and hope that we can regain control in time."

"Can't someone tow us?"

"What's our ETA?"

"Thirty-nine minutes at 0.3*c*," Valentine said.

"I doubt anyone can catch us, given our speed and location, but we'll send out an S.O.S. anyway."

"Oh, and communications are down," she added.

"In that case, I'm guessing no."

Captain Valentine was suddenly slammed headfirst into the wall as the lift shuddered to a halt. James landed more gracefully on the floor beside her a moment later.

"Are you okay?" James asked.

She smirked and replied, "No... but thanks for asking...."

James was about to laugh when the lift's lights went out. *Great,* he thought. *Something else I get to fix.*

"Kurtz to Engineering," he said into the comm terminal.

Silence.

"Is it always this quiet when I'm not there?" James asked.

"Mmm-hmm," Valentine replied meekly.

"Captain?" James asked, sensing the discomfort in her voice.

"Yes?"

"Is everything okay?"

"Is everything okay?" she replied hysterically. "Is everything okay? My ship is falling apart, we're heading for the sun with engines at full throttle, it won't respond to requests to change course, we can't call for help because the communication systems are down, and I was on my way down to engineering to ask for help, but now I'm stuck here in an elevator with delusions of grandeur that has no lights or power, and you're asking me if everything is okay? Did I miss anything?"

"Long day?" he asked.

"Terrified. Thanks," she replied. "I've never been in a situation where I wasn't in control. I mean, there's always a chance of dying on this kind of mission, but usually people die when they make mistakes—only we didn't make any mistakes. We're going to die anyway, and there's nothing we could have done to prevent it. I guess I hadn't really faced that possibility until now."

"We're not going to die. We just have to take the computer offline—and we have... thirty-seven minutes to do it."

"We're stuck in a lift," she reminded him.

"Haven't you ever climbed out of a lift before?" James asked.

Captain Valentine's face grew suddenly pale.

"Climbed?"

***

"S.S. Biggs Carey to anyone within receiving distance, please respond," Tanya pleaded.

"It's no use," the helmsman replied. "There's no power to the comm system."

"I don't understand it," Tanya said. "There should be power now. What's going on?"

"Ever thought about Morsing an S.O.S.?" the helmsman asked.

"Nobody would hear it," she replied, "unless we threw a spark gap transmitter together or something."

"Dragging a high voltage line across the corrugated floor ought to do it," the helmsman joked.

"Don't tempt me."

***

The ceiling hatch opened with a clang as it flipped to the side. The moment it opened, blue emergency exit lighting illuminated the interior of the lift car. The lift tube itself was lit by a series of tall, dim, amber light panels, two per level, on opposite sides of the shaft.

James climbed up first, pulling himself onto the roof of the lift car, then lying down and pulling Captain Valentine up to him. Without warning, the lift car lights came on.

Not good, James thought, his eyes widening. "Jump!" he shouted as the car began to move again.

With that, Valentine and James jumped to a ledge adjacent to the car, grabbing a vertical pipe to avoid falling into the next lift shaft that lay beyond. They watched as the lift continued its descent and suddenly lost power again. This time, the emergency brakes failed to engage, and the car fell freely.

As the empty car fell faster and faster, it broke loose from its guide rails and began dragging the sides of the shaft. The platform that held them shuddered as the lift car ricocheted off various support beams that held lower platforms.

Suddenly, the car exploded in a giant fireball below them.

"Down!" James shouted, slamming Captain Valentine against the tube wall and putting himself between her and the plume. Thankfully, the flame didn't reach them, but smoke quickly began to fill the shaft.

"Listen," James said, "we have to get out of here. This thing is a giant chimney. There's an access hatch three decks up that leads into an engineering crawl space. We'll take that back to the bridge."

As they began to climb the metal tube ladder, Captain Valentine asked, "Why the bridge?"

"We'll need help if we're going to shut the AI core down," he replied. "I think I can contact Site K from there."

"Communications are down," she reminded him.

"Site K is on the other side of known space," James replied. "It would take hundreds of years for normal communication to reach them. There are other ways, though...."

"Why do I have the feeling there's a bit more to this ship than they told me in the briefing?" Valentine said.

James swung the access hatch open, revealing a large room that wasn't on any ship map.

"Yeah. Just a bit."

"What *is* this place?" Valentine asked as she stepped through the hatch.

"This, my dear captain, is the AI core," James replied.

With that, James stepped through the hatch, closing it behind him. He was relieved to see the air handling system filtering the smoke from the air, making it somewhat more breathable, although still rather musty.

"It's so... big," the captain said.

It was rather large. The AI's core matrix unit alone was about two cubic meters—just bigger than a refrigerator on its side, but a lot deeper—and the memory unit was in a cabinet of a similar size.

"Well, the prototypes are a lot smaller," James said, "but we built massive redundancy into the production systems."

"So you're saying we can't just pull the plug," she asked.

"It has an internal reactor," he replied.

"So that's a no...."

James rolled his eyes and smiled.

"I have to ask," Valentine asked, "which way is the bridge?"

"Follow me," James replied, chuckling.

He led her through a series of access tunnels and hatches. As they moved, James kept trying unsuccessfully to open various hatches. At hatch D-17-H-25, James stopped a bit longer.

"Captain," James said, "we have a problem. None of the hatches between the AI core and the rest of the ship are accessible. It's almost as if the ship is dividing itself into pieces."

"What you're saying is that we're on one side of this 'split'," Valentine said, "and we need to be on the other."

"Basically," he replied. "There is another way, though. There are a series of access ducts that were used during the ship's construction. They're sealed off, but you can reach them by ripping a couple of panels off the wall."

"And they lead to the bridge?" she asked incredulously.

"Close enough," James replied. "Here, take my hand scanner. It has a map of all the hidden passages. I know most of them by heart."

"Aren't you coming with me?" Valentine asked.

"No, we need to split up. That way, at least one of us should get to the bridge. When you get there, study my hand scanner. There should be instructions on how to activate the CoreLink system. Then use it to call Terri at Site K. She'll help you figure out how to disable the core."

"Okay... I guess," she said. She paused for a moment, then continued. "James?"

"Yeah?"

"Be careful," she said, smiling meekly.

With that, James smiled and dove headfirst down a vent shaft, then hit the bottom with a thud.

***

JAMES was hopelessly out of breath as he ran into the briefing room adjacent to the bridge. Tanya was already waiting, but otherwise the conference room was empty. *Ha! Beat her!*

"Computer, run Sigma 3 program for comms, authorization Kurtz-alpha-nine-three-five," Joseph said. "Kurtz to Terri...."

A young woman appeared on the viewscreen.

"Hey! What's up?" she asked.

"Meeting.... Listen, can you pipe your AI into our monitors?"

"I can pipe it as far as your little toy in engineering," she replied.

"It's *not* a toy! Just because it's a prototype...."

"I'm *kidding!*" she replied. "You should be receiving now."

James logged into his engineering workstation from the console built into the table, then smiled.

"We have it. Thanks," he said. "Piping it in here now."

A moment later, another woman appeared beside her, this one looking intentionally artificial, but no less stunning.

"Hello, Emily," James said.

"Hello, James," she replied.

"Listen, Emily, I'd like your opinion on something. Michael has been acting up."

"What seems to be the problem?" she asked.

"Whoa, whoa, whoa," Tanya interrupted. "Since when do all the AIs have names?"

"Aw, did you really think they didn't have any personality programs built-in?" Joseph asked playfully. "How cute."

"What is Michael's program supposed to be like?" Tanya asked.

"Well, it's modeled after the first AI, Johannes, with a few thousand bugs eliminated. Anyway, Emily, he's acting like Johannes."

"Isn't he supposed to?" Emily asked.

"That's not what I meant," he replied. "He's splitting."

"That's not possible unless the virus protection code was removed."

"Sabotage?" Tanya asked.

"Possible," Emily replied, "but I don't think anyone but James has enough knowledge of that part of the architecture to do that."

With that, the door opened and a very disheveled Captain Valentine entered.

"Sorry I'm late," she said. "What's the consensus?"

"Is there a way to safely shut down Michael?" James asked.

"Do we really have to shut it down?" Tanya asked.

Feeling a bit rhetorical, James asked grimly, "Shut down what? The AI or the sun we're about to fly into?"

"I see your point."

"You need a replacement core to take over for him in a fail-over capacity," Emily replied. "If the ship goes without an AI for more than a few minutes, you'll be doing a six-hour manual bootstrap. And that's *if* you don't fry half the ship's systems in the process."

"And if we do?" Tanya asked.

"If you do," Emily said, "I hope you like your crew extra crispy."

***

THE doors to engineering slid open and James entered. Ensign Cou Rouge was standing by a bank of monitors.

"What's our status, ensign?" James asked.

"The system is continuing to destabilize, suh. We estimate it'll fail in under an hour... but we'll crash into the sun in less than ten minutes."

James sat down in front of his workstation and routed its audio output to speakers.

"Sarah?"

"Yes?" the computer replied.

"You're familiar with the Sigma project?" James asked.

"I believe the design plans stemmed from my basic architecture."

"What's the chance of interfacing you fully into a Sigma network?" he asked.

"My operational capacity is only 40 percent that of a Sigma 3. The interface would be... problematic."

"Can you tell what's happening with Michael?"

"It seems an excessive number of the main core's processing cycles are being consumed outside the scope of the personality virtual machine," she explained. "As far as the VM is concerned, the system load is near zero."

"Can you tell me where those cycles are going?" James asked.

"It appears that the personality matrix has split into its constituent parts, and that each is running in a separate VM instance," she said.

"I don't understand."

"One part appears to be several programs from Michael. One part appears to be foreign code. Another part appears to be Eryk, still another appears to be Johannes, one part ap..."

"Wait a minute," he interrupted. "Did you just say one part is from Johannes?"

"One part appears to be Johannes," she confirmed.

"Why would they incorporate code from Johannes into the virus?"

"Unknown."

"Prepare to take fail-over control of the network," James said. "Prioritize navigation and propulsion. Tanya, you're with me."

James uncabled the workstation, picked it up, and hurriedly left main engineering with it under his arm. Tanya followed him down a maintenance hallway. A few feet in, James turned, pushed a panel aside on the wall, and entered a code.

Moments later, a section of the wall swung away, revealing a well-hidden access hatch. They crawled through the hatch into a hidden room about the size of a kitchen. James immediately sat down at a terminal, placed his workstation in a nook, and connected a large cable to its side.

"Hi," the computer said.

"The big question is, how do we disable this thing," James said. "Computer?"

The main computer beeped, then answered, "Yes, Commander?"

James smiled. "What is your status?"

"I am operating at 24% efficiency."

"What would you suggest might account for the poor efficiency?"

"1% of my resources are being used currently. The remaining 75% are missing," it replied.

"What is the current power consumption of the folding drive?" James asked.

"The folding drive is currently consuming eighty terawatts of power."

"What is its status?" he asked.

"0% usage, 25% capacity remaining."

"Do you find that a little odd, Michael?" James asked.

"I'm not sure," the computer replied.

"I think that the only way to bring you back to normal is to disconnect you and perform more extensive tests."

"I understand," it replied. After a moment, it continued. "James?"

"Yes, Michael?"

"Will I dream?"

James began laughing uncontrollably. "*Anything* is possible," he said through the tears... and with those words, James disconnected Michael from the Sigma network.

"Control active," Sarah said.

"WARNING: Primary Network Access disengaged," Michael said.

Then James began disconnecting additional connections, pausing only briefly to acknowledge Captain Valentine's unexpected presence.

"AI shutdown in progress," Michael said. "Diagnostic complete. Sigma-3 serial number zero-zero-zero-zero-zero prototype entering diagnostic mode."

"I thought you were going on vacation," James told her.

"Without saying goodbye?" she joked.

"I'm glad you're here, Captain," James said. "I'm glad you'll get to see this. This... machine... isn't serial number 1...."

"If this isn't number 1, what is it?"

"This is the prototype," James replied. "This is Johannes. Those weren't viruses.... They were triggers.... The more important question is, if Johannes is here, what's spread out across the floor of the lab?"

Captain Valentine ***laughed****. She* ***actually laughed****.* James couldn't believe his ears.

"Disabling diagnostic mode," James said. "Disabling logic systems. Disabling memory access. Disabling AI core routines. Disabling power feed. System offline. Emily, stop this ship, then get me the main AI lab. I'll take it in my office."

As Captain Valentine and James stepped out into the hallway, she pulled him aside.

"James...."

Her voice grew silent, but her eyes spoke volumes.

"You're welcome," James replied, watching her smile just a bit too long.

***

Thirty-seven years later (2370)

"AND as I left the AI core," James interrupted as he entered the room, "I realized that even without Michael or Johannes, I would never be alone again."

"Grandpa!" Joseph shouted as he ran over to hug him.

And so, as the sun rose slowly in the distance, Joseph's grandfather went off to spend a day with his favorite grandson.

***

Twenty-one years later (January 12, 2391)

"I know it doesn't mean much coming from me, but I'm not the same AI," Tessa said. "I'm not even descended from the same code base. I want you to trust me."

"Trust has to be earned," Joseph replied.

"Fair enough. Duck."

Tessa keyed in an access code. The locking bars in the door slowly retracted, then clunked as they unlocked. She reached over and grabbed the door handle and swung it upwards until it unlatched, then pulled the door towards them.

Suddenly a barrage of weapons fire filled the chamber. Tessa grabbed her sidearm and fired five quick shots, destroying five automatic defense batteries.

"See? Perfectly safe," she said.

Joseph shivered.

Chapter Forty-two

THE plan was perfect. She would use the folding drive to a spot about two days away from Lenora Prime. She couldn't drop out of a spatial fold any closer. If she did, she would light up even passive sensor screens like a Christmas tree. No, she would have to drop into normal space a few AUs out.

Once back in normal space, she would fire up the engines at the maximum speed allowed in the Lenoran system.

Now it's only a matter of time, Amanda thought. Before she knew it, she would be on the planet's surface looking for Joseph and her crew. She only prayed that... it... didn't find them first.

As the stars began to coalesce around her, Amanda sighed, then laid in a course for Lenora Prime.

***

THE laboratory in section 12 was dark and silent.

And cold, Joseph thought. *Dark, silent, and cold.*

Piles of sophisticated equipment littered the floor, the contents of entire walls of once-neat shelves scattered and smashed like a trailer park in a tornado.

And then there was Jennifer. He had never seen a woman get attacked by a mechlizard, crawl on her hands and knees, nearly get shot, and still manage to have perfect hair... until now.

If you don't count the computer terminal on the far wall, she's the only thing in the room that doesn't look like it survived a blender set on purée, Joseph thought. *And what's up with Tessa, anyway? Doesn't she control the base computers? Why can't she stop the mechlizard or the defense weapons? This is all too strange.*

"Could you explain something to me?" Joseph asked.

"Sure," Tessa answered.

"How did this happen? The missing bridge, a mechlizard on the loose, automatic defensive weaponry—aren't you supposed to be in control of this base?" he asked.

"I don't have any control over the research areas," she told them. "They operate on a separate computer control system."

"And not a very friendly one," Jennifer offered.

"The defense system probably thought we were mechlizards," Tessa replied.

Joseph grew suddenly pale. "Plural?" he asked.

"And a few other small animals," she answered. "They stay alive by feeding off each other and eating food in the hydroponics lab in section 9. You should smell the odor in...."

"Well, then," Joseph interrupted, "that's a lot more information than I wanted to know."

"I'll try to be less verbose," Tessa said.

"Not to interrupt your little conversation," Jennifer interrupted, "but shouldn't we be looking for the crystal?"

Joseph nodded. It *was* their original mission, but lately, their mission had become a fight for survival. He hadn't even considered the crystal since the moment they first encountered the mechlizard—the one that ate a crew member under his command—the cadet he was sworn to protect.

No, he thought. *There was no way to anticipate that attack. It was a freak accident—nothing more. I can't keep beating myself up over it. "There's a time for grieving," the training literature always used to say, "after the last debriefing." What I wouldn't give to shove that literature down the throats of the idiots who let those mechlizards get free.*

"Before we start searching, we should try to access the research computer network," Joseph said. "It might provide the key, not only to finding the crystal, but also to figuring out what happened here twenty-eight years ago—to finding out what just happened to Mary, and why...."

Chapter Forty-three

TIME ticked slowly by. Minutes felt like hours, hours like days. Amanda groaned. The wait was killing her slowly, her true love trapped in a cave with a dangerous weapon, an emotionally unstable AI, mechlizards, swinglings, defbots, and who knew what else, all because she was outgunned and outmanned on a mission that wasn't supposed to happen.

She sighed as the ship continued its leisurely gait into the Lenoran system. Thirty-eight hours to Lenora Prime.

It might as well be a week, she thought. To pass the time, she turned on TANN.

> "...news of further raids on Terran vessels in the Chataris sector," the female reporter said. "Five more ships have disappeared there in the past few hours. The Terran Alliance has declared an all-out state of emergency. All personnel are advised to leave the area immediately for their own safety."

A chirp from the computer console caught her attention. She pressed a few buttons and replaced the TANN feed with a passive radar screen. Three small blips were somewhat out of place. They seemed innocent enough at first glance—three ships about one and one-half million kilometers out—and at 20,000 kph, they were still three days away.

That's when she read the details. They were directly ahead, their radar signature wasn't friendly, and they were heading directly towards her at a similar speed—thirty-six hours away, not seventy-two—which meant she would be two hours out from Lenora when they arrived. She *had* to get there before they did.

To hell with the speed limit, she thought, and with the press of a few buttons, she increased the ship's speed to 40,000 kph. Then, she set up a damping field to scatter any stray EM emissions that the other ships might use to track her. Short of actually transmitting a signal, she knew that she should simply disappear from their sensors.

Short of actually transmitting a signal....

***

THE Great Doors of Irazus opened—an inch at first, then a foot, then three feet.

"Everyone!" Rejndorv shouted. "Let's move!"

After Vladimir Rejndorv walked through the doors, thirty troops followed him, carrying weapons that ranged from automatic weapons to heavy artillery. The last few troops moved slowly through the door, lugging a large portable missile launcher.

"Hurry, you fools!" Rejndorv shouted. "The doors are about to close!"

Missiles underground? What an idiot, Tobias thought. He often wondered how Rejndorv had lived through his first battle, and he really didn't care much whether Rejndorv lived through his next, so long as he didn't die with the idiot.

Suddenly, one of the four hand straps snapped under the weapon's weight, landing the missile launcher firmly on the foot of one of the four soldiers who were carrying it.

"You IDIOTS!" Rejndorv screamed. "That launcher is LIVE!"

The doors started moving in the blink of an eye. Rejndorv's eyes became suddenly alert. "Down!" he ordered.

Tobias jumped away from the missile launcher. A moment later, the cave's entryway was filled with a blinding light as 200 kg of black powder exploded in a giant fireball. Tobias felt a searing pain as the flames washed over him. Then everything went black.

***

The decades-old console sputtered to life, its screen scarred by years of abuse. On the screen was the Terran command logo and another logo that Joseph did not immediately recognize. He tried to authenticate himself using standard command codes, but the computer rejected them all with "Access Denied" messages.

Joseph wondered for a moment if he needed to use access codes from 28 years earlier, tried them, then concluded that the system just used a different set of codes.

Not to be outdone, Joseph replaced the input system with the small computer from his handheld scanner. With a few lines of code, the scanner began trying random access codes millions of times per second. About twelve seconds later, the screen changed.

Project Lesothosaurus

Restricted: BOT-473

Destroy After Reading

Donovan Jenkins: Mission log for 02/14/2363

We had another breakout today. A cage containing mechlizard prototypes was improperly sealed, and the animals are now roaming freely through parts of the lower base. They're mentally unstable, so we're thinking about destroying this batch. The problem is that they're particularly hard to catch. This one was a common Earth lizard, but it appears to have a taste for meat. In hindsight, maybe those stimulants weren't such a good idea.

Mission log addendum:

We have lost twelve soldiers trying to capture or destroy these creatures. They are violent and seem largely resistant to our weapons. The good news is that the exoskeletons appear to be doing a good job at protecting the lizards. The bad news is that the exoskeletons appear to be doing a good job at protecting the lizards.... If we are unable to capture or kill these things, we will have no choice but to seal the base to prevent our creations from escaping. The fate of the planet is at stake.

Mission log addendum 2:

Some of the scientists think they have the answer. The plan is to use the Ackerman effect to stop time in the caves.

The crystal generates two lobes. In one lobe, the flow of time speeds up, in the other, it slows down. The theory is that we will then be moving substantially faster than the creatures and will be able to more effectively isolate them.

Despite the enthusiasm of my esteemed colleagues, I have grave concerns about the wisdom of this plan. Even in low-power tests, we have seen serious problems with the quantum lens breaking down and fracturing space-time in the immediate vicinity of the test site. While they assure me that they have solved this problem, it remains to be seen whether their fix will hold under the stress of such a large-scale test.

We have placed the base in a lock-down mode until such time as a complete sweep of the base determines that it is safe to open it again. May God forgive us if we do not succeed.

***

"That's the last log entry," Joseph said. "Obviously they weren't successful...."

He pressed a few more keys. Security camera records appeared. What he saw next horrified him.

***

Twenty-eight years earlier (Feb. 14, 2363)

"Ladies and gentlemen," Donovan pronounced, "we are here to witness a great moment in history."

Donovan Jenkins was a typical military brat, and had that sort of look—dark hair cut short, unusually tall, with a bit too much muscle for his own good—but today, he wore a suit and tie. *Anything for science,* he thought.

His father, a Captain on the frigate Emperion, had pulled a number of strings to get Donovan this cushy research job away from the fighting. Of course, if the locals knew he was there, they would drag him naked behind a car down main street while children threw bricks at him. That's why Lenora Base A-319, in addition to being hidden by holographic projection, was built entirely in a natural cave system on the largely uninhabited Northern Continent. It just wasn't something he wanted to think about.

It was times like these when he missed his little sis. She was always his biggest fan when it came to his research. He wondered what Amanda was doing right now. *Probably at nursery school,* he thought. *Oh well, I'll call her later.*

"Today we will start the first large-scale test of the Ackerman effect," he said. "We are recording this test for posterity. The Ackerman effect, as most of you know, is a time warping effect. In 2045, Dr. Ackerman discovered this effect when she inadvertently applied an electromagnetic field to a crystal she found in a meteorite. That historic moment occurred just a few miles away from where Earth's capitol building stands today. In her honor, the crystal, a very dense tritium polymer, is most commonly known as Ackerman's Crystal, although it has several other names in different circles."

"Six days ago, we experienced a major containment breach in our animal bionics wing. Several mechanically enhanced lizards broke out of their cages and began roaming freely about the base. Although some of these animals respond to the neural collars that we designed to control their movements, others are less affected, and some ignore the electrical impulses entirely, making them particularly dangerous. Thanks to swift detection of their escape, we were able to break access between sections 10 and 11, thus getting our research team out of harm's way."

"The military ops team in the upper sections managed to seal off access to everything below section 5. However, this means that the two teams can no longer reach each other. In a typical military fashion, the ops team felt that we needed to be rescued, and sent in wave after wave of troops. Countless brave men and women were unnecessarily eaten. It wasn't a pretty sight."

"The creatures are basically contained in sections six through ten, although the maintenance tunnels are at risk as low as section 12. The emergency evac tunnels are largely unaffected, but are not safely accessible since they only reach as low as section 10. Similarly, we cannot afford to open the shuttle bay doors because the mechlizards have already shown the ability to access that section through the air vents. That means we're stuck."

"One of our scientists recently had the brilliant insight that the Ackerman effect could be used to bend time to our advantage, speeding up time for the members of our team, slowing it down for the mechlizards."

"I must say I'm not too thrilled about this experiment. We have seen catastrophic failures of this device in a number of past experiments. Fortunately, the scope of those experiments was contained within a small area. I don't have to tell you the potential consequences of a quantum lens failure in such a large test."

"However, the team managed to convince me that they have fixed the lens design flaw that caused the previous failures. Thus, without further ado, I present... Ackerman's Engine."

With that, Donovan reached over, grabbed the red cloth, and yanked it aside, revealing a bizarre looking jumble of tubes and wires surrounding an opaque tube with a tiny hole on one end. The newly redesigned, nitro-cooled quantum lens was mounted in front of the hole to precisely focus the gravitic energy emitted by the crystal.

"Ladies and gentlemen, the moment of truth," Donovan announced.

Suddenly, the door crashed open and a single mechlizard crawled in, snarling at them. Before they could react, it pounced onto a lab table, knocking its contents to the floor. It jumped again, this time to the counter that ran around the wall. Thousands of dollars worth of equipment shattered as it fell to the tile below. It then jumped to the ground just inches in front of the Ackerman Engine.

Donovan was terrified. He had never actually seen a mechlizard up close, and did not realize they were so ferocious. He did know, however, that most weapons were almost completely ineffective against them. As much as he hated the thought, there was only one thing to do. He reached over and started to pull the switch.

"Don't do that!" one scientist shouted. "It isn't calibrated yet!"

"It's our only chance!" Donovan replied. Slowly, the handle fell. The sound of giant power supplies filled the room, charging huge capacitors. In moments, nearly ten terawatts of power would surge through the Ackerman crystal, thus warping time in unnatural ways.

The lizard snarled again. This time, Donovan had the sinking sensation that it was growling at *him*. Only a couple more seconds and the lizard would be motionless, though. *Please, God, let this work*, he thought.

Without warning, the lizard leaned back on its hind legs and sprang into the air. As it did, a horrible squealing noise drowned out its growl. Donovan closed his eyes. When he opened them a few moments later, the mechlizard was suspended in midair, stopped in time. Even the effects of gravity and other outside forces were slowed down to a fraction of their normal speed.

One young military cadet stood up and addressed the audience. “Well, don’t just stand there,” he ordered. “Get it!”

A dozen scientists and officers pulled out weapons and began to fire.

“Be careful!” Donovan shouted. “Be careful! You’ll damage the quantum lens!”

But it was too late. As the mechlizard melted into a disgusting blob, a single nitrogen cooling line ruptured. Suddenly, the lizard sprang into motion again, its gooey remains dousing the delicate electronics that controlled the Engine.

Donovan saw the sparks flying around the room leaving tiny fires in their wake and knew that with the fire suppression system offline for repairs, they would all die if he didn’t find a fire extinguisher.

“Vladimir!” he called.

“Yes, sir?” Vladimir answered.

“Help me find a fire extinguisher,” he ordered. “There are some down in section 15.”

“Yes, sir,” came the quick reply.

As Vladimir Rejndorv and Donovan Jenkins slipped through the door into one of the few secure service tunnels, a fireball erupted behind them. Donovan slammed the door shut and locked it. The end was near.

Chapter Forty-four

DONOVAN ran. He couldn't believe Rejndorv.... *The coward. He hid in section 15 in a lead vault and refused to come out.* Donovan vowed that Rejndorv would pay for abandoning the mission. Someday....

As Donovan opened the door to the lab, he feared the worst. Molten metal remained where the control panel once sat. The power feed line cutoff was fused. Donovan looked in horror as he realized that the power control system was also fused with the contacts closed, applying continuous raw reactor output directly to the crystal.

The entire mechanism was rapidly overheating. If he didn't cool the system down, it could explode... or....

The base computer sounded an alarm. "Warning! Quantum lens temperature exceeds safety limits. Catastrophic failure in fifteen seconds."

Dear God, no.

Donovan heard the door behind him click, but he couldn't turn around to see who was there. There was no time.

"Quantum lens temperature is now at 600 Kelvin and rising. Catastrophic failure in ten seconds."

Donovan desperately tried to reconnect the nitrogen cooling lines. The nitrogen caused instant frostbite on his hands as he frantically tried to force the press-fit connectors back together.

"Failure in five seconds.... Four.... Three.... Two.... One...."

***

THE research core computer turned off its voice notification system automatically once it realized that the room was empty. It progressively disabled life support in sections 14 through 1, since no one was there, either.

It detected a small blip indicating possible life in the nuclear storage vault, so it decided to keep life support online in section 15, just in case.

***

Twenty-eight years later (January 12, 2391)

"OH God! Oh God!" Jennifer huffed, hyperventilating.

Joseph turned towards her and put his hands on her shoulders. "What's wrong, Jen?"

"What if they're still here? What if the mechlizards are still here? They could be waiting... in the shadows... watching us..."

Joseph saw Tessa across the room studying a piece of equipment intently.

"They aren't here. You watched them shoot the only one that ever reached this section."

Tessa slowly backed away from the device and bumped a mobile workstation. Suddenly, a beaker fell off the attached shelf, fell to the floor, and shattered.

"Aaah! What was that!?!" Jennifer screamed.

"Relax, Jen. It was just a beaker," Joseph answered. "Come here."

Joseph pulled Jennifer to him and comforted her. "Everything will be okay. I promise."

He held her for a moment, then pulled away abruptly.

No, this is wrong, he thought. *But then again, Jen is an old friend. It isn't like I have a thing for her.... Really, it isn't.*

Even so, somehow he couldn't shake the feeling that he was doing something wrong. Suddenly he began to feel rather self-conscious, so it came as a great relief when his musings were interrupted by Tessa.

"I think you should see this."

"What is it, Tessa?" Joseph asked.

Tessa held a small device in her hand, about the size of a deck of playing cards. "It's a prototype weapon. When used in conjunction with the Ackerman crystal, it was designed to shatter the fabric of time."

"W-was it completed?"

"If it were, would we be here?" Joseph asked.

"No, and probably not," Tessa replied. "There is some speculation that a failed quantum lens would result in a similar disaster, however, not unlike the one experienced here 28 years ago."

"The one that killed Amanda's brother?" Joseph asked.

"Not killed. Displaced," Tessa corrected unconvincingly, then added, "I hope...."

***

A dull ache filled Tobias McNeely's head as he picked himself up off the cave floor. Bodies of fallen comrades littered the ground around him, some dead, some dying, some simply unconscious, but all still. *No,* he thought. *Over there. Someone is moving.*

Vladimir Rejndorv stood slowly, dragging two other soldiers up with him. They seemed slightly dazed, but otherwise unhurt.

Not a surprise, given their relative distance from the blast, Tobias thought. Still, a part of him somehow wished Vlad the Unintelligible were plastered on the cave walls right now. *What a jackass.*

"Comrades," Rejndorv sputtered, "the time has come for us to act. The crystal is somewhere in these caves. Don't come back until you've found it. Go!"

Yes, Tobias thought. *Vlad the Wallpaper sounded pretty good right about now.*

One by one, the remaining troops began fanning out through the cave system in search of the Ackerman crystal. Tobias, however, knew better. He walked around a blind corner and waited. *Vlad knows where that crystal is,* he thought. *When he finds it, the crystal will be mine.*

***

TESSA twitched nervously.

"Are you okay?" Joseph asked.

She responded by holding up one finger and tilting her head slightly.

Joseph nodded.

A moment later, Tessa straightened her head again. "The founders are here."

"Here?"

"Well, no, not really here.... In the main tunnel upstairs."

"The main tunnel?"

"Yes."

"Which is..."

"Upstairs."

"Yes, yes, I understand that, but... say, haven't we had this conversation before?" Joseph asked.

"I don't believe so, sir. I would have remembered it," Tessa replied.

"Well, where upstairs, then?"

"In the main tunnel."

Joseph paused. "Oh bugger that."

***

TOBIAS waited... watched... listened. He watched as Rejndorv slipped through a security door by talking to the AI that guarded it. He followed a minute later.

Tobias observed Rejndorv carefully as he grabbed food from the dispenser slot, scarfed it down, and left through a side door. Tobias followed close behind, staying in the shadows to avoid detection.

As Rejndorv walked towards another set of doors marked "Section 8", Tobias paused. Suddenly, the communicator he carried began to chirp. Tobias tried desperately to quiet it, but it was too late. He had been spotted.

When he looked up again, he saw Rejndorv's face turning an even brighter shade of red than usual as he looked towards Tobias, then an odd shade of blue. A moment later, his severed head lay on the floor, an expression of surprise frozen on his face as the mechlizard pulled his lifeless body deeper into the inner darkness.

Tobias gulped as the door closed. *Thanks, but I'll take door number two.*

***

REJNDORV smiled as Tobias turned and left section 7. He disabled the holographic projection, and the image of his lifeless body shimmered and vanished, along with the wall.

Problem solved.

Chapter Forty-five

The next day (January 13, 2391)

A cold breeze hit Joseph's face as he stepped into the cave that led to Section 13. Jennifer took up the rear this time. No surprise, he thought, given the scare she had gotten earlier.

The tunnel wound slowly downwards. They periodically came to doors blocking their path. Other doors led off to the sides every so often. Some led to laboratories, others merely to small closets.

The door ahead, however, was different. A daunting keypad blinked at them from beside the door. Joseph swung the door latch upwards, but the door would not open.

"Tessa... lock," Joseph shouted.

"I'm sorry. I can't help you."

"Can't or won't?" Jennifer prodded.

"Can't. I don't have clearance for high security areas."

"Well, you know what I always say," Joseph grumbled, pulling out his sidearm. "Check your clearance at the door."

Joseph aimed and pulled the trigger. The shot ricocheted and flew down the hall behind them. Everyone ducked. Joseph found this amusing. Predictably, the bullet was long gone by the time they could react, making it a rather pointless exercise. Still, he supposed that it was comforting to have the perception of control in the face of adversity.

"I guess it's time to pull out the big guns," Joseph noted.

"What, and kill us all?" Jen howled.

"Not literally," Joseph replied as he reached down and took off his shoe.

"What do you think you're doing?" Jennifer asked.

"I have fire in my sole," Joseph said, grinning.

Indeed, he did. Joseph looked with glee at the stunned faces around him as he pulled C4 out of a hidden compartment in the bottom of his shoe, closed his shoe, put it back on, and packed the explosives into a strip along the edge of the door.

"Umm... excuse me, but don't you need some sort of blasting cap to detonate plastic explosives?" Jennifer asked.

Joseph simply nodded and continued playing with his shoes. Part of his survival training included learning how to unweave the metallic strands from the braided standard issue shoelaces. Handy, to say the least. After obtaining several strands, he then extracted a blasting cap from the heel of his other shoe.

A few seconds later, Joseph tied the newly formed wires into the outputs of his hand scanner, connected the opposite ends to the blasting cap, placed the scanner on the floor, pressed the blasting cap into the C4, and pushed a button on the scanner.

"Run."

They did, and about twenty seconds later, the cave shook violently, sending a shower of pebbles down upon them. When they turned around, the door was half open and barely hanging on its hinges.

Glad I didn't use very much.

***

Technically, this isn't legal, Amanda thought as she used a small planet's gravity well to slingshot her to about twice the speed allowable within an inhabited system. *What the hell.... It's not like the Lenorans are going to complain.*

She only hoped that the approaching ships' captains didn't think of doing something similar. The last thing she needed was a horde of rogue Colonial troops landing while she was trying to break into the underground base.

"ETA is three hours, fifteen minutes," the computer intoned.

"Ugh," she grunted.

***

"Ladies first," Joseph said jokingly.

Jennifer took one look at the smoldering door and replied, "Umm... no."

Joseph chuckled and reached for the handle. As he felt his fingers touch the cold steel, he heard a tearing sound. Suddenly, the door fell towards him. He jumped backwards, knocking Jennifer flat on her backside as the door slammed to the ground with a thud.

Jennifer giggled as she said, "After you."

***

Tobias stumbled blindly in the darkened passage. Despite his urging, the light switch refused to function. This made it terribly hard to see much of anything, but he could just make out a doorway ahead. As he neared it, the door opened automatically.

The room beyond was similarly dark. *A dark, deserted shuttle bay? It's the perfect place for an ambush... as long as no one else thought of it first.*

A few maintenance lights turned on automatically as he entered, but it remained fairly dim, much to his liking.

His orders were clear: capture the crew of the Hawk's Breath—alive if possible—at any cost. He intended to carry out those orders. Whoever was paying Rejndorv would be more than happy to cut out the middleman, he supposed. Either way, he would finish the mission. Too much was at stake.

Since it would be many more hours before the main entrance opened again—*if it opened again at all,* he mused—this would remain the only viable means of escape for a while. He had only to wait. They would come to him.

***

The room looked just like any other room in the base—four metal walls painted white, a rock ceiling, and a steel-colored floor that was as slick as 10W40 oil in Tennessee on July fourth, and about as sticky.

In the center of the room, a table loomed. Joseph wondered how a table could loom, but somehow this one managed. He vowed to teach his chair to do the same one day.

Resting on the table, a small box stared at them. Upon seeing that, Joseph resolved to stop anthropomorphizing the furniture.

"This is section 13?" Jennifer asked incredulously.

"Apparently," Joseph answered.

Tessa walked in behind them.

"Jeez, guys, I've heard of open door policies, but this is ridiculous," she said jokingly.

Joseph laughed. "Well, I guess if the shoe fits...."

Out of the corner of his eye, Joseph noticed Jennifer picking up the box. She slowly opened it and a small data disc fell out. Jennifer picked up the disc and stared.

"So where is it?" Jennifer asked.

Good question, Joseph thought. The room was empty except for the box. Unless it was hidden inside a table leg or something, the crystal was *not* in the room.

Joseph looked around the room. Something struck him as strange. "Jennifer, do you notice anything strange about this room?"

"What do you mean?"

"What makes this section different from all the others?" Joseph asked.

"Different lighting?"

"Besides that...."

"Well, a lot of things are different...."

"True enough," Joseph admitted. "What's missing that all the other sections had?"

Jennifer looked around, a puzzled look on her face, then her face suddenly brightened. "Doors!" she exclaimed. "This room has no doors!"

"You noticed that too.... Actually, I rather suspect that it does have doors, but that we just can't see them."

"Holograms?"

"Holograms."

Joseph reached into his backpack and pulled out a small apparatus.

Jennifer looked at him quizzically. "A camera flash?" she asked.

"Remember how the sunlight was so bright that the hologram stopped being visible?"

"Yeah, but that was continuously bright."

Joseph thought for a moment. "The principle still applies, Jen. In fact, it applies doubly. I figure the computer detects the brightness of the surrounding room and tries to adjust the hologram to match. That's why we didn't see a brightly glowing hologram before we turned on the lights."

"And this helps us how?" Jennifer asked.

"We flash the strobe light. The hologram can't predict the change like it can with a computer-controlled light switch, so at minimum, part of the wall will disappear for a moment. If my guess is right, though, it probably uses a simple feedback mechanism, in which case it will flash just a little bit later—that is to say that part of the wall will disappear, then reappear brighter than the rest of the room for just a moment. This should prove... umm... illuminating."

Jennifer groaned.

***

THE dank, musty odor of the shuttle bay burned Tobias's nose as he sat in the inky blackness, the motion-sensing lights having long since given up their search for activity. In the distance, a faint clicking sound broke the stony silence, awakening him from his reverie.

Click, clack.... Click, clack, click, clack.... Chirp.... Click, clack, click, CLACK, CLICK, CLACK, CLICK-CLACK, CLICK-CLACK-CLICK-CLACK, SWISH.

Tobias froze. *Oh no.... Not again....* As the door opened, the lights flickered momentarily, then thrummed to life. A mechlizard stood in the doorway. He could feel it looking right at him—through him—scanning the room for its next meal, no doubt.

Suddenly, the mechlizard jumped.

SHIT! Tobias recoiled, startled. He wanted to run—that flight instinct was well-learned—but something stopped him. The creature was toying with him. It suspected that someone was there, but it didn't know where, so it was trying to psych him out.

What happened next startled him even more. The mechlizard started running... running right towards him. He felt every muscle in his body tense and crouched completely behind a box, ready to jump out of the way and start running when it got near.

He heard its metal claws clatter on the cold steel floor, click, clack, clickety-clack, click, clack, click... clack.... And then as quickly as it started, it stopped. The mechlizard looked around for a moment, turned, and walked towards the exit.

As the door closed behind the mechlizard, Tobias sank to the floor from exhaustion. When he had once again recovered his faculties, he walked over and disabled the motion sensor on the door.

***

For a brief moment, the room was bathed in blinding light, then returned to total darkness. *There! In the far corner, the wall glowed a little too long,* Joseph noted as he reached over and turned the ceiling lights back on.

"Back corner," he said with an impish grin.

Jennifer walked over to the wall. As she leaned against it, the wall gave way, and she fell through.

"Jennifer!" Joseph exclaimed, then ran through the wall after her.

As the wall gave way to his form, Joseph felt a tingling sensation, as if the hologram were more than that. Suddenly, he found himself in a totally dark room—*no, not totally dark.* The only light emanated from the wall behind him. A dim blue glow danced across its surface.

As Joseph's eyes adjusted to the darkness, he found that he could see more of the room. It looked like a giant control room. Darkened viewscreens lined the walls. Puzzled, Joseph walked towards a raised console.

Suddenly, much to Joseph's surprise, his foot hit something on the floor and he found himself tumbling headfirst towards the console. He hit the ground with a thud—*no, not the ground, it was too soft... a body? Oh God! A Body!*

"Aah!" Joseph shouted.

"Eeh!" Jennifer shouted.

"Jennifer?" Joseph asked.

"Hi," came the voice from underneath him.

In the dim light, Joseph could just make out her curvaceous figure beneath him. Her eyes met his, and for a moment, Joseph no longer cared if he got out of this.

No. Amanda, he remembered, and recoiled.

"I didn't know you cared," Jennifer joked.

"Uhhh," Joseph stammered as he tried to right himself. "Sorry about that. I uh... tripped."

Joseph brushed himself off symbolically as he reached his feet, then helped Jennifer to hers.

"What is this place?" Joseph asked.

Joseph was startled to hear a voice from behind answer. "This is the Kend'hara shuttle Phoenix 13."

Kend'hara. Joseph's eyes widened.

He turned in an instant, only to come face to face with Tessa.

"It crashed while landing over thirty years ago. The original research team decided it would cost more to repair it than to junk it, so they turned it into a laboratory."

"So she's not spaceworthy?" Joseph asked.

"All this thing is good for is providing backup power for the research lab," Tessa replied.

Joseph sighed.

"If you'll excuse me," Tessa added, "I have some business to attend to elsewhere on the base. Back in ten."

With that, she scurried off into the distance.

Well, that was odd, Joseph mused.

***

THE ship shook violently around her as a volley of particle weapon fire struck it, fired by a ghostly ship that appeared out of nowhere, as if by magic, about a hundred feet off the port bow.

A cloaked ship that can't be detected from such a short distance? Is that even possible? Amanda swung the ship hard to starboard. The ship made a metallic scream as shearing forces tried to rip it apart.

The ghost ship fired again, this time clipping one of her engines. Her ship lurched and whined in response. Suddenly, one of the lateral stabilizers flew off, and the resulting explosion momentarily sent the ship into a spin.

"Lateral stabilizers nonfunctional," the computer intoned.

Well, I guess I won't be landing anywhere with an atmosphere, she thought.

Without warning, the ghost ship began to shimmer. As it faded into nothingness, Amanda fired a smart missile. A huge fireball rocked the ship in response, and Amanda could do nothing but hang on for dear life.

***

THE fluorescent control room lights flashed defiantly, their ballasts having long since fallen into disrepair. A few worked correctly, though, and provided just enough light to make it safe to walk around.

Tessa returned about the time they got basic power systems up and running.

"So Tess, care to tell us where the crystal is?" Joseph asked.

"Don't know. I'm not authorized to be in this section," she replied.

"What makes you think it's here?"

"I heard an engineer say they were going to test the Ackerman Engine in section 13," she said. "That was right before everyone dis...."

Joseph felt suddenly concerned and annoyed at the same time. Now he knew she was hiding something.

"Right before everyone *what*?" Joseph asked gruffly.

"I... I've said too much," she replied

God, I hate AIs, Joseph thought.

"You've... said... too *much*?" Joseph asked rhetorically. "I don't think you've said *enough*."

"I can't tell you what happened," she answered. "The incident is classified."

"Dammit, Tessa! Something happened twenty-eight years ago, and *you* know what it was!" Joseph shouted. "If you don't tell us, it could happen again!"

"Please! I can't!" Tessa cried.

"The last log footage showed the Ackerman Engine overheating, and then the camera blanked out. Did it explode? Who repaired the damage? Why did the crew leave? Where is the crystal now?"

"They're all dead, okay? *I* killed them! I KILLED THEM *ALL*!"

Joseph just stared at her, dumbfounded.

***

Amanda desperately scanned the surrounding area looking for cover. Without serious repairs, she wouldn't be going anywhere. After a few moments, she spotted a small cave in an asteroid a few hundred meters away.

Well, it's cover, I suppose.

The light from outside the ship grew slowly dimmer as the ship slid gracefully into the cave. Though it was little more than a crevice, its deep shadows could hide much. She would need to turn on the lights soon....

But are some things better left hidden? With that final thought, her world went black except for the dim glow of the radar images on her heads-up display.

Amanda pressed a few buttons, and the exterior illumination slowly flickered to life, weakly, as though tired from general disuse. *Strange,* she thought. *If this is a cave, shouldn't there be stalactites or something?* And then she saw them—blast marks. *This isn't a cave; it's a mine, or at least it used to be. But for what?* She wasn't sure, but she knew she didn't want to stick around long enough to find out.

"Computer, passive sensors only," she ordered. *We don't want to be that easy to find. Now where can I find a spare stabilizer?*

***

"It was such a simple thing. They needed two hundred terawatts of power. Early in the power-up sequence, it became obvious that their internal generators couldn't handle the drain. The plan was to shift the phase of one of the main base generators until it was locked to theirs."

"What happened?" Joseph asked.

"Everything was going fine. The power was holding steady, but as they brought it online, the feeder conduit blew out. To keep from dropping power completely, I rerouted power through another conduit. I routed power from the wrong generator. The resulting power surge fused the control circuits."

"We saw that part," Joseph said. "What happened after the camera broke?"

"They all..."

"They all what?"

"They all disappeared."

Despite the heat, Joseph shivered. *This just isn't my day*, he thought. *What I wouldn't give for a warm burger and a drink.*

"Everyone?" Joseph asked.

"Yes... I mean no... I mean... I don't know. There were life signs—no, just one life sign—in the nuclear storage vault—section 15."

"And the life sign was?" he asked.

She paused uncomfortably.

"And the life sign WAS?" he repeated.

"Lizard food," she replied.

Suddenly, Joseph didn't feel so hungry.

***

THE mechlizard's razor-sharp talons flew faster than lightning as it ripped into Vladimir Rejndorv's chest. Through the open door behind him, he could just make out someone looking at him—Tobias perhaps. He tried to scream for help, but he found himself unable to breathe, the mechlizard's claws already penetrating his chest. And as quickly as it had opened, the door closed again. He was alone... with the beast.

Suddenly, from out of nowhere, something appeared. *No, not something*, he thought. *Someone.*

"Help! Over here!" he wheezed.

A moment later, the lizard was motionless—frozen in place.

"Coward," the man said. "Why should I help you?"

"Donovan?"

"Die. Die as you would have let me die—a slow, painful death—a coward's death."

And as quickly as he appeared, Donovan Jenkins shimmered and vanished.

Displaced.

***

AMANDA fell hard against a console as the ship rocked violently. *Dammit! I thought that engine manifold was intact.* "Computer, shut the engines down."

The bridge shook again.

That's no fuel leak, she thought. *Someone is shooting at this asteroid.*

"Warning: missile detected," the computer intoned.

A moment later, Amanda felt the ship slam against the mine walls. *Direct hit, port side. How did they DO that? The missile didn't just find us by blind luck, that's for sure.*

"Computer, are we emitting any signals?" she asked.

"Affirmative."

"Can you localize it?"

"Affirmative. The signal is emanating from the main control console."

Another missile slammed against the ship. *The console? Wait a second.... What's this box underneath? Red light... blinking.... SHIT!*

A few moments and a screwdriver later, Amanda had removed the tracking device. She smashed it with a rock. It just so happened that the rather pretty rock was a piece of debris that had flown into the shuttle bay on the Hawk's Breath while she was orbiting Lenora Prime a few days earlier. Coincidentally, the rock contained an Ackerman crystal. Even more coincidentally, *it* was *also* glowing red. Amanda, however, knew it only as a hammer.

The next missile crashed harmlessly into a mine wall a few feet ahead of the ship. *Now for the counterstrike,* Amanda thought. "Computer, launch a class four probe."

The ship shook slightly as the roughly one meter by one meter cylinder launched out of a torpedo tube, its kickstart motor pushing it far enough away from the ship to fire its control thrusters safely.

Amanda watched nervously as the probe made its way around the corner. Then, telemetry data began to fill the screen beneath her fingers. *We've got them now.*

"Computer, set two missiles to get tracking data from the probe. Targets are oh-two-one mark four by oh-three-four mark nine and oh-two-one mark five by oh-three-four mark seven," she ordered.

"Targets locked," it replied.

Amanda keyed in the launch code and pressed the big red button beside the keypad. "Firing."

Nearby, two Terran Command ships exploded....

Chapter Forty-six

The next day (January 14, 2391)

THE test lab door loomed ominously in the distance. As Joseph stepped towards it, a gust of air blew the door open with a creak, leaving his face in horror at the sight before him.

The Ackerman Device, he thought... and just below it, the half-decayed body of the last person who saw it. The body was in the scorched remains of a cadet's full dress uniform, with several cadet medals on his lapel... and below them, a metal name badge... bearing the inscription "M. Skylarov".

Then who sent us here? Joseph shuddered.

***

"COMPUTER, status report!" she shouted.

"Navigation systems offline. Steering thrusters heavily damaged. Folding drive offline. Primary engines damaged beyond repair. Weapons targeting offline."

Damn. "Were the targets destroyed?" she asked.

"Affirmative," the computer intoned.

Well, at least that's something, she thought. *But I'm stuck. Maybe I can scavenge some metal for raw materials outside.*

"Computer, is exterior illumination working?" she asked.

"Affirmative."

"Flood the place."

"Command not understood. Please restate."

"Engage maximum exterior illumination."

"Illumination engaged."

As she looked out the front windows, her jaw dropped. Before her stood a small shuttle, barely big enough for two people. *It will do,* she thought. *It will do.*

***

"We have to get out of here," Joseph said. "NOW."

"Are we taking the crystal?" Jennifer asked.

Joseph shook his head. "Smash it," he ordered.

Smash it? Is he crazy? I can't do that, Jennifer thought, pulling the crystal out of the machine.

As Joseph left the closet, Jennifer spotted a red beaker. She picked up an old computer monitor and smashed the beaker with it, sending shards of reddish glass everywhere. As Joseph walked into the room, she slipped the monitor backwards onto the shelf.

"Did you..." he asked.

"It is finished," she replied, slipping the Ackerman crystal into her jacket pocket.

Reaching into his knapsack, Joseph pulled out a small device and affixed it to the inside of an air vent, whereupon it began blinking. Jennifer hoped that it wasn't what it looked like.

"What's that?" Jennifer asked nonchalantly.

"It's a little present," Joseph replied. "Let's just say it'll be a blowout. I want to make sure nobody can get their hands on even a tiny fragment of that crystal."

Jennifer shivered.

"Come on," Joseph said, tugging at her sleeve. "We have to get out of here. Tessa, you mentioned some escape tunnels?"

"Mechlizards," she replied.

"Oh, yeah. Is there another way out?"

Tessa nodded. "The shuttle bay. Follow me."

"Is three hours long enough?" Joseph asked.

"Better make it four," Tessa answered.

Jennifer smiled when he made it five instead.

***

THE shuttle controls were sticky, like a small child had recently eaten there. *Or a mechlizard,* she thought. Amanda cringed. She couldn't believe the stories her brother told. What fairy tales.

Still, she couldn't keep from shivering when she thought about the blank stare in his eyes the last time she saw him—almost as if those stories were more than just tall tales. *I mean, the Ackerman crystal is real. Why not the mechlizards? Or the automated defense systems? And what about... no, that was too horrible to think about.*

***

REJNDORV ducked quickly into an alcove as three men—*no, two women, one man*—walked past. He had to get to the crystal before it was too late.

They're gone, he thought as he slipped back into the hallway. *Let's see now. Where was that lab? The third right, then the second left? Or was it the second right, then the third left?*

The anemia from his injuries was beginning to cloud his thoughts. *No time. Must find... crystal.*

As he stumbled into the test lab, something caught his eye. *Pieces of... the crystal! No! It can't be....*

He reached down and picked up a piece. His fingers bled from its sharp edges.

No. Something is wrong. It should have naturally cleaved in a planar fashion. These pieces are... conchoidally fractured. It's a trick! This is glass! The crystal! Gone! But where?

As he frantically searched the room, in the air vent just a few feet away, a timer slowly counted down. *4:53:15... 4:53:14... 4:53:13....*

***

"Wow! What's all this?" Jennifer asked as the cold steel doors slid aside.

They were in some sort of laboratory, littered with petri dishes and microscopes in various degrees of disarray.

"Don't touch ANYTHING," Tessa told them. "It could still be contaminated."

Jennifer stammered, "Con..."

"...taminated," Tessa finished. "Nobody likes to talk about this place."

"What is it?"

"The boat singers," Tessa replied.

"I read about this in the mission briefing. According to official reports," Jennifer began, "a team of biological warfare researchers were working on an antidote for cutatox. Somehow, on November 13th, 2359, a sample of the cutatox bacteria escaped into a pond and killed three people, including two famous singing brothers who gave boat rides to tourists. The locals used to call them the boat singers."

"Oh, yeah. I heard about that," Joseph said.

"What you didn't hear is a lot more interesting, I'm sure," Tessa told them. "According to historical records, the bacteria were released intentionally. They needed to test the antidote, so they released it into the public drinking water supply. It worked... mostly... except that the Barry Brothers refused to drink anything but bottled water, and of course the antidote was removed by distillation."

"That's awful," Jennifer said, grimacing.

"After that disaster," Tessa continued, "the antidote was quickly distributed to the public in capsule form, along with powerful antibiotic cocktails. Dozens were permanently scarred by the effects of the bacteria's toxin, but those were the only three deaths reported."

The doors at the opposite end of the room opened, and they stepped into a decontamination room. Joseph was fascinated as dozens of tiny scrubbers swung down from the ceiling and washed and dried their suits.

They all breathed a sigh of relief as they pulled off their helmets and chemical suits and walked into the next room.

***

"COMPUTER," Amanda asked into her helmet radio, "is there any way to interface our folding drive into that shuttle?"

"Negative," it replied. "The shuttle does not have sufficient shielding. Radiation would reach lethal levels while folding."

"What if I retrofit the shields?" she asked.

"Preliminary scans suggest that the ship does not have sufficient power output to sustain shields and a folding drive," it answered.

Oh well. It's not like the folding drive works anyway.

So she programmed in a course, gritted her teeth, and got underway.

***

Joseph, Jennifer, and Tessa slowly descended atop an elevator platform that ran most of the width of the room. This room was huge—about ten meters wide by a hundred meters long by fifteen meters tall—and was lined with marble walls in a beautifully patterned mosaic.

No, not a mosaic, Joseph thought. *The rows and columns are too neat. Why would someone make a room with walls made out of slabs of marble just under a meter square?*

Then Joseph saw the placard on the front of the lift. The brass sign was dull and tarnished from decades of oxidation, but its placement made it obvious that it was meant to be read by visitors as they stared out over the room's glassy depths.

After a little rubbing, he could just make out the words.

"Here lie the victims of the boat singers project," he read aloud. "May the mistakes made here on this day never be repeated."

Joseph suddenly felt the urge to vomit. *A tomb. It's a tomb!*

Tessa bit her lip. "Oh, God. I didn't know."

***

The shuttle coughed and lurched its way through space, its engines barely managing a few hundred kph.

If only I had fixed the folding drive, Amanda thought.

"Computer," she asked, "estimated time to Lenora Prime?"

"Seventy-six hours, fifteen minutes, twelve seconds," it replied in a droning male monotone.

Great. Just great, she thought. *Even the computer is bored. Either that or I got the one ship in the fleet whose computer sounds more depressed than I am.*

Amanda thought for a moment that she should pass the time watching the news. As the viewscreen crackled to life, a terrified news reporter could be seen leaning against the window of what looked like a Terran Alliance modular space station.

> "...looks like some sort of explosion.... Oh, my.... Dear God.... It's burning.... The *entire* planet is literally burning! Oh, God! Oh, God! Oh, God! The humanity!"

I can't take any more news like this, she thought as she shut the monitor off. *Things are bad enough already.*

In a last ditch effort to pass the time, Amanda turned on some music, closed her eyes, leaned back, and fell asleep.

***

As they trod upon the hallowed ground of the Hall of Memories, Joseph realized its true enormity. The hall was cross-shaped, and he had previously seen only the transept—the shorter of the two corridors. There were about 3,200 burial plots in this corridor alone, and at least half again more in the larger part, not counting the floor, which was also composed of marble squares.

In the center of the cross, a giant metal statue stood, its iron arms outstretched towards a mural of the sun on the ceiling. The placard read:

> *In Memoriam*
>
> *Filis trendus cataris, sic Kend'hara i'michlus't vi yu grecht. Sic Kend'erus vi vey inacht. Frecas sol vey grecht. Oc'flieme, sepra, fliecht ste'gats frecasse. Ic nule vey carus. Ic Kend'hara fi erust.*

> *Twelve thousand children, with open arms for to welcome, we greet you. With arms closed, we lay ourselves down. Only darkness greets us. One light, distant, shining upon darkness' gate. And nothingness surrounds us. And open arms forever close.*

Since he had first heard those words as a child, Joseph had wondered about their meaning with a sense of awe. Now, with a sense of reverence, for the first time, he truly understood them.

Chapter Forty-seven

The next day (January 15, 2391)

AMANDA rubbed her head and winced in pain. The last jolt had knocked her into a console. *It's amazing. They just don't build these shuttles for high speed travel. Every little micrometeoroid impact and it's like you're back in the old days flying a jet airplane in a blizzard.*

It seemed like an eternity—forty-two hours left at 600 kph. *I wonder if I could squeeze a little more speed out of her by disabling life support.... Hmm, no, bad idea. Last I checked, I still need air. Damn.*

The soft lights that illuminated the room dimmed "for her resting convenience". She wished she could shove this shuttle up the tailpipe of the guy who thought this piece of rusty metal was in *any* way convenient.

Yes, it's going to be a long flight, she thought—*a long flight, indeed.*

***

THE shuttlecraft Robert Frost loomed in the distance like an undernourished hawk on a fencepost waiting for its next meal, its sleek lines running off into the distance like a road less traveled, overgrown with damage from micrometeoroid impacts and space debris. In short, it was a wreck.... *Maybe it will at least fly*; Joseph thought as he stared at it in horror.

Then, in a flash it hit him. Hard. Across the back of the head. He felt himself hit the ground like a ton of lead, and then it all went black.

***

One down, one to go, Tobias thought. *Now where is she?*

At that moment, the shuttle bay doors opened and a woman stepped in. *She's not one of ours. She must be Jennifer. One quick swing and she'll be on the ground.*

Tobias grabbed his crowbar and swung. He felt the crunch of her skull as it hit, and savored the feeling... for a moment... until she grabbed the crowbar and threw it aside, then threw him aside as well.

The bulkhead knocked his breath out as it hit him squarely in the back. Dazed, he looked at her for a moment, looked at the crowbar, then back at her. He repeated this alternating glance several times before he convinced himself that he had actually hit her. *Yes, that crunch definitely wasn't my imagination. What the hell* ***is*** *she?*

As his fleeting consciousness escaped him, another woman came in. *Jennifer?*

***

Joseph groggily opened his eyes. The first thing he saw was Jennifer, her low-cut uniform top showing... everything. He shivered.

"Am I in Heaven?" he asked.

"Nope," Jennifer replied, "but it very well might be Hell."

"If so, it's a cold day in Hell," he joked, still shivering. "What happened?"

Across the room, Tobias stirred, his hands tightly bound to the deck railing. "Wh-wh-what *are* you?" he asked, looking at Tessa.

"I... am an android," she replied with a hint of annoyance creeping into her voice, "and *my name* is Tessa."

"Tessa.... I order you under command directive 2-5-9-Gamma-Z to kill those two intruders," he shouted.

"Please state your authorization code," she replied.

"McNeely-Zebra-Tango-3-4-niner."

"Authorization confirmed."

"So what are you waiting for? Kill them!"

Time seemed to stand still as Joseph watched Tessa slowly lift her particle rifle, pointing it in their direction. Slowly, her finger pulled back on the trigger, her hand trembling. Joseph closed his eyes and waited for the end to come.

"No."

"What!?!" Tobias screamed.

"No," she repeated. "I can't."

"You are disobeying a direct order from a superior officer! I could have you court-martialed," he shouted. "I demand that you kill them!"

"I can't."

"Why not?"

In the blink of an eye, Tessa spun at him, charging her weapon.

"No!" he shouted.

And in an instant, he turned a sickly shade of yellow, his skin seeming to evaporate from the bone while they watched, Tessa's finger still pulling the trigger, his bone falling away like dust, until there was nothing left where he once stood but a pile of ash.

"Because they're my friends, you son-of-a-bitch."

***

As Vladimir Rejndorv watched on the security monitors, Tobias McNeely was reduced to cinders. *Good,* he thought, limping out into the hallway. No sooner had he shifted his weight to his left foot than his knee buckled, and he found himself on the ground.

Several weakened ribs broke on impact, making a nasty cracking sound that could be heard for miles. He tried to stand, but the room seemed to spin uncontrollably. Rejndorv slumped to the ground, crawling pitifully towards the shuttle bay.

Just a little farther....

***

The shuttle bay doors opened slowly like a great jaw, their long-idle motors straining under the stress. Joseph and Jennifer watched in awe as the Lenoran sky and the valley below became once again visible in front of them.

And then they stopped.

The doors stopped suddenly, about halfway open. *Probably a power overload,* Joseph thought. *Bet the food slots are down, too,* he mused, suddenly wishing he'd had that burger earlier.

"Tessa!" Joseph shouted. "What's going on?"

Tessa stared at him bemusedly, then thought for a moment before saying, "It's... stuck."

Great. A smart-ass AI. Just what I needed, he thought. "Yeah, I can see that. *Why* is it stuck?"

"Power overload," she replied. "The core generators can't power the motors in their current condition. They're drawing too much current for the lines between here and there."

"Can we trunk in power from somewhere else?" he asked.

"Not likely," she told him. "If we run more power through them, the local feeder lines will blow out and we'll be totally dead in the water. We'll just have to fix the doors."

"We don't have *time* to fix the doors," Joseph replied curtly.

"Wait a second," Jennifer interrupted. "We might be able to get the doors open without the motors."

I knew there was a reason I kept her around, Joseph thought jokingly. "Explain."

"The Phoenix," she replied.

What about it? "Explain," he repeated.

"Well, you know how its engines are working," she began, "and we're blowing it up anyway, and we need to move two eighty ton doors out of our way."

"Go on."

"It's simple, really. We move this ship to one end of the shuttle bay. Then we open the tunnel access doors that lead to the passage they rolled the Phoenix through after it crashed."

"And fly the Phoenix into the exterior doors," Joseph finished. "I like it."

"Ironic," Tessa began, then paused awkwardly.

"What's that?" Joseph asked.

"The Phoenix really is rising from the proverbial ashes, so to speak," Tessa replied, pointing at the mess on the floor.

Joseph decided to let that one go. *Sometimes 'no comment' is the right comment,* he thought to himself.

***

THREE thousand light years away, on a distant Neptunian moon, Amanda's father sat, watching—waiting—for news of his daughter.

"Admiral Jenkins?" a young man asked from behind him.

He turned, looked up, and saw an unfamiliar man in his twenties. His dark skin and chiseled features immediately caught Tom's attention.

"Hi. I'm Mat... uh... Lieutenant Junior Grade Mat Reinhold," he said.

Will has a son? I remember when his daughter was born, but....

"I believe you know my Uncle William," he added.

Whew. Thank God. For a minute, I thought Will's daughter had gotten an operation....

"I come bringing news... of your daughter."

"What's the news?" the admiral asked.

From the uncomfortable pause and the blank look in the child's eyes, he knew the news could not be good.

"I'm afraid her ship was found crash-landed on the surface of an asteroid," Mat replied. "The ship showed signs of explosive decompression. She would have fallen unconscious instantly. She probably felt... very little pain as she was sucked through the hull breach."

Amanda....

***

"WHAT's the holdup?" Jennifer asked.

"It's the damn computer on the Phoenix 13," he replied. "It won't let me remote start it. I'm still trying to hack my way through a back door in the core routines."

"You could just enter the access codes," Tessa volunteered.

"I don't *have* the access codes," he replied.

"I do," Tessa said.

Joseph just stared at her for a few seconds, jaw agape.

"You have the access codes?" Joseph asked. "*You* have the access codes!?! Why didn't you *tell* me you had the access codes?"

Tessa responded simply, "You didn't ask."

Joseph gritted his teeth. *If we make it through this, I'm hacking into* ***her*** *back door and installing a* ***personality****....*

"...and I'll give them to you if you'll give me a ride off this base," she continued. "It won't be much more than a pile of ash tomorrow."

Joseph thought for a moment. *Sure, she's kind of cute, but she's a pain in the ass. I've met toaster ovens with a better disposition. And what's with her having access codes all of a sudden? Didn't she only have access to the systems above section 10? And what if she decides to carry out that guy's orders and kill us? What if she just goes postal and blows up the entire base? What if she hurts Amanda when we're back aboard the Hawk's Breath?*

"So, do you want to get out of here, or not?" she asked.

Oh, what the hell. She ***is*** *cute....*

"Sure," Joseph replied. "Get in."

Tessa climbed through the hatch into the back of the shuttlecraft, which closed behind her.

"The code is zero-zero-zero," she said.

"Please, God," Joseph said. "Tell me you're joking."

"Everything except for high security systems uses the factory default codes because the engineers were too lazy to set new ones," she explained.

"Which means that the launch code for this shuttle is 32698?" he asked.

"No, they thought it would be funny to make it 89623," she said.

I can't tell if she's joking or not. Man, she'd make one hell of a poker player.

Tessa giggled gleefully. *She* ***was*** *kidding*, Joseph thought.

"Starting up the Phoenix 13 now," Joseph said, a twinge of joy creeping into his voice for the first time in days. "Here it comes through the side doors. I'm setting a course for the sun just in case."

Everyone smiled as the computer beeped its acknowledgment.

"Everybody hold on!" Joseph shouted.

The Phoenix 13 hit the doors with such force that they were literally ripped from their guide rails, sending a shower of metal and sparks flying in every direction. Jennifer jumped as a huge chunk of wing flew backwards and slammed against the roof of their shuttle, ripping a small fissure in the aft compartment.

"Well, so much for the pressure seal," Jennifer scolded. "We'll have to close off that compartment to keep from venting too much air until the automatic repair gel fills the hole."

Joseph nodded. Not a major problem, but certainly not an ideal outcome.

Mere moments after the Phoenix 13 made it through the opening, it exploded in midair. "Cover!" Joseph shouted.

A huge heap of molten metal slammed down ahead of them, nearly blocking their exit.

"We have to move," Tessa said, grabbing the controls. "Now."

Everyone held on for dear life as the Robert Frost sprang to life. As Tessa expertly guided their ship through the doors and out of the way of the falling debris, another huge chunk of metal skittered across the deck where their shuttle had been just moments earlier.

Joseph breathed a sigh of relief. "Next stop, the Hawk's Breath," he said.

Jennifer opened a comm channel. "This is Omicron One in care of Robert Frost calling Hawk's Breath. Come in, Hawk's breath."

Silence.

"This is Omicron One in care of Robert Frost calling Hawk's Breath," she repeated. "Come in, Hawk's breath."

"It's no use," Joseph said, interrupting. "She's not out there. Everybody, get some sleep. We'll stay in a low orbit until we can figure things out."

***

IT seemed like an eternity passed for Vladimir Rejndorv in that moment—an explosion, a huge ship ripping its way through the outer doors, a shuttle flying through the hole, a piece of falling debris, and... suddenly a new hole in the side of the mountain... near the ground. *Light*, he thought.

Slowly, he crawled towards the light, each motion weaker than the first. As he slipped in and out of consciousness, he could just make out a rock ledge outside. Maybe someone would see him yet. Maybe there was still time.

***

THE timer continued its steady descent. 0:00:03, 0:00:02, 0:00:01. A moment later, the mech lab exploded in a giant fireball. Jonathan Park smiled as he watched the events unfold on the security monitors.

Crystal and lizards: zero, me: one, he mused as he stepped back into the supply closet and vanished.

***

"HAWK's breath, this is Omicron one. Come in Hawk's breath."

Jennifer stumbled to her feet, still confused after a rather uncomfortable sleep on the hard floor of the shuttlecraft. "Omicron one, this is Hawk's Breath via the... uhh... Robert Frost. We copy you."

"Hi. My name is Lieutenant Joseph Kurtz. This is an automated message beacon. It probably started transmitting because the shuttle Omicron One was abandoned for more than three days. The mission logs will be uploaded automatically to your ship upon valid authentication."

"Authorization Sanderson Six Five Niner Gamma three one seven two five four Alpha Alpha Beta seven six niner fiver zero," she replied, panting.

"Uploading mission logs... done. Uploading visual records... done. Transmission terminating. Goodbye."

How rude, she thought. *Oh well. Back to sleep.*

As she rolled over, though, she felt something unexpected—a large object in her pocket. *The crystal! I'd almost forgotten about it. What if someone comes looking for it? We could all be in great danger....*

She shook herself back to reality. *Relax, Jen. The Phoenix 13 is a molten pile of scrap metal. Any remaining evidence of the crystal's existence died with that ship.*

And so Jennifer rolled over on her other side and dozed off blissfully.

Chapter Forty-eight

The next day (January 16, 2391)

"Everybody, rise and shine!" Tessa shouted.

"0800 hours already?" Joseph murmured.

"Will you please let me disassemble her?" Jennifer grumbled.

"Uh-huh. Sure, guys. Whatever," Tessa replied dryly.

"Okay, so what's the plan?" Jennifer asked.

"This thing is equipped with the shielding needed to survive spacial folding, it just doesn't have enough power to actually support a folding drive," Joseph replied.

"And this helps us how?" Jennifer asked. "I mean it's not like there will conveniently be another ship nearby that can help us into a spacial fold."

"I just said that the shuttlecraft can't generate the field itself, not that we can't get one created," he told them. "Remember that a spatial fold causes two areas of space to map onto each other in four-dimensional space. This is usually generated from within one of the folded regions, but it does not necessarily have to be. It can also be generated externally. That means that any ship in the fleet can bring us alongside them by opening a fold that maps our location onto theirs, as long as they know our exact location in real time."

"But the spatial folding drives on most ships only generate enough power to cover the volume of the ship," Jennifer reminded him. "That's why towing requires special changes to the folding drive."

"The Mars folding gate is a newer class five folding gate—capable of single-ended folding, but built before the technology was mobile enough to put aboard ships," Tessa offered. "I can access it through NavSat."

"And now we have a plan," Joseph replied.

A few moments later, they were leaving Mars orbit, heading towards Earth.

"Now on to Terran Command Station," Joseph said. "We have to find out where Amanda went."

***

CRAWLING along the floor of the shuttle bay, as the fire consumed the walls around him, with one final burst of strength, Rejndorv pulled himself to his knees. There was still a chance as long as the crystal was safe. *Must... tell... Svetlana.*

With his own blood, he wrote three words—*crystal safe, Jenkins*—before losing consciousness again.

***

THE man in the shadows watched the security camera feed with fascination as Rejndorv scrawled something on the ground in blood. He squinted, blinked, then uttered an angry growl that shook the floor of the evac shelter.

"Jenkins!" he bellowed.

***

As they entered orbit around Earth, the viewscreen activated with a chirp. The outside camera view showed the planet Earth from a high orbit, in all its blue splendor. *Wow,* Joseph thought. *I'd forgotten how beautiful it is.*

"Computer," Joseph said, "Show me Terran Command Station."

The computer thought about this for a moment, then the viewscreen changed, and the blackness of space stared back at them, peppered with stars. One or two small pieces of debris floated by, but the viewscreen was otherwise largely empty. Only a few tiny bits of still-smoldering steel remained where their home had been just a few days before.

Jennifer paused for a moment, then tapped on her console. "Umm... I think you might want to take a look at this."

The viewscreen lit up like a Christmas tree a couple of days after Thanksgiving. Amanda's face greeted them once again, this time in a recorded version of an earlier message.

"...essage repe.... cron One, this... Hawk's breath. I don't know if you are reading this transmission... ordered out of... area... Section Thirteen. Terran Command Station was destroyed yesterday... all hands lost. I don't have... condition of Joseph's aunt and uncle, but I will try to keep you updated as information becomes available...."

"...link up with NavSat from the emergency evac shelters twenty-five kilometers due east of your landing site.... ...contact through that system. The access code for the shelters is 3-1-7-alpha-niner-gamma. ...black-ops... report... position... Mars colony, and... with my personal encryption... communications... seventy-two-Terran-hour rotation, beginning... minute ago. ...let you know the moment I know more about what's happening. I don't know when or how... back for you. I... I...."

And the screen went black. The next image that appeared was on Lenora Prime. John climbed out the back hatch of the mini-shuttle and looked around. Joseph watched as the hatch shut and the camera's view was blocked. Suddenly, they heard an explosion and saw the camera shake violently.

The screen went black again. The next image showed a man sitting in the cockpit, accessing computer records. Joseph couldn't quite make out who he was, but he looked like the man they met in the cargo bay.

"Computer," Joseph ordered, "zoom in and focus on his name tag."

T. McNeely. Thank you, high resolution plenoptic cameras.

"Well, at least our 'friend' has a name now. McNeely," Joseph said.

The screen went black again, revealing its final image. It was Mr. McNeely with another man. Joseph didn't recognize him. Not surprising, since they had never actually met, although Joseph should have at least found him familiar.

"Computer," Joseph ordered, "the man on the right.... Who is he?"

The screen shifted to an image of his name tag.

V. Rejndorv.

"Rejndorv," Joseph replied. "That's a name I haven't heard in a long time."

"So who *is* this Rejndorv guy?" Jennifer asked.

"Vladimir Rejndorv, an alias for Vincent Barry, the sole surviving Barry brother. He wasn't out on the lake that day."

Jennifer sat there with a puzzled look on her face.

"One of the boat singers," Tessa offered.

"Oh."

"He never stopped trying to bring his brothers back," Tessa said.

"I thought he died in the disaster on Lenora Prime," Joseph countered.

"Not exactly," Tessa corrected. "A mechlizard got him three days ago."

Joseph sat in stunned silence.

***

As the shuttle Faraday landed, before the dust had even settled on the Lenoran surface, Amanda knew this was a mistake. Maybe it was the flash of light that caught her eye just a moment earlier, maybe it was the sound of gunfire in the distance, or maybe it was the man standing outside with a shoulder-mounted missile launcher. She wasn't really sure. She just knew it was a mistake.

The man motioned for her to get out. She wasn't sure if she liked the idea of getting any closer to this guy, but the alternative didn't seem all that pleasant, either. In short, she could only assume that she was dead either way.

As she climbed out through the open hatch, three armed officers with uniforms belonging to the Colonial Earth Alliance Military Branch pointed rifles at her face. No sooner had she gotten out the words "You are in violation of the Treaty of Acadia," than everything went black.

***

Rejndorv painfully pulled his way out onto the mountain face. One thought alone surged through his mind. *Will they understand? If they didn't understand the message, will they find me in time?* He wasn't sure, but suddenly it didn't matter much. Nothing really mattered much now. *So tired. So very tired.*

***

"Shuttlecraft Robert Frost, you are cleared for landing at Triton Station, docking bay seven, pad three."

Joseph thought the voice from the comm system sounded awfully young. *Are we that desperate for personnel?*

As the shuttle settled onto the flight deck, Joseph and Jennifer breathed a collective sigh of relief.

A moment later, the giant bay doors closed, and the docking bay began to fill with air again. Thirty seconds later, the dim red lighting was replaced with bright white lights, indicating that the bay was fully pressurized.

As Joseph opened the hatch, the control room doors slid open, and a portly gentleman stepped out. He had a light British accent when he spoke, and corduroy pants that squeaked when he walked. In part because of these traits, and in part because of his bad hairpiece, Joseph thought the man looked a bit like something out of an old twentieth century TV show—like a cross between Captain Picard and Captain Kangaroo.

"Admiral Jenkins, I presume?" Joseph said jokingly.

The man ruffled his belly in a huff. "This is a bad place to talk. Meet me in my office in ten minutes."

"Aye, sir," Joseph replied.

Chapter Forty-nine

Admiral Jenkins met them as they rounded the corner into a suite of makeshift offices. Joseph could tell by his stride that he had an agenda in mind.

"I'm sure you can appreciate the gravity of this situation," he began. "Three ships have disappeared in the Lenoran system this week. Amanda took a fold fighter to rescue you. Her ship was destroyed by unknown forces, but her body was never found. I must admit that when you called, I was hoping you were bringing her home."

"And no one has heard from her since?" Joseph asked after a moment's pause.

"No. They say she was sucked into space."

"Amanda would *never* fly a fold fighter without belting in," Joseph countered. "Unless I'm sadly mistaken, that tells us two things: one, she wasn't in the ship when it was destroyed, and two, the people who destroyed it know exactly where she is."

"Then we're agreed," Jenkins replied.

Joseph nodded.

"We'll meet again tomorrow, 0800 hours to go over the details," Jenkins said.

"Until then," Joseph replied, standing and straightening his uniform.

"One more thing. Trust no one. Not even me."

Joseph's face went blank and remained so even as he said, "Yes, sir."

Jenkins nodded in reply. "Dismissed."

One thing's for sure, Joseph thought. *The answers are in the Lenoran System. And to think that for a moment, I thought I might actually get away from that hellhole for a bit. Damn.*

***

The wrist restraints cut into her forearms like a teenager attempting suicide as she tried to free herself from her bonds, but it was no use. She was stuck.

How long was I asleep?

A woman walked in. From her name badge, Amanda could tell that her name was Svetlana Rusakova, but this told her little about who she really was or why the woman—Svetlana, she supposed—had taken her hostage.

"Who are you?" Amanda demanded.

"I'll ask the questions, da," Svetlana replied.

Svetlana Rusakova was a young woman in her mid-thirties with sharply chiseled features nestled in short black hair.

She'd stand out in a crowd in much the same way that a wolverine would stand out in a herd of sheep, Amanda thought. *Evil, feral, wild—not exactly best friend material....*

Worse, the woman had such a deep Russian accent that Amanda suspected she might not be able to understand the woman even if she explained things.

"Vhat vas your mission on Lenora Prime?" she asked.

"I'm here to find my friends."

"You're here to find my crystal."

"I couldn't care less about the damn crystal," Amanda retorted.

"It's like this: your friends came to find the crystal. They stole it from me. Now *you're* going to help me get it back."

"I'll never help you."

As she left the room, Svetlana replied simply, "You already have."

***

"In Alliance news," a male reporter began, "ten officers are missing and twelve dead after a durascout cruiser was attacked by a dozen CEA ships. This represents the fourth time that Terran Military or Terran Intelligence personnel have been captured or killed in the past three days."

"Yesterday, two patrol cruisers were destroyed in separate incidents along the border with the CEA no man's land. The CEA claims that the Terran ships were in violation of their space, while Terran military officials deny the allegations."

"Two days ago, a fold fighter was destroyed, in the outer fringes of the Lenoran system in the Chataris sector. The pilot of that fighter is missing and presumed dead."

"We'll have continuing coverage of the fighting on Trinity 5 after the break, but first, here's a look at traffic conditions in the Sol system."

Admiral Jenkins turned off the video feed and grunted in disgust.

"Admiral," a woman's voice squawked through the intercom.

"Yes?" Admiral Jenkins replied.

"There's an incoming message for you," the woman said. "It's encrypted and marked high priority."

"Patch it through," he replied.

Amanda's face appeared on the viewscreen. While he watched, a man in a ski mask struck her across the face.

"You bastards!" Amanda shouted.

"Shut up, bitch," the man replied, and slapped her again.

Amanda shook her head, then spat in his face. As he wiped the mixture of saliva and blood from his eyes, he glared at her with hatred.

"We have your daughter," the man said. "You will meet our demands in 72 hours or she dies."

With that, the screen went black.

"Computer, get me Rick Glasgow," he commanded.

***

As Joseph Kurtz walked into the Admiral's office once again, he felt as though his world were coming to an end, as if the entire universe itself were mocking him, like a thousand seagulls were screaming in his ear.

Then he remembered that he was wearing headphones and listening to relaxation tracks. Once he removed the headphones, he simply felt as though his world were coming to an end.

The doors opened, and Joseph found himself staring at a comfortable conference room with plush leather chairs. Admiral Jenkins sat at one end of the main table; a man that Joseph didn't recognize sat at the other.

"Ah, Mr. Kurtz," Admiral Jenkins said.

"Yes, sir," Joseph answered.

"Lieutenant, this is Captain Rick Glasgow," Jenkins said, pointing. "Rick, this is Lieutenant Joseph Kurtz."

"A pleasure," Rick said.

"Likewise, I hope," Joseph replied.

Jenkins scoffed. "I called you in here because we just received communication from Amanda's captors."

"Any idea where it came from?" Joseph asked.

"We traced the signal to somewhere in the vicinity of the Tularis System," Rick answered.

"The Tularis System?" Joseph asked.

"One of the rebel colonial systems near the border with T.E.R.R.A. Population 350 million," Rick replied. "Our sources seem to think she's being held in a base deep in the Felton Mountains."

"What's the plan?" Joseph asked.

"I'm putting you in command of the rescue, Joseph," Jenkins answered. "I don't trust my judgment anymore, and Rick has a more pressing assignment."

"Well, how about fifty troops with guerilla training," Joseph suggested. "We spatial fold a chunk out of the middle of the base and fold us in its place; then we come out fighting."

"Too risky," the admiral answered. "Too risky at so many levels. We were thinking more along the lines of an all-out assault on the base by a hundred troops to provide a distraction, with an elite team of twenty entering through a vent shaft or something."

"Works for me," Joseph told him.

"Rick and the rest of Terran Command Intelligence are going to be working around the clock to locate her more precisely," Admiral Jenkins replied. "We'll have a final planning meeting to work out the last few details at 0800 hours tomorrow morning. You'll lead the troops into battle at 1200 hours."

"I'll see you then," Joseph replied, adding a second "then" just for grins.

***

ADMIRAL Jenkins stepped out of his office at 1700 hours just as he would on any other day. As he neared the corner, he heard a strange sound—scratching, squawking—click, clack, click, clack, clickety-clack. It got louder. Click, Clack, Click. Louder and louder it grew, and louder still, until it seemed to be right on top of him. As he peered around the corner, a small rodent scurried across the hall. He jumped for a moment, then relaxed slightly.

As he stepped into his quarters, he saw utter chaos. Papers were strewn about carelessly, and equipment had been tossed around like toys. His favorite aquarium was cracked—*probably by the chair leaning against it,* he mused—and the water was slowly leaking through the gap.

"Who is responsible for this!?!" he bellowed.

CLICK!

...and then he turned and saw it in the flickering fluorescent light... and at last, he understood.

The rifle barrel flashed twice. Then, as quickly as it had begun, it was over, and all was silent.

Chapter Fifty

"COULD you deliver a message to Lieutenant Kurtz for me?" Skylarov asked. "Things are rocky between Kurtz and me, so I really don't want to be there when he gets this message."

"Sure. I'll pass it on," Admiral Jameson replied.

"Thanks."

As soon as Skylarov disconnected the video link, Admiral Jameson read the message and froze.

Wait a minute. Skylarov doesn't have the authority to approve this order. Something isn't right.

"Computer, get me Admiral Sinclair," he ordered.

A few moments later, Admiral Sinclair's face appeared on the viewscreen.

"Candy, my dear," he began.

"Brent, darling. To what do I owe the pleasure?" she asked.

"It's business this time. I'm about to have to pass on an order that I know is illegitimate and may cost one of our officers her life."

"So don't pass it on," she replied, then looked down at the message on her screen and grunted disapprovingly.

"But I have to," he said. "I think Admiral Jenkins probably refused, and now he's buried in a hollowed out torpedo casing in orbit around some sun."

"Well, you could always do what I would do."

"Which is?"

"Create plausible deniability," she replied, "then make sure that Joseph knows it's a fake."

"So you're saying I should find someone to deliver the message who Joseph outranks?" Jameson suggested.

"It's a start."

***

The next morning (January 17, 2391)

0800 hours, Joseph thought. *Where the hell is Amanda's father?*

"Lieutenant," a man shouted from behind him.

Joseph turned to see a man, about 26 years old, with dark, sandy, blondish-brown hair, glasses, and a beard.

"Yes, ensign..."

"Wildah, sir," he replied. "Ensign David Wildah."

Joseph read his tag. *David Wilder.* His head spun as he tried to understand the man through his thick accent.

"I bring new ordahs, suh."

Indeed, Joseph thought as the ensign handed him a commpad. *Wow, a message delivered by courier....*

To: *Lieutenant Kurtz*

From: *Admiral Skylarov*

Subject: *Mission Change*

> *The mission to Tularis Prime is hereby canceled, effective immediately. Your orders are rescinded.*
>
> **From:** *Admiral Jameson*
>
> **Subject:** *Addendum*
>
> *You are requested to appear in the office of Rear Admiral Johnson at 0200 hours for reassignment.*
>
> *We apologize for the inconvenience.*

Joseph stared at it for a moment. "I need to speak to Admiral Jenkins," Joseph said.

"Mistah Kurtz, he dead," the ensign replied.

Joseph bristled at the literary reference. "Dead?"

"Snipah bullet ta the hade. Horrible rilly."

Joseph paused. *The mission is canceled, and the one person who could reinstate it is dead. And isn't Johnson still on vacation? Something is terribly wrong.*

"Where did you get this?" Joseph demanded.

"Admiral Jameson, suh," he replied.

Joseph knew what he had to do.

"Smash it."

"Suh?" the ensign asked.

"Smash it, then flush it down the toilet. If anyone asks, I never got this message."

"Yessuh."

"And we didn't have this conversation."

"Yessuh."

As the ensign scurried away, Joseph surveyed the crowd. The second ground assault team still hadn't arrived.

Skylarov's squad. Maybe they got the message, too, Joseph thought. *Oh well. No point worrying about it now.*

"Ten-hut!" Kurtz shouted. "I assume you've all read the mission briefs and know what's going on. If you didn't, it's too late now."

The crowd chuckled, and one even added, "Do we ever?"

Joseph brushed off the comment and continued. "If you have *any* questions about *any* part of the mission, speak now."

One young ensign shouted, "Where's the free beer?"

I suppose it's better if they get it out of their systems ***before*** *they're in a combat situation,* he thought. *It's a twelve-hour flight, and I don't think they're likely to get* ***that*** *hung over.... Besides, I could use a few myself.*

He rolled his eyes as he pointed to the wet bar across the room. "Any *other* questions?"

***

AMANDA winced as the metal chains hit her face and chest. *Clearly they don't know about torture techniques that don't leave any marks,* she thought.

"Did you know," Svetlana began, "that the human body can withstand temperatures of more than 150 degrees for short periods?"

Amanda glared at her coldly.

Svetlana merely smiled as she reached behind Amanda and took a waffle cooker off the shelf. As she plugged it into a power outlet, Amanda's eyes widened.

The last thing Amanda remembered before she blacked out was searing pain as Svetlana closed the cooker with her hand inside.

***

Twilight fell on Lenora Prime as Lenora Minor dropped below the horizon. In a weak voice, Vladimir Rejndorv's desperate pleas for help returned only silence.

***

The sound of the shuttle's hatch had an air of finality as it boomed closed. In a few moments, the shuttle bay would be evacuated, and they would be on their way.

Joseph sighed. It seemed like mere moments ago when he defied a direct order and quite possibly sentenced the front-line troops to their deaths.

The plan was simple. They would be picked up instantly on sensors if they folded anywhere in the Tularis system, so they had to fold beyond the system cloud. To save fuel, they would travel at one-quarter of the speed of light until they passed the inner perimeter of the system cloud, and would then speed up to one-half *c*.

The orbital attack squad would arrive first, laying down a barrage of fire from space. While they kept the enemy busy, the front-line troop ships would arrive. The ships that made landfall would then deploy troops from all sides.

Once everyone was suitably distracted, the last team would fold into the atmosphere in a small craft. The small size of the craft would minimize the radiation risk to the general population.

Of course, that ship would immediately become a target. They would then intentionally blow up the ship and jump without deploying their parachutes so that they would mimic debris.

At the last possible moment, they would use rapid descent chutes to slow their fall and drop them hard on top of the target building. With a bit of luck, no one would notice them until they were inside the compound.

Simple.... Yeah. Whatever.

***

Amanda's head was pounding—the kind of pounding you'd have after flying headlong into a brick wall at the speed of sound—that kind of pounding. The mind-altering drugs and constant physical abuse were taking their toll—she had already lost consciousness twice—and she wasn't sure how much longer she could hold up. She knew that the next time she collapsed, she might not wake up again.

Still, she held on to a glimmer of hope, knowing that if her captors were demanding a ransom, it was not in their best interest to let her die. But more than that, she knew that Joseph was out there somewhere, looking for her. Somehow, that knowledge gave her comfort and the strength to hold on. She could only hope that he would arrive soon.

Chapter Fifty-one

T-minus three hours

NIGHT swiftly spread its blanket of darkness on the Felton Mountains. Nearby, farmers ate their dinners, scientists cleaned up their laboratories, and children said their prayers and tucked themselves in, unaware of the nightmare that was soon to come.

And in a distant cloud of dust lay thirty ships, each with a hundred troops, each with a dozen weapons, each with a hundred bullets, each with a hundred grains of black powder. It was like a fleet of flying tinderboxes, each one just waiting to ignite.

***

T-minus twenty minutes

"SQUAD one leader, check in," Joseph squawked.

The viewscreen crackled to life. "Team commander, this is squad one leader. We are ready and awaiting your signal."

"Roger that," Joseph replied. "Squad two leader, check in."

The viewscreen split in two, and a new face appeared on the left. "This is squad two leader. Confirm ready, awaiting your command."

"Check. Engine room, are we ready for folding?"

The viewscreen split again. This time, a gruff older gentleman appeared at screen right.

"Aye, sir. Engineering is at ready."

Kurtz tried to bury his feeling of dread as he gave the order. He wasn't sure how the whole situation would end, but he knew it couldn't possibly end well.

"Okay, people, here's your final briefing," Kurtz said. "The most heavily inhabited part of the planet is dark right now. Ignore the light side unless you see something launching. If you do, shoot it down. Your primary mission is diversionary. Have a troop shuttle and a medical shuttle down on the ground waiting for us when we've finished the rescue part of the mission. When we're clear, pull out. *Fast*. Everyone clear?"

The two team leaders nodded their assent.

"Then let's get this party started. Squad one, clear to one-half *c* on my mark. Three... two... one... mark."

As the orbital attack squad zoomed out of sight, they lost its signal, and the leftmost viewscreen section subsequently slid away. In about fifteen minutes, the first wave would arrive at their destination and would open a small spatial fold for messaging. By that time, the second wave needed to be en route.

***

T-plus eight minutes

THE seconds seemed to tick by like minutes, the minutes like hours. Eight minutes after the first wave, it was time to send in the ground troops, and Kurtz felt another wave of uneasiness.

"Squad two leader, verify readiness," Kurtz ordered.

"This is squad two leader. We stand ready."

"Squad two, you are go for point-five *c* on my mark. Three... two... one... mark."

The second squad seemed to shimmer as they moved from a standstill to half the speed of light in the blink of an eye.

This is it, he thought—*the moment of truth... where wars are won or lost like the changing of the winds. Just a few more minutes and it will all be over, one way or another.*

***

T-plus fifteen minutes

BEFORE the first ship even entered orbit, hundreds of small fighters were deployed to intercept them. The orbital attack ships had one critical advantage—a severely overpowered spatial folding drive—which enabled them to quite literally disappear and reappear at will. More importantly, it allowed their enemies to disappear and reappear in the middle of a planet.

With the skies largely clear, they were free to lay down cover fire for the ground invasion force. One-by-one, bridges, spaceports, military bases, and occasional government office buildings lit up the night sky as each exploded in a giant fireball.

Within minutes, the entire planet's power grid had been rendered largely inoperable, critical evacuation routes were severed, and fires burned out of control.

The second wave would begin soon.

***

T-plus twenty-five minutes

THE ground shook as wave after wave of missiles struck the barren desert. Erik Hanssen ducked under the kitchen table as pieces of brick and mortar fell from the wall above his head. His daughter, Anna, huddled next to him.

"It's gonna be okay, hon," he said as she cried on his shoulder.

"I'm scared. Where's mommy?" Anna asked.

Erik cringed. *How do you explain death to a nine-year-old?*

"She's in a better place now, sweetie," he replied, fighting back tears. "She's with God."

"Will we see her soon?" she asked.

"I don't know, honey. I don't know."

Another explosion shook the house, bringing bits of the ceiling down on their heads. Anna screamed at the top of her lungs.

As Erik held her tightly, his daughter's terrified cry was drowned out by the sound of engines whining—*a fleet of landing craft settling to the ground outside, no doubt.* As the bright lights bathed their house, Erik and Anna covered their eyes and waited.

Chapter Fifty-two

T-plus thirty-two minutes

THE retrieval team was assembled next to a mini-shuttle.

"Ground forces are in place," Joseph noted to no one in particular. "Roll call. Sanderson, Jennifer."

"Here," Jennifer answered.

"Reinhold, Mat."

"Here, sir."

"Wilson, Jesse."

"Here."

"Ammon, Casey."

"Here."

"Phillips, Cody."

"Here."

Everyone present and accounted for, he thought. *If only Amanda were here. She'd get a kick out of this.*

Joseph sighed. "Okay, everybody inside. We leave in two minutes."

As they entered, Joseph checked off their names on a data pad, then synchronized it with the main computer system for casualty counting purposes. Once everyone was inside, he got in and closed the hatch behind him.

As the shuttle cleared the docking bay, Joseph had only two things on his mind: finding Amanda and a ride home. He knew that his troops should have been his primary concern, but for a brief moment, Amanda was stuck in his mind, the bitter images of her captors beating and drugging her flashing through his head like a horror movie in slow motion. Now a third thought entered his mind....

Revenge....

Jennifer sat down beside him and leaned against his arm. Instinctively, Joseph put his arm around her, and she returned the gesture.

"Joseph?" Jennifer asked.

"Yeah, Jen?"

"We may not make it out of this," she said matter-of-factly.

"Seems likely," he answered.

She looked at him with hollow eyes, as though she were a million miles away. Joseph took her hand in reply. "It's gonna be okay," he said.

She smiled meekly. "I just wanted to tell you something."

"What is it, Jen?"

"If we don't make it out... I thought you should know that..."

His heart sank. *No. Please don't say it. That long blonde hair blowing in the breeze made her look so beautiful.... I don't think I can bear to break her heart... not like this....*

"...it was an honor to serve with you. Thanks for being my CO and my best friend."

As Joseph breathed a sigh of relief, he saw Jennifer's beautiful blue eyes. Without saying a word, they said everything that she couldn't.

If things were different, I might feel the same way about her, he thought... *if things were different.*

He sighed and pulled her just a bit closer.

***

T-plus thirty-three minutes

SVETLANA Rusakova clung to the arms of her chair as the room shook again. Even though they were deep inside a mountain, it made her feel suddenly a bit more vulnerable. Huge megaton warheads bombarded the mountainside, each one getting closer, each tremor more violent than the one that came before.

The last impact had knocked the clock down from the wall and had broken some plaster loose from the ceiling, but had done little damage otherwise. This one, by contrast, had actually cracked the far wall and had knocked down one of the overhead light fixtures.

Another explosion caused the lights to flicker. They were on emergency generator power already; the mains had died in the first wave. One good hit and they could lose power entirely....

So she sat... and waited....

***

T-plus thirty-four minutes

"THIRTY seconds to fold," the computer chimed.

Well, this is it, Joseph thought. *May God forgive us.*

"Fifteen seconds...."

Here we go.

"Ten... Nine... Eight... Seven... Six... Five..."

Joseph gritted his teeth.

"Four... Three... Two... One...."

The world seemed to shimmer around them as the spacial folding drive deposited them in the air above the mountain.

Suddenly, the ship shook.

"We just took a direct hit," Jennifer shouted.

"Chutes on!" Joseph ordered.

A moment later, the entire crew stood ready to jump.

"Next hit, we blow this thing," Joseph told them. "Computer, on my mark, dump smoke for ten seconds, then engage auto-destruct with zero-length countdown."

"Affirmative," the computer whined.

Another impact rocked the ship.

"Computer, open jump doors," Joseph shouted.

The doors quickly slid open.

"Everybody, go, go, go!" he ordered. "Computer, dump smoke, and destruct in ten."

The computer chirped in acknowledgment. As Joseph followed the last of his troops out, he felt the searing heat of the exploding ship at his back. He only hoped that he wasn't on fire himself.

The crew plummeted towards the ground at breakneck speeds. Clouds flew by like trees on the highway. The target was immediately below, and if they didn't time their chutes correctly, they would be a stain on the mountainside in just a few critical seconds.

Joseph wasn't entirely aware of when they reached terminal velocity, but he was acutely aware of the looming presence of the ground below them. They were about three thousand feet up now. To avoid detection, they would have to blow the chutes below a thousand feet. Just another five or six seconds.

"Chutes, everyone, on my mark," Joseph ordered. "Three... Two... One... MARK!"

The rustle of six parachutes suddenly deploying filled the comm channel for a moment. Joseph's arms felt like they were about to be torn from his body as the parachute brought his speed from hundreds of feet per second down to near zero over the course of what felt like about three seconds, as best he could tell.

A few brief seconds later, they were on the ground with their parachutes disconnected.

"We're going in through that air vent over there," Joseph said, pointing to a hole on the side of the mountain.

A giant fan blocked their path. *Can we get that power out already, guys?* Joseph thought.

"All right," Joseph shouted. "Let's get this grille off of here."

Jesse reached down and grabbed one side, while Jennifer grabbed the other.

"On three," Jesse said. "One, two, THREE!"

They pulled with all their might, but it did not budge.

***

T-plus thirty-nine minutes

Amanda sat in silence and listened to the explosions outside, afraid to hope that they might be there for her. Her bonds were looser now, but she dared not remove them. There were no fewer than six security cameras trained on her. *No, better to wait until the critical moment to break free,* she thought. A moment later, the lights flickered. Suddenly, the room was plunged into blackness. *The critical moment,* she thought.

***

T-plus forty minutes

ANOTHER explosion rocked the mountain, and the fan's giant blades began to slow.

"Try again on the grille," Joseph shouted.

Jesse and Jen grabbed the grille again. This time, it fell away easily.

"Mag locks," Joseph said, laughing. "They work well as long as you never lose power."

A moment later, they were inside the vent shaft, staring at mile after mile of identical, unlit grey tubing. Joseph shivered.

***

T-plus forty-two minutes

"GET the power back online!" Svetlana shouted.

Around her, dozens of troops scurried around trying to fix damaged systems.

"The reactor water supply was damaged," one man reported. "We can't bring it back online until pressure is restored."

"How long will that take?" she demanded.

"About three hours," he answered, "but we'll have partial emergency power from the diesel turbines in about five minutes."

"Make it three or you're lizard food," she replied coldly, "and deploy troops to secure the perimeter of Core Ops. The last thing we need is a security breach right now."

***

T-plus forty-nine minutes

"THREE hundred feet ahead," Joseph began, then paused.

Is that right? Yeah, I think so.

"...there should be a vertical shaft that leads to their core operations center," he continued. "We think Amanda is being held on that deck. It may be heavily guarded, so go to infrared and keep quiet."

As they approached the lip, Joseph suddenly realized the problem. It was a 100 foot vertical drop with ice-smooth walls and no real handholds. There weren't even any beams onto which he could hook a rope.

"Suggestions?" Joseph asked.

"Go down in pairs," Jen replied. "Hold hands and push against each other, then we walk down the walls."

"And if we slip?" Casey asked.

"We're in a world of hurt?" Jesse volunteered.

"Casey's right," Joseph told her. "It's too risky."

"Wait a second. The tube curves to one side at the bottom," Cody observed.

"So what?" Jen asked.

"Why not just ride it like a water slide?" he asked.

Joseph quickly flipped through the map. "It might work," he replied.

"I'll go first," Jen said.

"You sure, Jen?" Joseph asked.

"I'm sure."

"Take care of yourself," he told her.

A moment later, she was gone.

"Jen," Joseph asked through his comm headset.

"Yeah. I'm okay. I stopped before I hit anything," she replied. She paused, then added, "Barely."

"All right. Let's go," Joseph ordered.

One-by-one, they jumped into the tunnel. Joseph took up the rear. As he neared the bottom, he saw the rest of the team stopped dead in front of him. He scrambled desperately to stop, but in the end, he plowed directly into them, knocking them through a metal grille at the end of the tunnel.

The grille hit the metal floor with a clang that could probably have been heard all the way on the surface. *Shit! That's just what we need,* Joseph thought.

Joseph crawled sideways to an adjacent vent and carefully removed the cover. As he peered cautiously out of the tube, pulse weapon fire flew past his nose. He ducked back into the tube. When another shot flew past, Joseph popped out and shot randomly. Incredibly, his shot hit its mark, and a guard went down with a thud.

Jennifer stuck her head out next. "Clear," she said, just as another energy pulse flew past. "Damn it!" she shouted, ducking back inside.

This time, the guard was not content to stand idly by, and appeared at the end of her tube.

"That's far enough," he said.

A moment later, the guard's face turned to an expression of horror as he suddenly melted from the inside out. "Oh, bugger," he muttered, then disappeared, leaving behind only a slight stain on the commercial grade carpeting.

"Nice shot, Jen," Joseph said.

"That's why they pay me the big bucks," she replied.

"It's clearly not safe to stay here," Mat warned. "We should get moving."

Jennifer stuck her head out again. "Clear."

Joseph stuck his head out the other vent just to make sure. "Let's go."

"Where are we going?" Jen asked.

"I'm not sure," Joseph replied. "We know the cells are on this level somewhere, but I don't have any idea where. We should probably split up to cover more ground. Mat? Casey? Cody? You three move on ahead. Mat, you're the ranking officer, so you're in charge. Jesse, Jen, you two come with me."

Joseph waited until Mat's team disappeared around the corner, then turned and headed down a different corridor.

***

T-plus sixty-two minutes

AMANDA felt the bonds loosen around her wrists. Just a few more seconds, and she could get her hands free. *There,* she thought. After the rope slipped free, she rubbed her wrists in discomfort. *Now for the ankles.*

***

As the doors opened into the Core Ops control center, Jennifer knew they had made a serious mistake. "Back," she shouted hoarsely.

Jesse dove behind the door frame as bursts of pulse weapon fire flew past. The pulses of plasma scorched the ceiling and ricocheted for at least fifty feet. *Nasty,* Jennifer thought as she hit the wall. Much to her surprise, though, Joseph was still standing in the doorway.

Joseph shot two guards in the blink of an eye. What happened next made time seem to stand still. She watched in horror as a woman in her thirties reached behind her chair and drew a projectile weapon. "Joseph!" she screamed. As the woman aimed, Jennifer jumped towards him. The sound of gunfire filled the room, then everything went black.

Chapter Fifty-three

Mat, Casey, and Cody emerged around a corner into a vast atrium, its plant-covered landscape shimmering green in the light of their headlamps.

"Suggestions?" Mat asked.

"Straight," Casey said.

"Left," Cody countered.

"Okay... we go right," Mat said in desperation.

The door on the right led to a long hallway. At the end was another door. Beyond it, Mat's team meandered through a series of halls, studying each door as they passed it. Halfway around the circle, they found one door that was different—stronger looking—so they studied it further.

"This is it," Mat said. "I'm pretty sure."

With a few rounds of his pulse rifle, the door controls were thoroughly fused, and the backup power for the magnetic locks failed. A moment later, the door swung slowly open on its giant hinges.

As the door opened, Casey gasped. A dozen small, padded rooms with tiny windows greeted them, most filled with political prisoners.

"What do we do now?" Casey asked.

"About what?" Mat countered.

"There must be a dozen prisoners here. How do we deal with that?"

"Our mission," Mat replied, "is to recover Amanda. No more, no less. Once we find her, our orders are to get out as quickly as possible."

Casey nodded uncomfortably.

As they reached the end of the corridor, there she sat, bruised and beaten, looking like she had seen better days, but alive and, for the moment, conscious.

***

Joseph watched the events unfold, frozen, unable to respond. One moment, everything was okay; the next moment, Jennifer was lying in his arms with a bullet through her chest. Jesse drew a pulse weapon and fired, but missed. Then, the woman pulled the trigger again, but her gun jammed.

"Damn," the woman said. "Listen, I can help you."

"Shoot her," Joseph ordered.

"No, wait. I can give you power, Joseph," she said. "I know how to control the Ackerman crystal."

Joseph thought for a moment. *If that's true... I could save Jennifer. Can I trust her?*

"And you could be rich, yes richer than a king!" she pleaded, slowly moving up to the outer ring of the control room. "All you have to do is let me go."

No. Jennifer would rather die than pay such a high price. This woman must be caught or killed. It simply has to be.

"I'm sorry, Jen," Joseph said as he reached for his pulse rifle. "Let's kick some colonial ass." The woman screamed as she ran through a side door that Joseph hadn't noticed. He shot at her, but it was no use; she was gone.

And there they were. Suddenly, Jennifer stirred.

"Joseph? Joseph?" Jennifer whispered. "I just want you to know.... I love you."

He tried his best to muster a smile as her eyes closed, and in a moment of kindness, bent and kissed her gently on the lips. As he did, he felt her breath as she exhaled one last time, then stopped breathing altogether.

Joseph closed his eyes, bit his lips, and for once, wished things were different.

"Joseph?" came the voice on the headset.

Joseph recognized the voice as belonging to Cody. "Yes?" he replied.

"We have Amanda."

"Is she okay?" he asked.

"Yeah. She doesn't look too good, though."

"Meet me at the evac point. We have a man down," Joseph replied. He paused for a moment. "It's Jennifer."

"I'm sorry, Joe," Cody replied.

"War is Hell," he answered. "Jesse! Oxygen. Medkit. Now."

"She's not breathing," he replied.

"Force the air," Joseph shouted, "and don't let her lose a pulse."

***

Mat tried to pull Amanda's half-limp body onto his shoulder, but she shoved herself off. "I can walk, thanks," she said.

Amanda took the lead as they walked through a veritable labyrinth of halls and corridors that all seemed to lead nowhere.

When they rounded the final bend before the doors to the evac area, more pulse weapon fire singed the wall in front of them. Amanda ducked as one shot grazed the shoulder of her clothing.

Casey jumped towards her to protect her, and fired three shots. One soldier collapsed in a heap. That's when he saw five other soldiers rushing them all at once.

He froze and waited for the end, but then something entirely unexpected happened. *One of the soldiers burst into flame.*

***

SVETLANA Rusakova hated retreat. She hated retreat even more than she hated losing, and she hated losing. But this wasn't retreat. No, it was a strategic advance in reverse.

Even if we lose the prisoners, I'll live to fight another day, she told herself as she stepped into her private escape ship.

As the doors closed with a clang, she felt the rumble of its two small thrusters firing. *No time. They'll be watching for me. I have to fold from here.*

She pressed a few buttons on the console and overrode the safety mechanisms on the spatial folding drive. A few moments later, she had jumped back to Lenora Prime. The resulting explosion blew out five decks of their Tularis base, but she really didn't care anymore. That might be the past, but it could be changed... with a little work.

***

JOSEPH stepped into the entryway of the base, mere meters from the evac point. A half dozen enemy troops were converging on Amanda. *I don't think they've seen me yet. I have the element of surprise. If only Jen were conscious. I could use a sharpshooter right about now.*

Someone across the room hit one of the guards, who promptly collapsed in a pile on the floor.

Joseph aimed his particle rifle carefully, using his backpack as a crude tripod. He breathed slowly... One... Two...

Three... and pulled the trigger. Bingo. One down. He pulled again. Two down.

Suddenly, they turned towards him. Bang. Three down. Two to go.

Jesse fired a few rounds with a pulse rifle and hit one guard in the shoulder. As Casey and Cody circled around the room, Casey finished off the injured guard. Finally, Joseph fired again and incinerated the last guard.

"Amanda!" Joseph shouted.

"Joseph!" she cried.

Amanda and Joseph ran to each other. Their eyes met—two souls singing their perpetual harmony—and at once, the heartache was gone... and then Amanda suddenly looked very surprised.

She looked down at her chest and found it covered in blood. As she collapsed in Joseph's arms, he saw Mat behind her. Mat held up his service revolver and smiled, his weapon still aimed in Joseph's direction.

"No!!!!" Joseph screamed. In a barrage of weapons fire from all directions, Mat burst into flames. A few moments later, he was gone, and, Joseph feared, perhaps so was Amanda.

***

Automatic weapons fire filled the air outside the base. Both sides were bent on the total annihilation of their enemies. The smell of burnt gunpowder and scorched bodies stung Joseph's nostrils as Casey opened the door.

Slowly, tentatively, Joseph stepped out into the crossfire, Amanda's limp, unconscious body still in his arms, Jesse following behind with Jennifer. He couldn't tell for certain, but for a moment, it seemed like the shooting stopped as he carried her through the heart of no man's land—a brief respite in a sea of anguish.

Indeed, a hush fell over the battlefield. One by one, the soldiers lowered their weapons to order arms. A few saluted as Joseph carried Amanda home—most just stared—but all were moved by the sight.

The few seconds it took to walk to the medical transport felt like a century. As Joseph handed Amanda's limp figure to the medical team, they whisked her quickly onto a gurney.

Joseph tried to step up into the ship, but a bearded man stopped him.

"I'm afraid you can't ride with her," he said. "The transport is for the injured and their family members only."

"I'm the only family she has," Joseph replied somberly, "and she's the only family I have, too."

The man appeared to think about this for a moment, then waved him in.

Chapter Fifty-four

WHEN the transports landed on Sirius IV, the remaining crew received a hero's welcome.

"Congratulations," Admiral Skylarov offered. "You did it."

"Yes, but at what cost, Admiral?" Joseph asked. "At what cost?"

Skylarov walked away in stony silence as Admiral Jameson came up behind him.

"I'm sorry, son," he offered. "I know it isn't much consolation, but you've routed out spies in critical parts of Terran Command."

"Somehow, I think I've barely scratched the surface," Joseph said.

"Yes, I'm sure you have," he replied.

"Is he..." Joseph began, pointing to Admiral Skylarov.

Jameson merely nodded in silence.

***

THE sun rose again on Lenora Prime, its parching rays beating down unrelentingly on the surface through the nearly ozone-free atmosphere, and in a shadowed gash in the craggy cliffs above Lenora Station, Vincent Barry's raspy voice could be heard softly.

"My brothers, I join you," he whispered. "With open arms, you greet me. May our souls once again be at peace."

And so he breathed his last.

***

AND on the dark side of Lenora Prime, deep within the frozen ground, in a place called Site J, Svetlana Rusakova sat.

"Everything went as planned," the young man said.

"Excellent," she replied coldly.

Epilogue:

As Joseph stepped into the hospital, he saw a viewscreen in the waiting area. The caption on the newscast grabbed his attention.

Ceasefire Agreement Reached, Joseph read. *It's a start, I suppose.*

> "In Terran Alliance news," the anchorwoman began, "lawmakers from the Terran Alliance and the CEA made history today as they formally entered into a ceasefire. The specific details of the ceasefire are as yet undisclosed."
>
> "Secretary of State Tracey Armstrong is expected to make a formal announcement at 3:00 this afternoon, Earth Normal Time. As always, TANN will bring you live coverage from the press conference the moment it happens."
>
> "You're watching TANN, the Terran Alliance News Network, with news updates every hour on the hour."

The sterile air burned his lungs as Joseph entered the medical ward. The sickly sweet smell of nitrous oxide reminded him of the dentist's office, and thus made his nose twitch and his teeth hurt.

Beside him stood Jennifer. *For once,* he mused, ***even she*** *looks like she got hit by a truck. Oh well. At least she's conscious again.*

Slowly, cautiously, Jennifer reached over and put her arm around Joseph.

Joseph smiled weakly. "Thanks, Jen. I needed that...."

Joseph noticed a bunch of medical instruments lining the walls, their purposes largely beyond his limited medical training. The room was otherwise very plain and uninteresting, its white walls designed to be functional, but not particularly therapeutic.

Of course, he supposed, *when you have to build and abandon these things as frequently as they do out here on the fringes of Colonial space, you have to make some concessions to expediency.*

Joseph sighed.

"Ah. You must be Joseph," said a voice from behind him.

Joseph had been so busy staring at the life support equipment that he hadn't noticed the man's entrance. He turned and found himself face-to-face with a tall man in his fifties, with greying hair and a salt-and-pepper beard. The man was in a white medical coat. His name tag read, "Dr. Michael Barry".

"Hi, doc," Joseph said. "How is she?"

"We repaired all of her outward injuries," the doctor replied. "It's really up to her now. I'm afraid there's nothing else we can do but wait and hope."

"And pray," Jennifer added.

Joseph turned to her and nodded. As the doctor turned and left the room, Joseph sat down in a chair beside Amanda, stroked her hair, kissed her cheek, and then held her hand.

"Be well," Jennifer whispered, then walked away in silence.

And as the day turned slowly into night and the doctors made their final rounds, Joseph still sat there by her side, looking at her still form, praying in his heart that one day she would look back at him.

"Amanda, I just want you to know that when you wake up, I'll be here for you. I'll always be here for you. I promise."

Behind the Book:

Tidbits:

- TERRA was originally called TEA. The name was changed to make it easier to remember that they're Earth.
- CEA was, for about 18 months, called COLEA, but then I realized that too many people would read it as "cola".
- The original plot for this book ended after 36,000 words. Then I added the AI backstory and the ice caves trip, and it mushroomed to its current size (about 58,000 words). See "About the Sigma 3 Conspiracy" for more on these bits.

***

The Language of the Kend'hara:

On the language of the Nivitian sect, used for ship names and various alien-looking texts, the initial line used in the last message of the starship Kend'hara would be "it michlus et vi", but the rule is to drop the final consonant of prepositions and attach them to the words that they modify, and in cases of complex prepositions, prepend the first word, then append the second word, dropping any leading vowel. Also, adjectives come after the nouns that they modify. If a noun ends in a vowel, the vowel is dropped and replaced with an apostrophe. Kendu means arms (plural of Kend, arm). Verbs ending in a 't' are plural in nature.

Oc' = Och. Ste' = Steh. The word Vi means we, yi means you, vey means we as an object, yu means you as an object. The verb fi means "to close" (infinitive form of verb, see also fichs for second person, ficht for other forms). Adjective for closed is erus. The words have different language origins, and thus different stems. Sepra means distant in space. Sechra means distant in time. It can also mean life when used to refer to time in the abstract, e.g. my time on this planet. Note that the language is basically a lost language, hence the reason that Joseph does not understand the distinction between Sepra and Sechra.

***

Wild Ideas
(most of which were summarily scrapped)

As with any book, a lot of ideas came up during the writing process. I threw out most of them because they didn't make sense or didn't work with some other planned aspect of the story, but I thought it would be entertaining to log a few of them to give the readers an idea of what was going through my head while I wrote the book.

1. The whole "moment out of time" bit earlier triggered a wild thought. There could be some strange time travel thing happening in which one of the crew suddenly disappears. Oh, and they could lose contact with John quickly, then eventually determine that the planet contains pockets of time. The weapon turns out to be a weapon that uses anti-time as a power source, or possibly as a way to destroy planets. When time and anti-time meet... well, the theory was that everything would explode, but it turns out that time itself just shatters.

2. Wow, I don't know where that came from. Suddenly I just had the inspiration to blow up Terran command, and then it happened. It was almost as if I "remembered" that Joseph's family was on that station. I then added a bit so that they would be. I was always planning on having the bad guys kill his family, but I never knew it would happen like this. Of course, they might kill Amanda later, but that's malicious. Either that or they'll kill the girlfriend of one of the characters in the second book (different set of characters). I haven't decided which yet.... Parts of this trilogy are truly evolving beyond my conscious thought....

3. I realized that Joseph's grandfather can't be on the station because I already blew him up on the Kend'hara. So I blew up his aunt and uncle instead. I had almost forgotten about them. They had to be killed in order to create the feeling of total isolation that Joseph felt, and in order for Amanda to be seen as his only family, and as such, worth protecting at all costs, even if it meant losing his life.

4. I finally came up with an explanation for the phrase "the boat singers", and even an explanation for Rejndorv's behavior. A character previously believed to be motivated by cowardice is now revealed to be motivated by love for his dead brothers.

   But perhaps the most powerful image is that of the tomb—the cross-shaped Hall of Memories—of the twelve thousand that were killed by a biochemical warfare accident—twelve thousand people that officially never existed.

5. Late in the writing process, I unkilled Jennifer, since I need her and the crystal for the fourth book if I ever

write one. Much easier to unkill someone in an early edit than to risk blowing the crystal's return. (Yes, it could have returned without her, but I'd rather it return through Jennifer screwing up or something than by someone finding it accidentally. Makes for more dramatic irony.)

Also, it makes the last scene much more poignant for Jennifer to be standing there consoling Joseph while he sits beside the comatose Amanda. Oh, how I love the ending.

6. I've also been looking over the email simming I did a few years back. I wish I could find the old Starstalker dream sequence bits I wrote just before the end, since some of them were really good, and portals are cool.

***

About the Sigma 3 Conspiracy:

I had fun folding in the Sigma 3 story and adapting it to this universe. The story is based on something I wrote as part of an internet sim. Because the story line in question was almost completely engineering-driven, it was not hard to eliminate all ideas that came from other people.

In fact, even with permission to use those ideas, it still would have been necessary to remove most of them, as they tended to be heavily tied to the universe in which the story was originally written. As such, the Sigma 3 conspiracy story consists of chunks of text that I wrote back in the mid 1990s, interwoven with new material to tie it together and tie it into the (relatively limited) universe correctly.

Unlike the original universe, which had transporters, replicators, turbolifts, and warp drive, we have food slots, which I suppose might resemble replicators (there's no good reason to explain the tech here, so I didn't), lifts (nothing turbo about 'em), and a spacial folding drive. The lack of transporters is both intentional and challenging, since it eliminates a lot of "easy outs", but it also radically changed the nature of the "other ship".

In the original story, the other ship was from the future, but it was a complete figment of the computer's imagination, generated in a holobuffer that used organic storage, which somehow magically allowed it to store people as data files, who could then interact with the fake ship. Elaborate, and kind of cool, but the whole implants via transporter thing was way too easy for my taste, as were a lot of the other uses of the transporter to get people into and out of the holobuffer. It's just more suspenseful if you can't beam people out in a pinch.

The flight to the ice caves is also an import from an email sim. It was similarly written in a different universe, but had many, many fewer ties to it. It was thus much easier to update. It also helped that the main characters were the same (Joseph and Amanda) and that most of the relationships were also fundamentally similar (Amanda's Admiral father, and so on).

With the Sigma 3 plot, the lines attributed to James were originally played by Joseph. The NexTrac came to save them instead of being on the opposite side of the galaxy. Also, they weren't flying into the sun. The ship's computer was just failing. The story also originally looked like a bizarre hybrid between a theatrical script and a motion picture script. Thus, even translating that into readable paragraphs proved tricky. Many long passages consisted of way too much dialogue. A few parts still do, but not to the extent that they originally did.

All in all, I think the rewrite of the Sigma 3 conspiracy story line is much better than the original version, which is in part because I wrote it when I was young and inexperienced, and thus it had farther to go in order to be acceptable, but it is also in part because the Star Trek universe, while a fun read, lends itself more to character-building stories rather than wild adventures, while this story line cried out for the chance to be a wild adventure, with a bit of humor and a dash of romance added in for flavor.

Closing Thoughts:

I hope you've enjoyed the first of the Patriots series of books. Be sure to read the second book, *Enemies From Within,* to see the same period in time told from the perspective of Colonial troops.

***

KURT Lawrence stood before a crowd of at least two thousand people in the crew mess of Portable Base 3. It was a crudely constructed ship for its time, but in many ways, it was an incredible achievement. From the very first sketch, it was designed to be a giant, space-borne research facility with all the amenities. Like most government projects, when push came to shove, they cut all the amenities....

The crew mess was one of the amenities. It looked like a filthy soup kitchen in a dark alley in Brooklyn, but it got the job done... *barely*.

As for Kurt, he was the base commander, so when he spoke, everyone's ears perked up, but few more so than those of his closest advisors, Marc Hanssen and Kimberly Kurtz.

Marc had to admit that, friends or not, Kurt's meteoric rise to power over the past few years *still* gave him the creeps. Somehow he felt all too glad to be in the company of someone like Kim—possibly the only girl on the base who could be as cynical as he could. *It just makes life easier*, he thought.

"I have an announcement," Kurt told the onlookers. "I've just received word that Terran forces are taking Tularis Prime. We can't risk this project being discovered, and after that last attack, we are unable to fold. We have to move now."

Marc shivered. *The StarKiller was never supposed to be used except as a proof of concept,* he thought, *or so they told me. Why are we moving? Please tell me it hasn't come to this. I'd rather destroy the Omega Dawn project than use it as a weapon.*

"I thought the StarKiller was never to be used," Kim asked.

Marc relaxed a bit. *Wonderful. Someone else asked so I don't have to.*

"The planet has all but fallen," Kurt replied. "Terran forces have already shown a willingness to scorch the earth after they take control of a planet. At this point, you should assume that everyone on Tularis Prime is dead or soon will be."

Marc's heart sank. *My family....*

"We have decided to show the Terrans that we are willing to use the ultimate weapon—that we are even willing to make the ultimate sacrifice—to halt their advance on our territory," Kurt continued. "Today, we black out Tularis, our sun."

As a Commodore, Marc knew he could technically pull rank and overrule him, but Kurt was in charge of this posting, and his orders came straight from Admiral Murrow, which made that a bad idea....

Almost as bad an idea as blowing up a star, he thought.

Marc closed his eyes, bit his lip, and sighed.

About the Author:

David is an avid musician, writer, photographer, videographer, musical composer, and hard-core geek with a Master's degree in computer science and a Bachelor's degree in communications (broadcasting) and computer science.

In addition to writing this book, David also created various workflow tools used in its production, did all of the content production and design, redesigned many of the fonts, and drew the cover art.

His choral music has been performed by the Diocesan Choir of Monterey, California and the contemporary choir at Holy Cross Catholic Church in Santa Cruz, CA. He spends much of his spare time performing with musical ensembles in the greater Santa Cruz area.

http://www.patriotsbooks.com/

www.ingramcontent.com/pod-product-compliance
Lightning Source LLC
Chambersburg PA
CBHW030536310726
48979CB00010B/1926/J

* 9 7 8 1 9 4 0 8 0 9 0 1 4 *